A HARLEM MOON CLASSIC

OTHER HARLEM MOON CLASSICS

The Heart of Happy Hollow
by Paul Laurence Dunbar

Pride of Family: Four Generations of American Women of Color by Carole Ione

The Quest of the Silver Fleece by W.E.B. Du Bois

Soulscript: A Collection of African American Poetry
edited by June Jordan

THE COLONEL'S DREAM

*

A Novel

CHARLES W. CHESNUTT

HARLEM MOON

Broadway Books

New York

Published by Harlem Moon, an imprint of Broadway Books, a division of Random House, Inc.

A hardcover edition of this book was originally published in 1905 by Doubleday, New York.

Reader's Companion by Richard Anthony Blint.

PRINTED IN THE UNITED STATES OF AMERICA

Harlem Moon Classics Series Advisor: Gina Dent, Associate Professor of Women's Studies and History of Consciousness, University of California, Santa Cruz

Visit our website at www.harlemmoon.com

First Harlem Moon trade paperback edition published 2005.

Book design by Amanda Dewey

Cataloging-in-Publication Data is on file with the Library of Congress.

ISBN 0-7679-1951-3

10 9 8 7 6 5 4 3 2 1

Contents

Introduction

Charles Chesnutt's remarkable life spanned a number of crucial periods in American history, from the Civil War to Reconstruction, Confederate Restoration (referred to by some as the Southern Redemption) and World War I to the rise of Franklin Roosevelt and the New Deal. Rather than becoming a neutral observer, Chesnutt, following the lead of his father, the elected official Andrew Jackson Chesnutt, became an active participant in the events of his time as community leader, essayist, and organizer.

Born in Cleveland, Ohio, in 1858, Chesnutt attended Howard School, a public school for black children built with Freedman's Bureau funds, until he was forced to discontinue his studies as a result of his father taking up farming after a failed grocery business. The young Chesnutt was invited by Robert Harris, his mentor and Howard's principal, to take a pupil-teacher job so to, thereby, spare a bright student from farm work. Chesnutt later became Howard's principal.

In 1881, he became a leader in the Fayetteville, North Carolina,

A.M.E. Zion church, serving as choirmaster and organist. In 1901, he chaired the Committee on Colored Troops for the 35th National Encampment of the Grand Army of the Republic, and, in 1905, he became a member of the Committee of Twelve, a group of advisers to Booker T. Washington who were organized to promote "the advancement of the Interests of the Negro race."

In 1913, he persuaded the Mayor of Cleveland, Newton Baker, to oppose a bill prohibiting interracial marriage. (His advocacy might have been partially attributable to, like millions of African Americans, the white-skinned Chesnutts having European ancestors. Some even referred to him as "a voluntary Negro" because of his ability to pass if he so chose.)

In 1914, Chesnutt helped to establish Playhouse Settlement in Cleveland, which later became one of the nation's premier African-American theaters, Karamu House. And in the early 1920s, Chesnutt's politicking included protests against the American occupation of Haiti and Harvard University's attempt to exclude black students from its freshman dormitories and dining halls.

Charles Chesnutt's activism included his literary endeavors; he was a major American writer of his period, who, had he been white, would have been canonized long before now. He was a prolific writer, publishing between 1885 and 1931 sixty-one pieces of short fiction, one biography, thirty-one speeches, articles, and essays, and three novels: *The House behind the Cedars, The Marrow of Tradition*, and *The Colonel's Dream*.

Chesnutt did everything that was required of him to become one of the leading writers of his time. He studied the classics and attuned his ear to a variety of American speech patterns through his work as a court stenographer, feats that enabled him to portray a wide range of characters convincingly, whether they were black or white, Northern or Southern, rich, poor, or middle class.

Armed with these tools, he challenged the prevailing attitudes of his time, writing in a period when Americans were undergoing a reconciliation after one of the bloodiest wars in world history, and when some influential opinion makers were remembering with affection the plantation, an institution that some current congress and cabinet members still pine for.

The setting for the 1905 work, *The Colonel's Dream*, is the post–Civil War South, represented by a town called Clarendon, the birthplace of Colonel French, a former Confederate officer who has returned to the town after making his fortune in the North. The landed aristocracy has been stripped of its power and finds itself at the mercies of a new class of businessmen, composed of those who were once their surrogates:

> "The mayor . . . had sprung from the same class as Fetters, that of the aspiring poor whites, who, freed from the moral incubus of slavery, had by force of numbers and ambition secured political control of the State and relegated not only Negroes, but the old master class, to political obscurity."

Unscrupulous overseers, ex–indentured servants and former slave traders like William Fetters, "a mortgage shark, labor contractor and political boss," are now in charge and treat their former bosses in a manner that would have been considered insolent in antebellum times. The colonel is a member of this fallen aristocracy and discovers upon his return that members of his class lack the clout they once possessed.

Throughout the novel, those who once held his kind in awe abuse him with ridicule and sarcasm. When the colonel seeks the release of Bud Johnson, the novel's "Bad Nigger," who resists being "sold" to Fetters, Turner, Fetter's agent, the colonel's inferior in a former time, insults the colonel with vindictive relish: "Fetters has got this county where he wants it, an' I'll bet dollars to bird shot he ain't goin' to let no coon-flavoured No'the'n interloper come down here an' mix up with arrangements, even if he did hail from this town way back yonder. This here nigger problem is a South'en problem, and outsiders might's well keep their han's off."

One reviewer, writing in Lousville, Kentucky's, *Courier-Journal* (September 16, 1905), agreed with Turner's sentiments, saying that after the colonel returned to the North, he hoped that he would remain there. Another reviewer, writing in the *Globe and Commercial Advertiser* (September 9, 1905) perhaps finding some of Chesnutt's white characters an embarrassment, suggested that he stick to writing about blacks, a standard that obviously wasn't applied to white writers such as Mark Twain. The reviewer said, "Mr. Chesnutt has been more successful when taking for his principal characters the people of his own race," advice that is still given to black writers who, in the mind of white reviewers, dare to wander off the literary plantation.

Thankfully, Chesnutt's imagination was far more democratic. He maintained that the end of slavery was beneficial not only for the African captives, but for the ersatz aristocracy that prospered from their labor. Of the loyal ex-slave, Peter, who was given to the colonel when he was a child, and passed on to Phillip, the colonel's son, after the colonel returned to the South, the narrator says: "How easy the conclusion that the slave's lot had been more fortunate! But no, Peter had been better free. There were plenty of poor white men, and no one had suggested slavery as an improvement of their condition. Had Peter remained a slave, then the colonel would have remained a master, which was only another form of slavery. The colonel had been emancipated by the same token that made Peter free. Peter had returned home poor and broken, not because he had been free, but because nature first, and society next, in distributing their gifts, had been niggardly with old Peter."

This is one of the milder observations *The Colonel's Dream* makes about the treatment of African Americans; elsewhere in the novel,

Chesnutt's indictment of the South, during the backlash on Reconstruction, is restrained but merciless. Just as Anne Frank's powerful diary challenged the revisionist opinion that sought to minimize the suffering of the European Holocaust victims, Chesnutt was able to provide a different witness to the South, both before and after the war, than the one that continues to either sympathize with the rebellion or justify the way of life it sought to defend. This effort continues to this day in films like *Gods and Generals*, where we view mass murderers like Robert E. Lee and Stonewall Jackson becoming tearful as they sing Christmas carols by the fireplace, and PBS's "The Civil War," which earned its producer, Ken Burns, a membership in the Sons of the Confederacy.

In both *Dream* and his other works, Chesnutt allowed those responsible for the South remaining backwards to hang themselves through their words and actions. In *The Marrow of Tradition*, Miller, a black doctor, makes his way through the riot-torn streets, only to be stopped by a white man who declares, "Sorry to have had to trouble you, doctuh, but them's the o'ders. It ain't men like you that we're after, but the vicious and criminal class of niggers."

The narrator continues: "Miller smiled bitterly as he urged his horse forward. He was quite well aware that the virtuous citizen who had stopped him had only a few weeks before finished a term in the penitentiary, to which he had been sentenced for stealing. Miller knew that he could have bought all the man owned for fifty dollars, and his soul for as much more."

This passage exemplifies why Chesnutt's stories are literary predecessors to later novels that have courageously exposed institutional hypocrisy and exploded popular myths: *And Then We Heard the Thunder* (1962) by John O' Killens, skewered the racist and antidemocratic aspects of the Greatest Generation that fought for democracy abroad yet segregated blacks at home; the masterwork, *The Man Who Cried I Am* (1967), by John A. Williams weaves the tale of a fascist plan that advocates the internment of African-American leaders; and Kristin Hunter Lattany's *Breaking Away* (2003) details the plight of a black female professor who deals with death threats and campus ostracism after she aids a black sorority in filing a sexual harassment suit.

As a leader of this canon, Chesnutt's portrait of the white supremacists who thwarted the ambitions of black citizens could be withering. After Colonel French defies Southern custom by integrating a burial vault, a white mob that has already lynched a black man makes its objections known by digging up the corpse of the loyal ex-slave, Uncle Peter.

Members of the new Master race leave a note alongside the coffin that they have deposited on the colonel's porch. "Kurnell French; Take notis. Berry yore ole nigger sonewhar else. He can't stay in Oak Semitary. The majority of white people of this town, who dident tend yore nigger funarl, woant have him there. Niggers by there selves, white peepul by there selves, and them that lives in our town must bide by our rules. By order of Cumitty."

Such a depiction of whites as illiterate by a black writer was not likely to garner sales among white audiences; the same could be said for his depiction of miscegenation, the rabble-rousing white media, police brutality, and economic injustice. Looking at Chesnutt's thematic concerns helps to clarify why *Dream* received such a mixed, lukewarm, or even hostile reception from white critics and audiences of the time, despite his earnest desire to connect with that audience. With that agenda in mind, he makes his hero a white ex-confederate colonel, an unlikely one for black writers for whom the Confederate Army ranks right up there with the SS and other nefarious, brutal institutions.

The angry rhetoric that offended white critics who judged the novels and poetry written by black male writers in the '60s is absent in Chesnutt's work. The prose is polite and even deferential as he attempted to woo the white book-buying public of his time. Chesnutt's empathy extends to whites as well as blacks. Of the cotton mill operated by Fetters, the book's villain, he writes: ". . . he had seen the operation of Fetter's convict labour plantation, where white humanity, in its fairest and tenderest form, was stunted and blighted and destroyed."

Chesnutt's experience as a novelist demonstrates that whether black novelists' prose is florid like Victorian Chesnutt's style, or whether they are prone to stridency, their views often are at odds with the "mainstream" book-buying public, which today, as in Chesnutt's time, becomes uncomfortable when black writers expose the bigotry and ugly side of the American experience. They prefer being soothed by a neoconservative black intellectual elite that proposes that racism is a thing of the past, and that the problems of blacks are "structural" and "behavioral."

But it's imperative that we look at Chesnutt's work with an eye that's not clouded by the lens of conservatism and bias, allowing us to see just how remarkably prophetic his ideas were,* and just how long lasting racism would be. In one section, the narrator observes ". . . this [white] supremacy must be made permanent. Negroes must be taught that they need never look for any different state of things. New definitions were given to old words, new pictures set in old frames, new wine poured into old bottles."

Other issues which Chesnutt's colonel grapples with continue to nag the nation. They are the new pictures set in old frames. Racial profiling, employment discrimination, a racist criminal justice system, disenfranchisement of African Americans—all major themes in *Dream*—exist alongside a collected media many times more powerful than Clarendon's newspaper *Anglo Saxon* (or the *Morning Chronicle* for that matter in *The Marrow of Tradition*), continuing to portray African Americans in an unfavorable light and stir hateful passions against us in order to boost ratings.

Additionally, the convict labor industry, one of the main issues

* Long before Richard Nixon's "Southern Strategy," Chesnutt has a character predict a time when the Republican Party will become a white man's party!

addressed by *The Colonel's Dream,* has become big business. In a recent *Black Enterprise* article, it was reported that a Justice Department study found that 12.9% of black men between the ages of 25 and 29 were incarcerated in 2002, whereas the incarceration rate for Hispanic males in the same age group was 4.3%, and for white men, 1.6%. Like the convict labor system of Chesnutt's novel, what Angela Davis refers to as the Prison-Industrial Complex is targeted to ensnare young African-American men.

In *Dream,* the town's law enforcers, Fetter's henchmen, ensnare blacks into a cheap labor pool by using vagrancy laws. Historian Leon F. Litwack describes this system in his acclaimed nonfiction work *Trouble in Mind—Black Southerners in the Age of Jim Crow*: "Replacing the discipline of slavery, vagrancy laws, contract laws, and a variety of local ordinances reinforced the power of employers to procure, maintain, and exploit black workers."

Moreover, the privatization of the prison system has the same result as the old corrupt convict labor system; it places private interests above that of the general public and leads to the exploitation of cheap labor. Yet it seems that only when abuses of prisoners occur abroad as in the case of Abu Ghraib Prison, where Iraqi prisoners were tortured and abused sexually, does the public become repulsed by the actions of sadistic prison personnel, while such abuses of black prisoners even before Chesnutt's time have been greeted with silence.

Other issues addressed by the novel have remained contemporary as well. Chesnutt's prose soars when he writes about the Southern landscape. An early environmentalist, he deplores the ravaging of the land by developers in passages that are unsparing: "When the colonel had traveled that road in his boyhood, great forests of primeval pine had stretched for miles on either hand, broken at intervals by thriving plantations. Now all was changed. The tall and stately growth of the long-leaf pine had well nigh disappeared; fifteen years before, the turpentine industry, moving southward from Virginia, along the upland counties of the Appalachian slope, had swept through Clarendon County, leaving behind it a trail of blasted trunks and abandoned stills. Ere these had yielded to decay, the sawmill has followed, and after the sawmill the tar kiln, so that the dark-green forest was now only a waste of blackened stumps and undergrowth."

Today, environmental preservation is a dire social concern. As a result of the kind of reckless development depicted in *The Colonel's Dream*, the ecology of the planet is in peril.

Chesnutt's message of social reform apparently did not receive wide circulation. According to *To Be an Author: Letters of Charles W. Chestnutt, 1889–1905*, "Chesnutt pressured the Doubleday, Page & Co. about the advertising and promotion they were responsible for. The tone in many of his letters to the publishing company regarding his new book was written with disappointment and misunderstanding."

Charles Chesnutt's complaint to his publisher about the lack of promotion for *The Colonel's Dream* reflects a problem also faced by contemporary African-American writers who belong to the tradition of Gwendolyn Brooks, Richard Wright, Margaret Walker, Chester Himes, and Charles Wright—The Tradition of Serious Concerns. This tradition is in serious jeopardy as the market is saturated with escapist chick lit and booty bling-bling books, titles that are little more than advertisements for brand names in which bad fiction serves as filler.

But unlike Chesnutt, a black novelist in the Tradition of Serious Concerns is no longer totally dependent upon large publishers. As a result of E book and Print-on-Demand technology, writers like Michael Ross and Fred Beauford have been able to publish their books. Moreover, the rise of a multicultural readership, black book clubs, and black literary fairs, such as the Harlem Book Fair, free the writer from having to accommodate a more limited readership.

Chesnutt rose to the challenge that black writers have always faced, and he did it magnificently. Regardless of the monopoly that those opposed to African-American progress have over the dissemination of ideas and opinion, Chesnutt's example proves that a good writer can always present a version of history that challenges the official one, and if the writer is as extraordinary and as talented as Chesnutt, their appeal will transcend their times and address the needs of many generations after they have come and gone.

ISHMAEL REED
Oakland, California
August 16, 2004

Ishmael Reed is a celebrated and prolific writer, editor, and activist. He has published nine novels, including Yellow Back Radio Broke-Down, The Last Days of Louisiana Reed, *and* The Freelance Pallbearers, *in addition to his books of essays and poetry. A MacArthur Fellow, he has taught at the University of California at Berkeley for more than 30 years.*

THE **COLONEL'S** DREAM

DEDICATION

To the great number of those who are seeking, in whatever manner or degree, from near at hand or far away, to bring the forces of enlightenment to bear upon the vexed problems which harass the South, this volume is inscribed, with the hope that it may contribute to the same good end.

If there be nothing new between its covers, neither is love new, nor faith, nor hope, nor disappointment, nor sorrow. Yet life is not the less worth living because of any of these, nor has any man truly lived until he has tasted of them all.

LIST OF CHARACTERS

Colonel Henry French, A RETIRED MERCHANT

Mr. Kirby,
Mrs. Jerviss, } HIS FORMER PARTNERS

Philip French, THE COLONEL'S SON

Peter French, HIS OLD SERVANT

Mrs. Treadwell, AN OLD LADY

Miss Laura Treadwell, HER DAUGHTER

Graciella Treadwell, HER GRANDDAUGHTER

Malcolm Dudley, A TREASURE-SEEKER

Ben Dudley, HIS NEPHEW

Viney, HIS HOUSEKEEPER

William Fetters, A CONVICT LABOUR CONTRACTOR

Barclay Fetters, HIS SON

Bud Johnson, A CONVICT LABOURER

Caroline, HIS WIFE

Henry Taylor, A NEGRO SCHOOLMASTER

William Nichols, A MULATTO BARBER

Haynes, A CONSTABLE

One

Two gentlemen were seated, one March morning in 189—, in the private office of French and Company, Limited, on lower Broadway. Mr. Kirby, the junior partner—a man of thirty-five, with brown hair and mustache, clean-cut, handsome features, and an alert manner, was smoking cigarettes almost as fast as he could roll them, and at the same time watching the electric clock upon the wall and getting up now and then to stride restlessly back and forth across the room.

Mr. French, the senior partner, who sat opposite Kirby, was an older man—a safe guess would have placed him somewhere in the debatable ground between forty and fifty; of a good height, as could be seen even from the seated figure, the upper part of which was held erect with the unconscious ease which one associates with military training. His closely cropped brown hair had the slightest touch of gray. The spacious forehead, deep-set gray eyes, and firm chin, scarcely concealed by a light beard, marked the thoughtful man of affairs. His face indeed might have seemed austere, but for a sensitive mouth, which suggested a reserve of humour and a capacity for deep feeling. A man of well-balanced character, one would have said, not apt to undertake anything lightly, but sure to go far in whatever he took in hand; quickly responsive to a generous impulse, and capable of a righteous indignation; a good friend, a dangerous enemy; more likely to be misled by the heart than by the head; of the salt of the earth, which gives it savour.

Mr. French sat on one side, Mr. Kirby on the other, of a handsome, broad-topped mahogany desk, equipped with telephones and push buttons, and piled with papers, account books and letter files in orderly array. In marked contrast to his partner's nervousness, Mr. French scarcely moved a muscle, except now and then to take the cigar from his lips and knock the ashes from the end.

"Nine fifty!" ejaculated Mr. Kirby, comparing the clock with his watch. "Only ten minutes more."

Mr. French nodded mechanically. Outside, in the main office, the same air of tense expectancy prevailed. For two weeks the office force had been busily at work, preparing inventories and balance sheets. The firm of French and Company, Limited, manufacturers of crashes and burlaps and kindred stuffs, with extensive mills in Connecticut, and central offices in New York, having for a long time resisted the siren voice of the promoter, had finally faced the alternative of selling out, at a sacrifice, to the recently organised bagging trust, or of meeting a disastrous competition. Expecting to yield in the end, they had fought for position—with brilliant results. Negotiations for a sale, upon terms highly favourable to the firm, had been in progress for several weeks; and the two partners were awaiting, in their private office, the final word. Should the sale be completed, they were richer men than they could have hoped to be after ten years more of business stress and struggle; should it fail, they were heavy losers, for their fight had been expensive. They were in much the same position as the player who had staked the bulk of his fortune on the cast of a die. Not meaning to risk so much, they had been drawn into it; but the game was worth the candle.

"Nine fifty-five," said Kirby. "Five minutes more!"

He strode over to the window and looked out. It was snowing, and the March wind, blowing straight up Broadway from the bay, swept the white flakes northward in long, feathery swirls. Mr. French preserved his rigid attitude, though a close observer might have wondered whether it was quite natural, or merely the result of a supreme effort of will.

Work had been practically suspended in the outer office. The clerks were also watching the clock. Every one of them knew that the board of directors of the bagging trust was in session, and that at ten o'clock it was to report the result of its action on the proposition of French and Company, Limited. The clerks were not especially cheerful; the impending change meant for them, at best, a change of masters, and for many of them, the loss of employment. The firm, for relinquishing its business and good will, would receive liberal compensation; the clerks, for their skill, experience, and prospects of advancement, would receive their discharge. What else could be expected? The principal reason for the trust's existence was economy of administration; this was stated, most convincingly, in the prospectus. There was no suggestion, in that model document, that competition would be crushed, or that, monopoly once established, labour must sweat and the public groan in order that a few captains, or chevaliers, of industry, might double their dividends. Mr. French may have known it, or guessed it, but he was between the devil and the deep sea—a victim rather than an accessory—he must take what he could get, or lose what he had.

"Nine fifty-nine!"

Kirby, as he breathed rather than spoke the words, threw away his scarcely lighted cigarette, and gripped the arms of his chair spasmodically. His partner's attitude had not varied by a hair's breadth; except for the scarcely perceptible rise and fall of his chest he might have been a wax figure. The pallor of his countenance would have strengthened the illusion.

Kirby pushed his chair back and sprung to his feet. The clock marked the hour, but nothing happened. Kirby was wont to say, thereafter, that the ten minutes that followed were the longest day of his life. But everything must have an end, and their suspense was terminated by a telephone call. Mr. French took down the receiver and placed it to his ear.

"It's all right," he announced, looking toward his partner. "Our figures accepted—resolution adopted—settlement to-morrow. We are——"

The receiver fell upon the table with a crash. Mr. French toppled over, and before Kirby had scarcely realised that something was the matter, had sunk unconscious to the floor, which, fortunately, was thickly carpeted.

It was but the work of a moment for Kirby to loosen his partner's collar, reach into the recesses of a certain drawer in the big desk, draw out a flask of brandy, and pour a small quantity of the burning liquid down the unconscious man's throat. A push on one of the electric buttons summoned a clerk, with whose aid Mr. French was lifted to a leather-covered couch that stood against the wall. Almost at once the effect of the stimulant was apparent, and he opened his eyes.

"I suspect," he said, with a feeble attempt at a smile, "that I must have fainted—like a woman—perfectly ridiculous."

"Perfectly natural," replied his partner. "You have scarcely slept for two weeks—between the business and Phil—and you've reached the end of your string. But it's all over now, except the shouting, and you can sleep a week if you like. You'd better go right up home. I'll send for a cab, and call Dr. Moffatt, and ask him to be at the hotel by the time you reach it. I'll take care of things here to-day, and after a good sleep you'll find yourself all right again."

"Very well, Kirby," replied Mr. French, "I feel as weak as water, but I'm all here. It might have been much worse. You'll call up Mrs. Jerviss, of course, and let her know about the sale?"

When Mr. French, escorted to the cab by his partner, and accompanied by a clerk, had left for home, Kirby rang up the doctor, and requested him to look after Mr. French immediately. He then called for another number, and after the usual delay, first because the exchange girl was busy, and then because the line was busy, found himself in communication with the lady for whom he had asked.

"It's all right, Mrs. Jerviss," he announced without preliminaries. "Our terms accepted, and payment to be made, in cash and bonds, as soon as the papers are executed, when you will be twice as rich as you are to-day."

"Thank you, Mr. Kirby! And I suppose I shall never have another happy moment until I know what to do with it. Money is a great trial. I often envy the poor."

Kirby smiled grimly. She little knew how near she had been to ruin. The active partners had mercifully shielded her, as far as possible, from the knowledge of their common danger. If the worst happened, she must know, of course; if not, then, being a woman whom they both liked—she would be spared needless anxiety. How closely they had skirted the edge of disaster she did not learn until afterward; indeed, Kirby himself had scarcely appreciated the true situation, and even the senior partner, since he had not been present at the meeting of the trust managers, could not know what had been in their minds.

But Kirby's voice gave no hint of these reflections. He laughed a cheerful laugh. "If the world only knew," he rejoined, "it would cease to worry about the pains of poverty, and weep for the woes of wealth."

"Indeed it would!" she replied, with a seriousness which seemed almost sincere. "Is Mr. French there? I wish to thank him, too."

"No, he has just gone home."

"At this hour?" she exclaimed, "and at such a time? What can be the matter? Is Phil worse?"

"No, I think not. Mr. French himself had a bad turn, for a few minutes, after we learned the news."

Faces are not yet visible over the telephone, and Kirby could not see that for a moment the lady's grew white. But when she spoke again the note of concern in her voice was very evident.

"It was nothing—serious?"

"Oh, no, not at all, merely overwork, and lack of sleep, and the suspense—and the reaction. He recovered almost immediately, and one of the clerks went home with him."

"Has Dr. Moffatt been notified?" she asked.

"Yes, I called him up at once; he'll be at the Mercedes by the time the patient arrives."

There was a little further conversation on matters of business, and Kirby would willingly have prolonged it, but his news about Mr. French had plainly disturbed the lady's equanimity, and Kirby rang off, after arranging to call to see her in person after business hours.

Mr. Kirby hung up the receiver with something of a sigh.

"A fine woman," he murmured, "I could envy French his chances, though he doesn't seem to see them—that is, if I were capable of envy toward so fine a fellow and so good a friend. It's curious how clear-sighted a man can be in some directions, and how blind in others."

Mr. French lived at the Mercedes, an uptown apartment hotel overlooking Central Park. He had scarcely reached his apartment, when the doctor arrived—a tall, fair, fat practitioner, and one of the best in New York; a gentleman as well, and a friend of Mr. French.

"My dear fellow," he said, after a brief examination, "you've been burning the candle at both ends, which, at your age won't do at all. No, indeed! No, indeed! You've always worked too hard, and you've been worrying too much about the boy, who'll do very well now, with care. You've got to take a rest—it's all you need. You confess to no bad habits, and show the signs of none; and you have a fine constitution. I'm going to order you and Phil away for three months, to some mild climate, where you'll be free from business cares and where the boy can grow strong without having to fight a raw Eastern spring. You might try the Riviera, but I'm afraid the sea would be too much for Phil just yet; or southern California—but the trip is tiresome. The South is nearer at hand. There's Palm Beach, or Jekyll Island, or Thomasville, Asheville, or Aiken—somewhere down in the pine country. It will be just the thing for the boy's lungs, and just the place for you to rest. Start within a week, if you can get away. In fact, you've *got* to get away."

Mr. French was too weak to resist—both body and mind seemed strangely relaxed—and there was really no reason why he should not go. His work was done. Kirby could attend to the formal transfer of the business. He would take a long journey to some pleasant, quiet spot, where he and Phil could sleep, and dream and ride and drive and grow strong, and enjoy themselves. For the moment he felt as though he would never care to do any more work, nor would he need to, for he was rich enough. He would live for the boy. Phil's education, his health, his happiness, his establishment in life—these would furnish occupation enough for his well-earned retirement.

It was a golden moment. He had won a notable victory against greed and craft and highly trained intelligence. And yet, a year later, he was to recall this recent past with envy and regret; for in the meantime he was to fight another battle against the same forces, and others quite as deeply rooted in human nature. But he was to fight upon a new field, and with different weapons, and with results which could not be foreseen.

But no premonition of impending struggle disturbed Mr. French's pleasant reverie; it was broken in a much more agreeable manner by the arrival of a visitor, who was admitted by Judson, Mr. French's man. The visitor was a handsome, clear-eyed, fair-haired woman, of thirty or thereabouts, accompanied by another and a plainer woman, evidently a maid or companion. The lady was dressed with the most expensive simplicity, and her graceful movements were attended by the rustle of unseen silks. In passing her upon the street, any man under ninety would have looked at her three times, the first glance instinctively recognising an attractive woman, the second ranking her as a lady; while the third, had there been time and opportunity, would have been the long, lingering look of respectful or regretful admiration.

"How is Mr. French, Judson?" she inquired, without dissembling her anxiety.

"He's much better, Mrs. Jerviss, thank you, ma'am."

"I'm very glad to hear it; and how is Phil?"

"Quite bright, ma'am, you'd hardly know that he'd been sick. He's gaining strength rapidly; he sleeps a great deal; he's asleep now, ma'am. But, won't you step into the library? There's a fire in the grate, and I'll let Mr. French know you are here."

But Mr. French, who had overheard part of the colloquy, came forward from an adjoining room, in smoking jacket and slippers.

"How do you do?" he asked, extending his hand. "It was mighty good of you to come to see me."

"And I'm awfully glad to find you better," she returned, giving him her slender, gloved hand with impulsive warmth. "I might have telephoned, but I wanted to see for myself. I felt a part of the blame to be mine, for it is partly for me, you know, that you have been overworking."

"It was all in the game," he said, "and we have won. But sit down and stay awhile. I know you'll pardon my smoking jacket. We are partners, you know, and I claim an invalid's privilege as well."

The lady's fine eyes beamed, and her fair cheek flushed with pleasure. Had he only realised it, he might have claimed of her any privilege a woman can properly allow, even that of conducting her to the altar. But to him she was only, thus far, as she had been for a long time, a very good friend of his own and of Phil's; a former partner's widow, who had retained her husband's interest in the business; a wholesome, handsome woman, who was always excellent company and at whose table he had often eaten, both before and since her husband's death. Nor, despite Kirby's notions, was he entirely ignorant of the lady's partiality for himself.

"Doctor Moffatt has ordered Phil and me away, for three months," he said, after Mrs. Jerviss had inquired particularly concerning his health and Phil's.

"Three months!" she exclaimed with an accent of dismay. "But you'll be back," she added, recovering herself quickly, "before the vacation season opens?"

"Oh, certainly; we shall not leave the country."

"Where are you going?"

"The doctor has prescribed the pine woods. I shall visit my old home, where I was born. We shall leave in a day or two."

"You must dine with me to-morrow," she said warmly, "and tell me about your old home. I haven't had an opportunity to thank you for making me rich, and I want your advice about what to do with the money; and I'm tiring you now when you ought to be resting."

"Do not hurry," he said. "It is almost a pleasure to be weak and helpless, since it gives me the privilege of a visit from you."

She lingered a few moments and then went. She was the embodiment of good taste and knew when to come and when to go.

Mr. French was conscious that her visit, instead of tiring him, had

had an opposite effect; she had come and gone like a pleasant breeze, bearing sweet odours and the echo of distant music. Her shapely hand, when it had touched his own, had been soft but firm; and he had almost wished, as he held it for a moment, that he might feel it resting on his still somewhat fevered brow. When he came back from the South, he would see a good deal of her, either at the seaside, or wherever she might spend the summer.

When Mr. French and Phil were ready, a day or two later, to start upon their journey, Kirby was at the Mercedes to see them off.

"You're taking Judson with you to look after the boy?" he asked.

"No," replied Mr. French, "Judson is in love, and does not wish to leave New York. He will take a vacation until we return. Phil and I can get along very well alone.

Kirby went with them across the ferry to the Jersey side, and through the station gates to the waiting train. There was a flurry of snow in the air, and overcoats were comfortable. When Mr. French had turned over his hand luggage to the porter of the Pullman, they walked up and down the station platform.

"I'm looking for something to interest us," said Kirby, rolling a cigarette. "There's a mining proposition in Utah, and a trolley railroad in Oklahoma. When things are settled up here, I'll take a run out, and look the ground over, and write to you."

"My dear fellow," said his friend, "don't hurry. Why should I make any more money? I have all I shall ever need, and as much as will be good for Phil. If you find a good thing, I can help you finance it; and Mrs. Jerviss will welcome a good investment. But I shall take a long rest, and then travel for a year or two, and after that settle down and take life comfortably."

"That's the way you feel now," replied Kirby, lighting another cigarette, "but wait until you are rested, and you'll yearn for the fray; the first million only whets the appetite for more."

"All aboard!"

The word was passed along the line of cars. Kirby took leave of Phil, into whose hand he had thrust a five-dollar bill, "To buy popcorn on the train," he said, kissed the boy, and wrung his ex-partner's hand warmly.

"Good-bye," he said, "and good luck. You'll hear from me soon. We're partners still, you and I and Mrs. Jerviss."

And though Mr. French smiled acquiescence, and returned Kirby's hand clasp with equal vigour and sincerity, he felt, as the train rolled away, as one might feel who, after a long sojourn in an alien land, at last takes ship for home. The mere act of leaving New York, after the severance of all compelling ties, seemed to set in motion old currents of feeling, which, moving slowly at the start, gathered momentum as the miles rolled by, until his heart leaped forward to the old Southern town which was his destination, and he soon felt himself chafing impatiently at any delay that threatened to throw the train behind schedule time.

"He'll be back in six weeks," declared Kirby, when Mrs. Jerviss and he next met. "I know him well; he can't live without his club and his counting room. It is hard to teach an old dog new tricks."

"And I'm sure he'll not stay away longer than three months," said the lady confidently, "for I have invited him to my house party."

"A privilege," said Kirby gallantly, "for which many a man would come from the other end of the world."

But they were both mistaken. For even as they spoke, he whose future each was planning, was entering upon a new life of his own, from which he was to look back upon his business career as a mere period of preparation for the real end and purpose of his earthly existence.

Two

The hack which the colonel had taken at the station after a two-days' journey, broken by several long waits for connecting trains, jogged in somewhat leisurely fashion down the main street toward the hotel. The colonel, with his little boy, had left the main line of railroad leading north and south and had taken at a certain way station the one daily train for Clarendon, with which the express made connection. They had completed the forty-mile journey in two or three hours, arriving at Clarendon at noon.

It was an auspicious moment for visiting the town. It is true that the grass grew in the street here and there, but the sidewalks were separated from the roadway by rows of oaks and elms and china-trees in early leaf. The travellers had left New York in the midst of a snowstorm, but here the scent of lilac and of jonquil, the song of birds, the breath of spring, were all about them. The occasional stretches of brick sidewalk under their green canopy looked cool and inviting; for while the chill of winter had fled and the sultry heat of summer was not yet at hand, the railroad coach had been close and dusty, and the noonday sun gave some slight foretaste of his coming reign.

The colonel looked about him eagerly. It was all so like, and yet so different—shrunken somewhat, and faded, but yet, like a woman one loves, carried into old age something of the charm of youth. The old town, whose ripeness was almost decay, whose quietness was scarcely distinguishable from lethargy, had been the home of his youth, and he saw it, strange to say, less with the eyes of the lad of sixteen who had gone to the war, than with those of the little boy to whom it had been, in his tenderest years, the great wide world, the only world he knew in the years when, with his black boy Peter, whom his father had given to him as a personal attendant, he had gone forth to field and garden, stream and forest, in search of childish adventure. Yonder was the old academy, where he had attended school. The yellow brick of its walls had scaled away in places, leaving the surface mottled with pale splotches; the shingled roof was badly dilapidated, and overgrown here and there with dark green moss. The cedar trees in the yard were in need of pruning, and seemed, from their rusty trunks and scant leafage, to have shared in the general decay. As they drove down the street, cows were grazing in the vacant lot between the bank, which had been built by the colonel's grandfather, and the old red brick building, formerly a store, but now occupied, as could be seen by the row of boxes visible through the open door, by the post-office.

The little boy, an unusually handsome lad of five or six, with blue eyes and fair hair, dressed in knickerbockers and a sailor cap, was also keenly interested in the surroundings. It was Saturday, and the little two-wheeled carts, drawn by a steer or a mule; the pigs sleeping in the shadow of the old wooden market-house; the lean and sallow pinelanders and listless negroes dozing on the curbstone, were all objects of novel interest to the boy, as was manifest by the light in his eager eyes and an occasional exclamation, which in a clear childish treble, came from his perfectly chiselled lips. Only a glance was needed to see that the child, though still somewhat pale and delicate from his recent illness, had inherited the characteristics attributed to good blood. Features, expression, bearing, were marked by the signs of race; but a closer scrutiny was required to discover, in the blue-eyed, golden-haired lad, any close resemblance to the shrewd, dark man of affairs who sat beside him, and to whom this little boy was, for the time being, the sole object in life.

But for the child the colonel was alone in the world. Many years before, when himself only a boy, he had served in the Southern army, in a regiment which had fought with such desperate valour that the honour of the colonelcy had come to him at nineteen, as the sole survivor of the group of young men who had officered the regiment. His father died during the last year of the Civil War, having lived long enough to see the conflict work ruin to his fortunes. The son had been offered employment in New York by a relative who had sympathised with the South in her struggle; and he had gone away from Clarendon. The old family "mansion"—it was not a very imposing structure, except by comparison with even less pretentious houses—had been sold upon foreclosure, and bought by an ambitious mulatto, who only a few years before had himself been an object of barter and sale. Entering his uncle's office as a clerk, and following his advice, reinforced by a sense of the fitness of things, the youthful colonel had dropped his military title and become plain Mr. French. Putting the past behind him, except as a fading memory, he had thrown himself eagerly into the current of affairs. Fortune favoured one both capable and energetic. In time he won a partnership in the firm, and when death removed his relative, took his place at its head.

He had looked forward to the time, not very far in the future, when he might retire from business and devote his leisure to study and travel, tastes which for years he had subordinated to the pursuit of wealth; not entirely, for his life had been many sided; and not so much for the money, as because, being in a game where dollars were the counters, it was his instinct to play it well. He was winning already, and when the bagging trust paid him, for his share of the business, a sum double his investment, he found himself, at some years less than fifty, relieved of business cares and in command of an ample fortune.

This change in the colonel's affairs—and we shall henceforth call him the colonel, because the scene of this story is laid in the South, where titles are seldom ignored, and where the colonel could hardly have escaped his own, even had he desired to do so—this change in the colonel's affairs coincided with that climacteric of the mind, from which, without ceasing to look forward, it turns, at times, in wistful retrospect, toward the distant past, which it sees thenceforward through a mellowing glow of sentiment. Emancipated from the counting room, and ordered South by the doctor, the colonel's thoughts turned easily and naturally to the old town that had given him birth; and he felt a twinge of something like remorse at the reflection that never once since leaving it had he set foot within its borders. For years he had been too busy. His wife had never manifested any desire to visit the South, nor was her temperament one to evoke or sympathise with sentimental reminiscence. He had married, rather late in life, a New York woman, much younger than himself; and while he had admired her beauty and they had lived very pleasantly together, there had not existed between them the entire union of souls essential to perfect felicity, and the current of his life had not been greatly altered by her loss.

Toward little Phil, however, the child she had borne him, his feeling was very different. His young wife had been, after all, but a sweet and pleasant graft upon a sturdy tree. Little Phil was flesh of his flesh and bone of his bone. Upon his only child the colonel lavished all of his affection. Already, to his father's eye, the boy gave promise of a noble manhood. His frame was graceful and active. His hair was even more brightly golden than his mother's had been; his eyes more deeply blue than hers; while his features were a duplicate of his father's at the same age, as was evidenced by a faded daguerreotype among the colonel's few souvenirs of his own childhood. Little Phil had a sweet temper, a loving disposition, and endeared himself to all with whom he came in contact.

The hack, after a brief passage down the main street, deposited the passengers at the front of the Clarendon Hotel. The colonel paid the black driver the quarter he demanded—two dollars would have been the New York price—ran the gauntlet of the dozen pairs of eyes in the heads of the men leaning back in the splint-bottomed armchairs under the shade trees on the sidewalk, registered in the book pushed forward by a clerk with curled mustaches and pomatumed hair, and accompanied by Phil, followed the smiling black bellboy along a passage and up one flight of stairs to a spacious, well-lighted and neatly furnished room, looking out upon the main street.

Three

When the colonel and Phil had removed the dust and disorder of travel from their appearance, they went down to dinner. After they had eaten, the colonel, still accompanied by the child, left the hotel, and following the main street for a short distance, turned into another thoroughfare bordered with ancient elms, and stopped for a moment before an old gray house with high steps and broad piazza—a large, square-built, two-storied house, with a roof sloping down toward the front, broken by dormer windows and buttressed by a massive brick chimney at either end. In spite of the gray monotone to which the paintless years had reduced the once white weatherboarding and green Venetian blinds, the house possessed a certain stateliness of style which was independent of circumstance, and a solidity of construction that resisted sturdily the disintegrating hand of time. Heart-pine and live-oak, mused the colonel, like other things Southern, live long and die hard. The old house had been built of the best materials, and its woodwork dowelled and mortised and tongued and grooved by men who knew their trade and had not learned to scamp their work. For the colonel's grandfather had built the house as a town residence, the family having owned in addition thereto a handsome country place upon a large plantation remote from the town.

The colonel had stopped on the opposite side of the street and was looking intently at the home of his ancestors and of his own youth, when a neatly dressed coloured girl came out on the piazza, seated herself in a rocking-chair with an air of proprietorship, and opened what the colonel perceived to be, even across the street, a copy of a woman's magazine whose circulation, as he knew from the advertising rates that French and Co. had paid for the use of its columns, touched the million mark. Not wishing to seem rude, the colonel moved slowly on down the street. When he turned his head, after going a rod or two, and looked back over his shoulder, the girl had risen and was reentering the house. Her disappearance was promptly followed by the notes of a piano, slightly out of tune, to which some one—presumably the young woman—was singing in a high voice, which might have been better had it been better trained,

"I dreamt that I dwe-elt in ma-arble halls
With vassals and serfs at my si-i-ide."

The colonel had slackened his pace at the sound of the music, but, after the first few bars, started forward with quickened footsteps which he did not relax until little Phil's weight, increasing momentarily, brought home to him the consciousness that his stride was too long for the boy's short legs. Phil, who was a thoroughbred, and would have dropped in his tracks without complaining, was nevertheless relieved when his father's pace returned to the normal.

Their walk led down a hill, and, very soon, to a wooden bridge which spanned a creek some twenty feet below. The colonel paused for a moment beside the railing, and looked up and down the stream. It seemed narrower and more sluggish than his memory had pictured it. Above him the water ran between high banks grown thick with underbrush and over-arching trees; below the bridge, to the right of the creek, lay an open meadow, and to the left, a few rods away, the ruins of the old Eureka cotton mill, which in his boyhood had harboured a flourishing industry, but which had remained, since Sherman's army laid waste the country, the melancholy ruin the colonel had seen it last, when twenty-five years or more before, he left Clarendon to seek a wider career in the outer world. The clear water of the creek rippled harmoniously down a gentle slope and over the site where the great dam at the foot had stood, while birds were nesting in the vines with which kindly nature had sought to cloak the dismantled and crumbling walls.

Mounting the slope beyond the bridge, the colonel's stride now carefully accommodated to the child's puny step, they skirted a low brick wall, beyond which white headstones gleamed in a mass of verdure. Reaching an iron gate, the colonel lifted the latch, and entered the cemetery which had been the object of their visit.

"Is this the place, papa?" asked the little boy.

"Yes, Phil, but it is farther on, in the older part."

They passed slowly along, under the drooping elms and willows, past the monuments on either hand—here, resting on a low brick wall, a slab of marble, once white, now gray and moss-grown, from which the hand of time had well nigh erased the carved inscription; here a family vault, built into the side of a mound of earth, from which only the barred iron door distinguished it; here a pedestal, with a time-worn angel holding a broken fragment of the resurrection trumpet; here a prostrate headstone, and there another bending to its fall; and among them a profusion of rose bushes, on some of which the early roses were already blooming—scarcely a well-kept cemetery, for in many lots the shrubbery grew in wild unpruned luxuriance; nor yet entirely neglected, since others showed the signs of loving care, and an effort had been made to keep the walks clean and clear.

Father and son had traversed half the width of the cemetery, when they came to a spacious lot, surrounded by large trees and containing several monuments. It seemed less neglected than the lots about it, and as they drew nigh they saw among the tombs a very black and seemingly aged Negro engaged in pruning a tangled rose tree. Near him stood a dilapidated basket, partially filled with weeds and leaves, into which he was throwing the dead and superfluous limbs. He seemed very intent upon his occupation, and had not noticed the colonel's and Phil's approach until they had paused at the side of the lot and stood looking at him.

When the old man became aware of their presence, he straightened himself up with the slow movement of one stiff with age or rheumatism and threw them a tentatively friendly look out of a pair of faded eyes.

"Howdy do, uncle," said the colonel. "Will you tell me whose graves these are that you are caring for?"

"Yas, suh," said the old man, removing his battered hat respectfully—the rest of his clothing was in keeping, a picturesque assortment of rags and patches such as only an old Negro can get together, or keep together—"dis hyuh lot, suh, b'longs ter de fambly dat I useter b'long ter—de ol' French fambly, suh, de fines' fambly in Beaver County."

"Why, papa!" cried little Phil, "he means——"

"Hush, Phil! Go on, uncle."

"Yas, suh, de fines' fambly in Cla'endon, suh. Dis hyuh headstone hyuh, suh, an' de little stone at de foot, rep'esents de grave er ol' Gin'al French, w'at fit in de Revolution' Wah, suh; and dis hyuh one nex' to it is de grave er my ol' marster, Majah French, w'at fit in de Mexican Wah, and died endyoin' de wah wid de Yankees, suh."

"Papa," urged Phil, "that's my——"

"Shut up, Phil! Well, uncle, did this interesting old family die out, or is it represented in the present generation?"

"Lawd, no, suh, de fambly did n' die out—'deed dey did n' die out! dey ain't de kind er fambly ter die out! But it's mos' as bad, suh—dey's moved away. Young Mars Henry went ter de Norf, and dey say he's got rich; but he ain't be'n back no mo', suh, an' I don' know whether he's ever comin' er no."

"You must have been very fond of them to take such good care of their graves," said the colonel, much moved, but giving no sign.

"Well, suh, I b'longed ter de fambly, an' I ain' got no chick ner chile er my own, livin', an' dese hyuh dead folks 'pears mo' closer ter me dan anybody e'se. De cullud folks don' was'e much time wid a ole man w'at ain' got nothin', an' dese hyuh new w'ite folks wa't is come up sence de wah, ain' got no use fer niggers, now dat dey don' b'long ter nobody no mo'; so w'en I ain' got nothin' e'se ter do, I comes roun' hyuh, whar I knows ev'ybody and ev'ybody knows me, an' trims de rose bushes an' pulls up de weeds and keeps de grass down jes' lak I s'pose Mars Henry'd 'a' had it done ef he'd 'a' lived hyuh in de ole home, stidder 'way off yandah in de Norf, whar he so busy makin' money dat he done fergot all 'bout his own folks."

"What is your name?" asked the colonel, who had been looking closely at the old man.

"Peter, suh—Peter French. Most er de niggers change' dey names after de wah, but I kept de ole fambly name I wuz raise' by. It wuz good 'nuff fer me, suh; dey ain' none better."

"Oh, papa," said little Phil, unable to restrain himself longer, "he must be some kin to us; he has the same name, and belongs to the same family, and you know you called him 'Uncle.' "

The old Negro had dropped his hat, and was staring at the colonel and the little boy, alternately, with dawning amazement, while a look of recognition crept slowly into his rugged old face.

"Look a hyuh, suh," he said tremulously, "is it?—it can't be!—but dere's de eyes, an' de nose, an' de shape er de head—why, it *must* be my young Mars Henry!"

"Yes," said the colonel, extending his hand to the old man, who grasped it with both his own and shook it up and down with unconventional but very affectionate vigour, "and you are my boy Peter; who took care of me when I was no bigger than Phil here!"

This meeting touched a tender chord in the colonel's nature, already tuned to sympathy with the dead past of which Peter seemed the only survival. The old man's unfeigned delight at their meeting; his retention of the family name, a living witness of its former standing; his respect for the dead; his "family pride," which to the unsympathetic outsider might have seemed grotesque; were proofs of loyalty that moved the colonel deeply. When he himself had been a child of five or six, his father had given him Peter as his own boy. Peter was really not many years older than the colonel, but prosperity had preserved the one, while hard luck had aged the other prematurely. Peter had taken care of him, and taught him to paddle in the shallow water of the creek and to avoid the suck-holes; had taught him simple woodcraft, how to fish, and how to hunt, first with bow and arrow, and later with a shotgun. Through the golden haze of memory the colonel's happy childhood came back to him with a sudden rush of emotion.

"Those were good times, Peter, when we were young," he sighed regretfully, "good times! I have seen none happier."

"Yas, suh! yas, suh! 'Deed dem wuz good ole times! Sho' dey wuz, suh, sho' dey wuz! 'Member dem co'n-stalk fiddles we use' ter make, an' dem elderberry-wood whistles?"

"Yes, Peter, and the robins we used to shoot and the rabbits we used to trap?"

"An' dem watermillions, suh—um-m-m, um-m-m-m!"

"Y-e-s," returned the colonel, with a shade of pensiveness. There had been two sides to the watermelon question. Peter and he had not always been able to find ripe watermelons, early in the season, and at times there had been painful consequences, the memory of which came back to the colonel with surprising ease. Nor had they always been careful about boundaries in those early days. There had been one occasion when an irate neighbour had complained, and Major French had thrashed Henry and Peter both—Peter because he was older, and knew better, and Henry because it was important that he should have impressed upon him, early in life, that of him to whom much is given, much will be required, and that what might be lightly regarded in Peter's case would be a serious offence in his future master's. The lesson had been well learned, for throughout the course of his life the colonel had never shirked responsibility, but had made the performance of duty his criterion of conduct. To him the line of least resistance had always seemed the refuge of the coward and the weakling. With the twenty years preceding his return to Clarendon, this story has nothing to do; but upon the quiet background of his business career he had lived an active intellectual and emotional life, and had developed into one of those rare natures of whom it may be truly said that they are men, and that they count nothing of what is human foreign to themselves.

But the serenity of Peter's retrospect was unmarred by any passing cloud. Those who dwell in darkness find it easier to remember the bright places in their lives.

"Yas, suh, yas, suh, dem watermillions," he repeated with unction, "I kin tas'e 'em now! Dey wuz de be's watermillions dat evuh growed, suh—dey doan raise none lack 'em dese days no mo'. An' den dem chinquapin bushes down by de swamp! 'Member dem chinquapin bushes, whar we killt dat water moccasin dat day? He wuz 'bout ten foot long!"

"Yes, Peter, he was a whopper! Then there were the bullace vines, in the woods beyond the tanyard!"

"Sho' 'nuff, suh! an' de minnows we use' ter ketch in de creek, an' dem perch in de mill pon'?"

For years the colonel had belonged to a fishing club, which preserved an ice-cold stream in a Northern forest. For years the choicest fruits of all the earth had been served daily upon his table. Yet as he looked back to-day no shining trout that had ever risen to his fly had stirred his emotions like the diaphanous minnows, caught, with a crooked pin, in the crooked creek; no luscious fruit had ever matched in sweetness the sour grapes and bitter nuts gathered from the native woods—by him and Peter in their far-off youth.

"Yas, suh, yas, suh," Peter went on, "an' 'member dat time you an' young Mars Jim Wilson went huntin' and fishin' up de country tergether, an' got ti'ed er waitin' on yo'se'ves an' writ back fer me ter come up ter wait on yer and cook fer yer, an' ole Marster say he did n' dare ter let me go 'way off yander wid two keerliss boys lak you-all, wid guns an' boats fer fear I mought git shot, er drownded?"

"It looked, Peter, as though he valued you more than me! more than his own son!"

"Yas, suh, yas, suh! sho' he did, sho' he did! old Marse Philip wuz a monstus keerful man, an' *I* wuz winth somethin', suh, dem times; I wuz wuth five hundred dollahs any day in de yeah. But nobody would n' give five hundred cents fer me now, suh. Dey'd want pay fer takin' me, mos' lakly. Dey ain' none too much room fer a young nigger no mo', let 'lone a' ol' one."

"And what have you been doing all these years, Peter?" asked the colonel.

Peter's story was not a thrilling one; it was no tale of inordinate ambition, no Odyssey of a perilous search for the prizes of life, but the bald recital of a mere struggle for existence. Peter had stayed by his master until his master's death. Then he had worked for a railroad contractor, until exposure and overwork had laid him up with a fever. After his recovery, he had been employed for some years at cutting turpentine boxes in the pine woods, following the trail of the industry southward, until one day his axe had slipped and wounded him severely. When his wound was healed he was told that he was too old and awkward for the turpentine, and that they needed younger and more active men.

"So w'en I got my laig kyo'ed up," said the old man, concluding his story, "I come back hyuh whar I wuz bo'n, suh, and whar my w'ite folks use' ter live, an' whar my frien's use' ter be. But my w'ite folks wuz all in de graveya'd, an' most er my frien's wuz dead er moved away, an' I fin's it kinder lonesome, suh. I goes out an' picks cotton in de fall, an' I does arrants an' little jobs roun' de house fer folks w'at 'll hire me; an' w'en I ain' got nothin' ter eat I kin gor oun' ter de ole house an' wo'k in de gyahden er chop some wood, an' git a meal er vittles f'om ole Mis' Nichols, who's be'n mighty good ter me, suh. She's de barbuh's wife, suh, w'at bought ouah ole house. Dey got mo' dan any yuther colored folks roun' hyuh, but dey he'ps de po', suh, dey he'ps de po'."

"Which speaks well for them, Peter. I'm glad that all the virtue has not yet gone out of the old house."

The old man's talk rambled on, like a sluggish stream, while the colonel's more active mind busied itself with the problem suggested by this unforeseen meeting. Peter and he had both gone out into the world, and they had both returned. He had come back rich and independent. What good had freedom done for Peter? In the colonel's childhood his father's butler, old Madison, had lived a life which, compared to that of Peter at the same age, was one of ease and luxury. How easy the conclusion that the slave's lot had been the more fortunate! But no, Peter had been better free. There were plenty of poor white men, and no one had suggested slavery as an improvement of their condition. Had Peter remained a slave, then the colonel would have remained a master, which was only another form of slavery. The colonel had been emancipated by the same token that had made Peter free. Peter had returned home poor and broken, not because he had been free, but because nature first, and society next, in distributing their gifts, had been niggardly with old Peter. Had he been better equipped, or had a better chance, he might have made a better showing. The colonel had prospered because, having no Peters to work for him, he had been compelled to work for himself. He would set his own success against Peter's failure; and he would take off his hat to the memory of the immortal statesman, who in freeing one race had emancipated another and struck the shackles from a Nation's mind.

Four

While the colonel and old Peter were thus discussing reminiscences in which little Phil could have no share, the boy, with childish curiosity, had wandered off, down one of the shaded paths. When, a little later, the colonel looked around for him, he saw Phil seated on a rustic bench, in conversation with a lady. As the boy seemed entirely comfortable, and the lady not at all disturbed, the colonel did not interrupt them for a while. But when the lady at length rose, holding Phil by the hand, the colonel, fearing that the boy, who was a child of strong impulses, prone to sudden friendships, might be proving troublesome, left his seat on the flat-topped tomb of his Revolutionary ancestor and hastened to meet them.

"I trust my boy hasn't annoyed you," he said, lifting his hat.

"Not at all, sir," returned the lady, in a clear, sweet voice, some haunting tone of which found an answering vibration in the colonel's memory. "On the contrary, he has interested me very much, and in nothing more than in telling me his name. If this and my memory do not deceive me, *you* are Henry French!"

"Yes, and you are—you are Laura Treadwell! How glad I am to meet you! I was coming to call this afternoon."

"I'm glad to see you again. We have always remembered you, and knew that you had grown rich and great, and feared that you had forgotten the old town—and your old friends."

"Not very rich, nor very great, Laura—Miss Treadwell."

"Let it be Laura," she said with a faint colour mounting in her cheek, which had not yet lost its smoothness, as her eyes had not faded, nor her step lost its spring.

"And neither have I forgotten the old home nor the old friends—since I am here and knew you the moment I looked at you and heard your voice."

"And what a dear little boy!" exclaimed Miss Treadwell, looking down at Phil. "He is named Philip—after his grandfather, I reckon?"

"After his grandfather. We have been visiting his grave, and those of all the Frenches; and I found them haunted—by an old retainer, who had come hither, he said, to be with his friends."

"Old Peter! I see him, now and then, keeping the lot in order. There are few like him left, and there were never any too many. But how have you been these many years, and where is your wife? Did you bring her with you?"

"I buried her," returned the colonel, "a little over a year ago. She left me little Phil."

"He must be like her," replied the lady, "and yet he resembles you."

"He has her eyes and hair," said his father. "He is a good little boy and a lad of taste. See how he took to you at first sight! I can always trust Phil's instincts. He is a born gentleman."

"He came of a race of gentlemen," she said. "I'm glad it is not to die out. There are none too many left—in Clarendon. You are going to like me, aren't you, Phil?" asked the lady.

"I like you already," replied Phil gallantly. "You are a very nice lady. What shall I call you?"

"Call her Miss Laura, Phil—it is the Southern fashion—a happy union of familiarity and respect. Already they come back to me, Laura—one breathes them with the air—the gentle Southern customs. With all the faults of the old system, Laura—it carried the seeds of decay within itself and was doomed to perish—a few of us, at least, had a good time. An aristocracy is quite endurable, for the aristocrat, and slavery tolerable, for the masters—and the Peters. When we were young, before the rude hand of war had shattered our illusions, we were very happy, Laura."

"Yes, we were very happy."

They were walking now, very slowly, toward the gate by which the colonel had entered, with little Phil between them, confiding a hand to each.

"And how is your mother?" asked the colonel. "She is living yet, I trust?"

"Yes, but ailing, as she has been for fifteen years—ever since my father died. It was his grave I came to visit."

"You had ever a loving heart, Laura," said the colonel, "given to duty and self-sacrifice. Are you still living in the old place?"

"The old place, only it is older, and shows it—like the rest of us."

She bit her lip at the words, which she meant in reference to herself, but which she perceived, as soon as she had uttered them, might apply to him with equal force. Despising herself for the weakness which he might have interpreted as a bid for a compliment, she was glad that he seemed unconscious of the remark.

The colonel and Phil had entered the cemetery by a side gate and their exit led through the main entrance. Miss Laura pointed out, as they walked slowly along between the elms, the graves of many whom the colonel had known in his younger days. Their names, woven in the tapestry of his memory, needed in most cases but a touch to restore them. For while his intellectual life had ranged far and wide, his business career had run along a single channel, his circle of intimates had not been very large nor very variable, nor was his memory so overlaid that he could not push aside its later impressions in favour of those graven there so deeply in his youth.

Nearing the gate, they passed a small open space in which stood a simple marble shaft, erected to the memory of the Confederate Dead. A wealth of fresh flowers lay at its base. The colonel took off his hat as he stood before it for a moment with bowed head. But for the mercy of God, he might have been one of those whose deaths as well as deeds were thus commemorated.

Beyond this memorial, impressive in its pure simplicity, and between it and the gate, in an obtrusively conspicuous spot stood a florid monument of granite, marble and bronze, of glaring design and strangely out of keeping with the simple dignity and quiet restfulness of the surroundings; a monument so striking that the colonel paused involuntarily and read the inscription in bronze letters on the marble shaft above the granite base:

" '*Sacred to the Memory of*
Joshua Fetters and Elizabeth Fetters, his Wife.
" '*Life's work well done,*
Life's race well run,
Life's crown well won,
Then comes rest.' "

"A beautiful sentiment, if somewhat trite," said the colonel, "but an atrocious monument."

"Do you think so?" exclaimed the lady. "Most people think the monument fine, but smile at the sentiment."

"In matters of taste," returned the colonel, "the majority are always wrong. But why smile at the sentiment? Is it, for some reason, inappropriate to this particular case? Fetters—Fetters—the name seems familiar. Who was Fetters, Laura?"

"He was the speculator," she said, "who bought and sold negroes, and kept dogs to chase runaways; old Mr. Fetters—you must remember old Josh Fetters? When I was a child, my coloured mammy used him for a bogeyman for me, as for her own children."

" 'Look out, honey,' she'd say, 'ef you ain' good, ole Mr. Fettuhs 'll ketch you.' "

Yes, he remembered now. Fetters had been a character in Clarendon—not an admirable character, scarcely a good character, almost a bad character; a necessary adjunct of an evil system, and, like other parasites, worse than the body on which he fed; doing the dirty work of slavery, and very naturally despised by those whose instrument he was, but finding consolation by taking it out of the Negroes in the course of his business. The colonel would have expected Fetters to lie in an unmarked grave in his own back lot, or in the potter's field. Had he so far escaped the ruin of the institution on which he lived, as to leave an estate sufficient to satisfy his heirs and also pay for this expensive but vulgar monument?

"The memorial was erected, as you see from the rest of the inscription, 'by his beloved and affectionate son.' That either loved the other no one suspected, for Bill was harshly treated, and ran away from home at fifteen. He came back after the war, with money, which he lent out at high rates of interest; everything he touched turned to gold; he has grown rich, and is a great man in the State. He was a large contributor to the soldiers' monument."

"But did not choose the design; let us be thankful for that. It might have been like his father's. Bill Fetters rich and great," he mused, "who would have dreamed it? I kicked him once, all the way down Main Street from the schoolhouse to the bank—and dodged his angry mother for a whole month afterward!"

"No one," suggested Miss Laura, "would venture to cross him now. Too many owe him money."

"He went to school at the academy," the colonel went on, unwinding the thread of his memory, "and the rest of the boys looked down on him and made his life miserable. Well, Laura, in Fetters you see one thing that resulted from the war—the poor white boy was given a chance to grow; and if the product is not as yet altogether admirable, taste and culture may come with another generation."

"It is to be hoped they may," said Miss Laura, "and character as well. Mr. Fetters has a son who has gone from college to college, and will graduate from Harvard this summer. They say he is very wild and spends ten thousand dollars a year. I do not see how it can be possible!"

The colonel smiled at her simplicity.

"I have been," he said, "at a college football game, where the gate receipts were fifty thousand dollars, and half a million was said to have changed hands in bets on the result. It is easy to waste money."

"It is a sin," she said, "that some should be made poor, that others may have it to waste."

There was a touch of bitterness in her tone, the instinctive resentment (the colonel thought) of the born aristocrat toward the upstart who had pushed his way above those no longer strong enough to resist. It did not occur to him that her feeling might rest upon any personal ground. It was inevitable that, with the incubus of slavery removed, society should readjust itself in due time upon a democratic basis, and that poor white men, first, and black men next, should reach a level representing the true measure of their talents and their ambition. But it was perhaps equally inevitable that for a generation or two those who had suffered most from the readjustment, should chafe under its seeming injustice.

The colonel was himself a gentleman, and the descendant of a long line of gentlemen. But he had lived too many years among those who judged the tree by its fruit, to think that blood alone entitled him to any special privileges. The consciousness of honourable ancestry might make one clean of life, gentle of manner, and just in one's dealings. In so far as it did this it was something to be cherished, but scarcely to be boasted of, for democracy is impatient of any excellence not born of personal effort, of any pride save that of achievement. He was glad that Fetters had got on in the world. It justified a fine faith in humanity, that wealth and power should have been attained by the poor white lad, over whom, with a boy's unconscious brutality, he had tyrannised in his childhood. He could have wished for Bill a better taste in monuments, and better luck in sons, if rumour was correct about Fetters's boy. But, these, perhaps, were points where blood *did* tell. There was something in blood, after all, Nature might make a great man from any sort of material: hence the virtue of democracy, for the world needs great men, and suffers from their lack, and welcomes them from any source. But fine types were a matter of breeding and were perhaps worth the trouble of preserving, if their existence were compatible with the larger good. He wondered if Bill ever recalled that progress down Main Street in which he had played so conspicuous a part, or still bore any resentment toward the other participants?

"Could your mother see me," he asked, as they reached the gate, "if I went by the house?"

"She would be glad to see you. Mother lives in the past, and you would come to her as part of it. She often speaks of you. It is only a short distance. You have not forgotten the way?"

They turned to the right, in a direction opposite to that from which the colonel had reached the cemetery. After a few minutes' walk, in the course of which they crossed another bridge over the same winding creek, they mounted the slope beyond, opened a gate, climbed a short flight of stone steps and found themselves in an enchanted garden, where lilac bush and jessamine vine reared their heads high, tulip and daffodil pushed their way upward, but were all dominated by the intenser fragrance of the violets.

Old Peter had followed the party at a respectful distance, but, seeing himself forgotten, he walked past the gate, after they had entered it, and went, somewhat disconsolately, on his way. He had stopped, and was looking back toward the house—Clarendon was a great place for looking back, perhaps because there was little in the town to which to look forward—when a white man, wearing a tinned badge upon his coat, came up, took Peter by the arm and led him away, despite some feeble protests on the old man's part.

Five

At the end of the garden stood a frame house with a wide, columned porch. It had once been white, and the windows closed with blinds that still retained a faded tint of green. Upon the porch, in a comfortable arm chair, sat an old lady, wearing a white cap, under which her white hair showed at the sides, and holding her hands, upon which she wore black silk mits, crossed upon her lap. On the top step, at opposite ends, sat two young people—one of them a rosy-cheeked girl, in the bloom of early youth, with a head of rebellious brown hair. She had been reading a book held open in her hand. The other was a long-legged, lean, shy young man, of apparently twenty-three or twenty-four, with black hair and eyes and a swarthy complexion. From the jack-knife beside him, and the shavings scattered around, it was clear that he had been whittling out the piece of pine that he was adjusting, with some nicety, to a wooden model of some mechanical contrivance which stood upon the floor beside him. They were a strikingly handsome couple, of ideally contrasting types.

"Mother," said Miss Treadwell, "this is Henry French—Colonel French—who has come back from the North to visit his old home and the graves of his ancestors. I found him in the cemetery; and this is his dear little boy, Philip—named after his grandfather."

The old lady gave the colonel a slender white hand, thin almost to transparency.

"Henry," she said, in a silvery thread of voice, "I am glad to see you. You must excuse my not rising—I can't walk without help. You are like your father, and even more like your grandfather, and your little boy takes after the family." She drew Phil toward her and kissed him.

Phil accepted this attention amiably. Meantime the young people had risen.

"This," said Miss Treadwell, laying her hand affectionately on the girl's arm, "is my niece Graciella—my brother Tom's child. Tom is dead, you know, these eight years and more, and so is Graciella's mother, and she has lived with us."

Graciella gave the colonel her hand with engaging frankness. "I'm sure we're awfully glad to see anybody from the North," she said. "Are you familiar with New York?"

"I left there only day before yesterday," replied the colonel.

"And this," said Miss Treadwell, introducing the young man, who, when he unfolded his long legs, rose to a rather imposing height, "this is Mr. Ben Dudley."

"The son of Malcolm Dudley, of Mink Run, I suppose? I'm glad to meet you," said the colonel, giving the young man's hand a cordial grasp.

"His nephew, sir," returned young Dudley. "My uncle never married."

"Oh, indeed? I did not know; but he is alive, I trust, and well?"

"Alive, sir, but very much broken. He has not been himself for years."

"You find things sadly changed, Henry," said Mrs. Treadwell. "They have never been the same since the surrender. Our people are poor now, right poor, most of them, though we ourselves were fortunate enough to have something left."

"We have enough left for supper, mother," interposed Miss Laura quickly, "to which we are going to ask Colonel French to stay."

"I suppose that in New York every one has dinner at six, and supper after the theatre or the concert?" said Graciella, inquiringly.

"The fortunate few," returned the colonel, smiling into her eager face, "who can afford a seat at the opera, and to pay for and digest two meals, all in the same evening."

"And now, colonel," said Miss Treadwell, "I'm going to see about the supper. Mother will talk to you while I am gone."

"I must be going," said young Dudley.

"Won't you stay to supper, Ben?" asked Miss Laura.

"No, Miss Laura; I'd like to, but uncle wasn't well to-day and I must stop by the drug store and get some medicine for him. Dr. Price gave me a prescription on my way in. Good-bye, sir," he added, addressing the colonel. "Will you be in town long?"

"I really haven't decided. A day or two, perhaps a week. I am not bound, at present, by any business ties—am foot-loose, as we used to say when I was young. I shall follow my inclinations."

"Then I hope, sir, that you'll feel inclined to pay us a long visit and that I shall see you many times."

As Ben Dudley, after this courteous wish, stepped down from the piazza, Graciella rose and walked with him along the garden path. She was tall as most women, but only reached his shoulder.

"Say, Graciella," he asked, "won't you give me an answer."

"I'm thinking about it, Ben. If you could take me away from this dead old town, with its lazy white people and its trifling niggers, to a place where there's music and art, and life and society—where there's something going on all the time, I'd *like* to marry you. But if I did so now, you'd take me out to your rickety old house, with your daffy old uncle and his dumb old housekeeper, and I should lose my own mind in a week or ten days. When you can promise to take me to New York, I'll promise to marry you, Ben. I want to travel, and to see things, to visit the art galleries and libraries, to hear Patti, and to look at the millionaires promenading on Fifth Avenue—and I'll marry the man who'll take me there!"

"Uncle Malcolm can't live forever, Graciella—though I wouldn't wish his span shortened by a single day—and I'll get the plantation. And then, you know," he added, hesitating, "we may—we may find the money."

Graciella shook her head compassionately. "No, Ben, you'll never find the money. There isn't any; it's all imagination—moonshine. The war unsettled your uncle's brain, and he dreamed the money."

"It's as true as I'm standing here, Graciella," replied Ben, earnestly, "that there's money—gold—somewhere about the house. Uncle couldn't imagine paper and ink, and I've seen the letter from my uncle's uncle Ralph—I'll get it and bring it to you. Some day the money will turn up, and then may be I'll be able to take you away. Meantime some one must look after uncle and the place; there's no one else but me to do it. Things must grow better some time—they always do, you know."

"They couldn't be much worse," returned Graciella, discontentedly.

"Oh, they'll be better—they're bound to be! They'll just have to be. And you'll wait for me, won't you, Graciella?"

"Oh, I suppose I'll have to. You're around here so much that every one else is scared away, and there isn't much choice at the best; all the young men worth having are gone away already. But you know my ultimatum—I must get to New York. If you are ready before any one else speaks, you may take me there."

"You're hard on a poor devil, Graciella. I don't believe you care a bit for me, or you wouldn't talk like that. Don't you suppose I have any feelings, even if I ain't much account? Ain't I worth as much as a trip up North?"

"Why should I waste my time with you, if I didn't care for you?" returned Graciella, begging the question. "Here's a rose, in token of my love."

She plucked the flower and thrust it into his hand.

"It's full of thorns, like your love," he said ruefully, as he picked the sharp points out of his fingers.

" 'Faithful are the wounds of a friend,' " returned the girl. "See Psalms, xxvii: 6."

"Take care of my cotton press, Graciella; I'll come in to-morrow evening and work on it some more. I'll bring some cotton along to try it with."

"You'll probably find some excuse—you always do."

"Don't you want me to come?" he asked with a trace of resentment. "I can stay away, if you don't."

"Oh, you come so often that I—I suppose I'd miss you, if you didn't! One must have some company, and half a loaf is better than no bread."

He went on down the hill, turning at the corner for a lingering backward look at his tyrant. Graciella, bending her head over the wall, followed his movements with a swift tenderness in her sparkling brown eyes.

"I love him better than anything on earth," she sighed, "but it would never do to tell him so. He'd get so conceited that I couldn't manage him any longer, and so lazy that he'd never exert himself. I must get away from this town before I'm old and gray—I'll be seventeen next week, and an old maid in next to no time—and Ben must take me away. But I must be his inspiration; he'd never do it by himself. I'll go now and talk to that dear old Colonel French about the North; I can learn a great deal from him. And he doesn't look so old either," she mused, as she went back up the walk to where the colonel sat on the piazza talking to the other ladies.

Six

The colonel spent a delightful evening in the company of his friends. The supper was typically Southern, and the cook evidently a good one. There was smothered chicken, light biscuit, fresh eggs, poundcake and tea. The tablecloth and napkins were of fine linen. That they were soft and smooth the colonel noticed, but he did not observe closely enough to see that they had been carefully darned in many places. The silver spoons were of fine, old-fashioned patterns, worn very thin—so thin that even the colonel was struck by their fragility. How charming, he thought, to prefer the simple dignity of the past to the vulgar ostentation of a more modern time. He had once dined off a golden dinner service, at the table of a multi-millionaire, and had not enjoyed the meal half so much. The dining-room looked out upon the garden and the perfume of lilac and violet stole in through the open windows. A soft-footed, shapely, well-trained negro maid, in white cap and apron, waited deftly upon the table; a woman of serious countenance—so serious that the colonel wondered if she were a present-day type of her race, and if the responsibilities of freedom had robbed her people of their traditional light-heartedness and gaiety.

After supper they sat out upon the piazza. The lights within were turned down low, so that the moths and other insects might not be attracted. Sweet odours from the garden filled the air. Through the elms the stars, brighter than in more northern latitudes, looked out from a sky of darker blue; so bright were they that the colonel, looking around for the moon, was surprised to find that luminary invisible. On the green background of the foliage the fireflies glowed and flickered. There was no strident steam whistle from factory or train to assault the ear, no rumble of passing cabs or street cars. Far away, in some distant part of the straggling town, a sweet-toned bell sounded the hour of an evening church service.

"To see you is a breath from the past, Henry," said Mrs. Treadwell. "You are a fine, strong man now, but I can see you as you were, the day you went away to the war, in your new gray uniform, on your fine gray horse, at the head of your company. You were going to take Peter with you, but he had got his feet poisoned with poison ivy, and couldn't walk, and your father gave you another boy, and Peter cried like a baby at being left behind. I can remember how proud you were, and how proud your father was, when he gave you his sword—your grandfather's sword, and told you never to draw it or sheath it, except in honour; and how, when you were gone, the old gentleman shut himself up for two whole days and would speak to no one. He was glad and sorry—glad to send you to fight for your country, and sorry to see you go—for you were his only boy."

The colonel thrilled with love and regret. His father had loved him, he knew very well, and he had not visited his tomb for twenty-five years. How far away it seemed too, the time when he had thought of the Confederacy as his country! And the sword, his grandfather's sword, had been for years stored away in a dark closet. His father had kept it displayed upon the drawing-room wall, over the table on which the family Bible had rested.

Mrs. Treadwell was silent for a moment.

"Times have changed since then, Henry. We have lost a great deal, although we still have enough—yes, we have plenty to live upon, and to hold up our heads among the best."

Miss Laura and Graciella, behind the colonel's back, exchanged meaning glances. How well they knew how little they had to live upon!

"That is quite evident," said the colonel, glancing through the window at the tasteful interior, "and I am glad to see that you have fared so well. My father lost everything."

"We were more fortunate," said Mrs. Treadwell. "We were obliged to let Belleview go when Major Treadwell died—there were debts to be paid, and we were robbed as well—but we have several rentable properties in town, and an estate in the country which brings us in an income. But things are not quite what they used to be!"

Mrs. Treadwell sighed, and nodded. Miss Laura sat in silence—a pensive silence. She, too, remembered the time gone by, but unlike her mother's life, her own had only begun as the good times were ending. Her mother, in her youth, had seen something of the world. The daughter of a wealthy planter, she had spent her summers at Saratoga, had visited New York and Philadelphia and New Orleans, and had taken a voyage to Europe. Graciella was young and beautiful. Her prince might come, might be here even now, if this grand gentleman should chance to throw the handkerchief. But she, Laura, had passed her youth in a transition period; the pleasures neither of memory nor of hope had been hers—except such memories as came of duty well performed, and such hopes as had no root in anything earthly or corruptible.

Graciella was not in a reflective mood, and took up the burden of the conversation where her grandmother had dropped it. Her thoughts were not of the past, but of the future. She asked many eager questions of New York. Was it true that ladies at the Waldorf-Astoria always went to dinner in low-cut bodices with short sleeves, and was evening dress always required at the theatre? Did the old Knickerbocker families recognise the Vanderbilts? Were the Rockefellers anything at all socially? Did he know Ward McAllister, at that period the Beau Brummel of the metropolitan smart set? Was Fifth Avenue losing its pre-eminence? On what days of the week was the Art Museum free to the public? What was the fare to New York, and the best quarter of the city in which to inquire for a quiet, select boarding house where a Southern lady of refinement and good family might stay at a reasonable price, and meet some nice people? And would he recommend stenography or magazine work, and which did he consider preferable, as a career which such a young lady might follow without injury to her social standing?

The colonel, with some amusement, answered these artless inquiries as best he could; they came as a refreshing foil to the sweet but melancholy memories of the past. They were interesting, too, from this very pretty but very ignorant little girl in this backward little Southern town. She was a flash of sunlight through a soft gray cloud; a vigorous shoot from an old moss-covered stump—she was life, young life, the vital principle, breaking through the cumbering envelope, and asserting its right to reach the sun.

After a while a couple of very young ladies, friends of Graciella, dropped in. They were introduced to the colonel, who found that he had known their fathers, or their mothers, or their grandfathers, or their grandmothers, and that many of them were more or less distantly related. A little later a couple of young men, friends of Graciella's friends—also very young, and very self-conscious—made their appearance, and were duly introduced, in person and by pedigree. The conversation languished for a moment, and then one of the young ladies said something about music, and one of the young men remarked that he had brought over a new song. Graciella begged the colonel to excuse them, and led the way to the parlour, followed by her young friends.

Mrs. Treadwell had fallen asleep, and was leaning comfortably back in her armchair. Miss Laura excused herself, brought a veil, and laid it softly across her mother's face.

"The night air is not damp," she said, "and it is pleasanter for her here than in the house. She won't mind the music; she is accustomed to it."

Graciella went to the piano and with great boldness of touch struck the bizarre opening chords and then launched into the grotesque words of the latest New York "coon song," one of the first and worst of its kind, and the other young people joined in the chorus.

It was the first discordant note. At home, the colonel subscribed to the opera, and enjoyed the music. A plantation song of the olden time, as he remembered it, borne upon the evening air, when sung by the tired slaves at the end of their day of toil, would have been pleasing, with its simple melody, its plaintive minor strains, its notes of vague longing; but to the colonel's senses there was to-night no music in this hackneyed popular favourite. In a metropolitan music hall, gaudily bedecked and brilliantly lighted, it would have been tolerable from the lips of a black-face comedian. But in this quiet place, upon this quiet night, and in the colonel's mood, it seemed like profanation. The song of the coloured girl, who had dreamt that she dwelt in marble halls, and the rest, had been less incongruous; it had at least breathed aspiration.

Mrs. Treadwell was still dozing in her armchair. The colonel, beckoning Miss Laura to follow him, moved to the farther end of the piazza, where they might not hear the singers and the song.

"It is delightful here, Laura. I seem to have renewed my youth. I yield myself a willing victim to the charm of the old place, the old ways, the old friends."

"You see our best side, Henry. Night has a kindly hand, that covers our defects, and the starlight throws a glamour over everything. You see us through a haze of tender memories. When you have been here a week, the town will seem dull, and narrow, and sluggish. You will find us ignorant and backward, worshipping our old idols, and setting up no new ones; our young men leaving us, and none coming in to take their place. Had you, and men like you, remained with us, we might have hoped for better things."

"And perhaps not, Laura. Environment controls the making of men. Some rise above it, the majority do not. We might have followed in the well-worn rut. But let us not spoil this delightful evening by speaking of anything sad or gloomy. This is your daily life; to me it is like a scene from a play, over which one sighs to see the curtain fall—all enchantment, all light, all happiness."

But even while he spoke of light, a shadow loomed up beside them. The coloured woman who had waited at the table came around the house from the back yard and stood by the piazza railing.

"Miss Laura!" she called, softly and appealingly. "Kin you come hyuh a minute?"

"What is it, Catherine?"

"Kin I speak just a word to you, ma'am? It's somethin' partic'lar—mighty partic'lar, ma'am."

"Excuse me a minute, Henry," said Miss Laura, rising with evident reluctance.

She stepped down from the piazza, and walked beside the woman down one of the garden paths. The colonel, as he sat there smoking—with Miss Laura's permission he had lighted a cigar—could see the light stuff of the lady's gown against the green background, though she was walking in the shadow of the elms. From the murmur which came to him, he gathered that the black woman was pleading earnestly, passionately, and he could hear Miss Laura's regretful voice, as she closed the interview:

"I am sorry, Catherine, but it is simply impossible. I would if I could, but I cannot."

The woman came back first, and as she passed by an open window, the light fell upon her face, which showed signs of deep distress, hardening already into resignation or despair. She was probably in trouble of some sort, and her mistress had not been able, doubtless for some good reason, to help her out. This suspicion was borne out by the fact that when Miss Laura came back to him, she too seemed troubled. But since she did not speak of the matter, the colonel gave no sign of his own thoughts.

"You have said nothing of yourself, Laura," he said, wishing to divert her mind from anything unpleasant. "Tell me something of your own life—it could only be a cheerful theme, for you have means and leisure, and a perfect environment. Tell me of your occupations, your hopes, your aspirations."

"There is little enough to tell, Henry," she returned, with a sudden courage, "but that little shall be the truth. You will find it out, if you stay long in town, and I would rather you learned it from our lips than from others less friendly. My mother is—my mother—a dear, sweet woman to whom I have devoted my life! But we are not well off, Henry. Our parlour carpet has been down for twenty-five years; surely you must have recognised the pattern! The house has not been painted for the same length of time; it is of heart pine, and we train the flowers and vines to cover it as much as may be, and there are many others like it, so it is not conspicuous. Our rentable property is three ramshackle cabins on the alley at the rear of the lot, for which we get four dollars a month each, when we can collect it. Our country estate is a few acres of poor land, which we rent on shares, and from which we get a few bushels of corn, an occasional load of firewood, and a few barrels of potatoes. As for my own life, I husband our small resources; I keep the house, and wait on mother, as I have done since she became helpless, ten years ago. I look after Graciella. I teach in the Sunday School, and I give to those less fortunate such help as the poor can give the poor."

"How did you come to lose Belleview?" asked the colonel, after a pause. "I had understood Major Treadwell to be one of the few people around here who weathered the storm of war and emerged financially sound."

"He did; and he remained so—until he met Mr. Fetters, who had made money out of the war while all the rest were losing. Father despised the slavetrader's son, but admired his ability to get along. Fetters made his acquaintance, flattered him, told him glowing stories of wealth to be made by speculating in cotton and turpentine. Father was not a business man, but he listened. Fetters lent him money, and father lent Fetters money, and they had transactions back and forth, and jointly. Father lost and gained and we had no inkling that he had suffered greatly, until, at his sudden death, Fetters foreclosed a mortgage he held upon Belleview. Mother has always believed there was something wrong about the transaction, and that father was not indebted to Fetters in any such sum as Fetters claimed. But we could find no papers and we had no proof, and Fetters took the plantation for his debt. He changed its name to Sycamore; he wanted a post-office there, and there were too many Belleviews."

"Does he own it still?"

"Yes, and runs it—with convict labour! The thought makes me shudder! We were rich when he was poor; we are poor and he is rich. But we trust in God, who has never deserted the widow and the fatherless. By His mercy we have lived and, as mother says, held up our heads, not in pride or haughtiness, but in self-respect, for we cannot forget what we were."

"Nor what you are, Laura, for you are wonderful," said the colonel, not unwilling to lighten a situation that bordered on intensity. "You should have married and had children. The South needs such mothers as you would have made. Unless the men of Clarendon have lost their discernment, unless chivalry has vanished and the fire died out of the Southern blood, it has not been for lack of opportunity that your name remains unchanged."

Miss Laura's cheek flushed unseen in the shadow of the porch.

"Ah, Henry, that would be telling! But to marry me, one must have married the family, for I could not have left them—they have had only me. I have not been unhappy. I do not know that I would have had my life different."

Graciella and her friends had finished their song, the piano had ceased to sound, and the visitors were taking their leave. Graciella went with them to the gate, where they stood laughing and talking. The colonel looked at his watch by the light of the open door.

"It is not late," he said. "If my memory is true, you too played the piano when you—when I was young."

"It is the same piano, Henry, and, like our life here, somewhat thin and weak of tone. But if you think it would give you pleasure, I will play—as well as I know how."

She readjusted the veil, which had slipped from her mother's face, and they went into the parlour. From a pile of time-stained music she selected a sheet and seated herself at the piano. The colonel stood at her elbow. She had a pretty back, he thought, and a still youthful turn of the head, and still plentiful, glossy brown hair. Her hands were white, slender and well kept, though he saw on the side of the forefinger of her left hand the telltale marks of the needle.

The piece was an arrangement of the well-known air from the opera of *Maritana:*

"Scenes that are brightest,
May charm awhile,
Hearts which are lightest
And eyes that smile.
Yet o'er them above us,
Though nature beam,
With none to love us,
How sad they seem!"

Under her sympathetic touch a gentle stream of melody flowed from the old-time piano, scarcely stronger toned in its decrepitude, than the spinet of a former century. A few moments before, under Graciella's vigorous hands, it had seemed to protest at the dissonances it had been compelled to emit; now it seemed to breathe the notes of the old opera with an almost human love and tenderness. It, too, mused the colonel, had lived and loved and was recalling the memories of a brighter past.

The music died into silence. Mrs. Treadwell was awake.

"Laura!" she called.

Miss Treadwell went to the door.

"I must have been nodding for a minute. I hope Colonel French did not observe it—it would scarcely seem polite. He hasn't gone yet?"

"No, mother, he is in the parlour."

"I must be going," said the colonel, who came to the door. "I had almost forgotten Phil, and it is long past his bedtime."

Miss Laura went to wake up Phil, who had fallen asleep after supper. He was still rubbing his eyes when the lady led him out.

"Wake up, Phil," said the colonel. "It's time to be going. Tell the ladies good night."

Graciella came running up the walk.

"Why, Colonel French," she cried, "you are not going already? I made the others leave early so that I might talk to you."

"My dear young lady," smiled the colonel, "I have already risen to go, and if I stayed longer I might wear out my welcome, and Phil would surely go to sleep again. But I will come another time—I shall stay in town several days."

"Yes, *do* come, if you *must* go," rejoined Graciella with emphasis. "I want to hear more about the North, and about New York society and—oh, everything! Good night, Philip. *Good* night, Colonel French."

"Beware of the steps, Henry," said Miss Laura, "the bottom stone is loose."

They heard his footsteps in the quiet street, and Phil's light patter beside him.

"He's a lovely man, isn't he, Aunt Laura?" said Graciella.

"He is a gentleman," replied her aunt, with a pensive look at her young niece."

"Of the old school," piped Mrs. Treadwell.

"And Philip is a sweet child," said Miss Laura.

"A chip of the old block," added Mrs. Treadwell. "I remember——"

"Yes, mother, you can tell me when I've shut up the house," interrupted Miss Laura. "Put out the lamps, Graciella—there's not much oil—and when you go to bed hang up your gown carefully, for it takes me nearly half an hour to iron it."

"And you are right good to do it! Good night, dear Aunt Laura! Good night, grandma!"

Mr. French had left the hotel at noon that day as free as air, and he slept well that night, with no sense of the forces that were to constrain his life. And yet the events of the day had started the growth of a dozen tendrils, which were destined to grow, and reach out, and seize and hold him with ties that do not break.

Seven

The constable who had arrested old Peter led his prisoner away through alleys and quiet streets—though for that matter all the streets of Clarendon were quiet in midafternoon—to a guardhouse or calaboose, constructed of crumbling red brick, with a rusty, barred iron door secured by a heavy padlock. As they approached this structure, which was sufficiently forbidding in appearance to depress the most lighthearted, the strumming of a banjo became audible, accompanying a mellow Negro voice which was singing, to a very ragged ragtime air, words of which the burden was something like this:

"W'at's de use er my wo'kin' so hahd?
I got a' 'oman in de white man's yahd.
W'en she cook chicken, she save me a wing;
W'en dey 'low I'm wo'kin', I ain' doin' a thing!"

The grating of the key in the rusty lock interrupted the song. The constable thrust his prisoner into the dimly lighted interior, and locked the door.

"Keep over to the right," he said curtly, "that's the niggers' side."

"But, Mistah Haines," asked Peter, excitedly, "is I got to stay here all night? I ain' done nuthin'."

"No, that's the trouble; you ain't done nuthin' fer a month, but loaf aroun'. You ain't got no visible means of suppo't, so you're took up for vagrancy."

"But I does wo'k we'n I kin git any wo'k ter do," the old man expostulated. "An' ef I kin jus' git wo'd ter de right w'ite folks, I'll be outer here in half a' hour; dey'll go my bail."

"They can't go yo' bail to-night, fer the squire's gone home. I'll bring you some bread and meat, an' some whiskey if you want it, and you'll be tried to-morrow mornin'."

Old Peter still protested.

"You niggers are always kickin'," said the constable, who was not without a certain grim sense of humour, and not above talking to a Negro when there were no white folks around to talk to, or to listen. "I never see people so hard to satisfy. You ain' got no home, an' here I've give' you a place to sleep, an' you're kickin'. You doan know from one day to another where you'll git yo' meals, an' I offer you bread and meat and whiskey—an' you're kickin'! You say you can't git nothin' to do, an' yit with the prospect of a reg'lar job befo' you to-morrer—you're kickin'! I never see the beat of it in all my bo'n days."

When the constable, chuckling at his own humour, left the guardhouse, he found his way to a nearby barroom, kept by one Clay Jackson, a place with an evil reputation as the resort of white men of a low class. Most crimes of violence in the town could be traced to its influence, and more than one had been committed within its walls.

"Has Mr. Turner been in here?" demanded Haines of the man in charge.

The bartender, with a backward movement of his thumb, indicated a door opening into a room at the rear. Here the constable found his man—a burly, bearded giant, with a red face, a cunning eye and an overbearing manner. He had a bottle and a glass before him, and was unsociably drinking alone.

"Howdy, Haines," said Turner, "How's things? How many have you got this time?"

"I've got three rounded up, Mr. Turner, an' I'll take up another befo' night. That'll make fo'—fifty dollars fer me, an' the res' fer the squire."

"That's good," rejoined Turner. "Have a glass of liquor. How much do you s'pose the Squire'll fine Bud?"

"Well," replied Haines, drinking down the glass of whiskey at a gulp, "I reckon about twenty-five dollars."

"You can make it fifty just as easy," said Turner. "Niggers are all just a passell o' black fools. Bud would 'a' b'en out now, if it had n't be'n for me. I bought him fer six months. I kept close watch of him for the first five, and then along to'ds the middle er the las' month I let on I'd got keerliss, an' he run away. Course I put the dawgs on 'im, an' followed 'im here, where his woman is, an' got you after 'im, and now he's good for six months more."

"The woman is a likely gal an' a good cook," said Haines. "*She'd* be wuth a good 'eal to you out at the stockade."

"That's a shore fact," replied the other, "an' I need another good woman to help aroun'. If we'd 'a' thought about it, an' give' her a chance to hide Bud and feed him befo' you took 'im up, we could 'a' filed a charge ag'inst her for harborin' 'im."

"Well, I kin do it nex' time, fer he'll run away ag'in—they always do. Bud's got a vile temper."

"Yes, but he's a good field-hand, and I'll keep his temper down. Have somethin' mo'?"

"I've got to go back now and feed the pris'ners," said Haines, rising after he had taken another drink; "an' I'll stir Bud up so he'll raise h—ll, an' to-morrow morning I'll make another charge against him that'll fetch his fine up to fifty and costs."

"Which will give 'im to me till the cotton crop is picked, and several months more to work on the Jackson Swamp ditch if Fetters gits the contract. You stand by us here, Haines, an' help me git all the han's I can out o' this county, and I'll give you a job at Sycamo' when yo'r time's up here as constable. Go on and feed the niggers, an' stir up Bud, and I'll be on hand in the mornin' when court opens."

When the lesser of these precious worthies left his superior to his cups, he stopped in the barroom and bought a pint of rotgut whiskey—a cheap brand of rectified spirits coloured and flavoured to resemble the real article, to which it bore about the relation of vitriol to lye. He then went into a cheap eating house, conducted by a Negro for people of his own kind, where he procured some slices of fried bacon, and some soggy corn bread, and with these various purchases, wrapped in a piece of brown paper, he betook himself to the guard-house. He unlocked the door, closed it behind him, and called Peter. The old man came forward.

"Here, Peter," said Haines, "take what you want of this, and give some to them other fellows, and if there's anything left after you've got what you want, throw it to that sulky black hound over yonder in the corner."

He nodded toward a young Negro in the rear of the room, the Bud Johnson who had been the subject of the conversation with Turner. Johnson replied with a curse. The constable advanced menacingly, his hand moving toward his pocket. Quick as a flash the Negro threw himself upon him. The other prisoners, from instinct, or prudence, or hope of reward, caught him, pulled him away and held him off until Haines, pale with rage, rose to his feet and began kicking his assailant vigorously. With the aid of well-directed blows of his fists he forced the Negro down, who, unable to regain his feet, finally, whether from fear or exhaustion, lay inert, until the constable, having worked off his worst anger, and not deeming it to his advantage seriously to disable the prisoner, in whom he had a pecuniary interest, desisted from further punishment.

"I might send you to the penitentiary for this," he said, panting for breath, "but I'll send you to h—ll instead. You'll be sold back to Mr. Fetters for a year or two tomorrow, and in three months I'll be down at Sycamore as an overseer, and then I'll learn you to strike a white man, you——"

The remainder of the objurgation need not be told, but there was no doubt, from the expression on Haines's face, that he meant what he said, and that he would take pleasure in repaying, in overflowing measure, any arrears of revenge against the offending prisoner which he might consider his due. He had stirred Bud up very successfully—much more so, indeed, than he had really intended. He had meant to procure evidence against Bud, but had hardly thought to carry it away in the shape of a black eye and a swollen nose.

Eight

When the colonel set out next morning for a walk down the main street, he had just breakfasted on boiled brook trout, fresh laid eggs, hot muffins and coffee, and was feeling at peace with all mankind. He was alone, having left Phil in charge of the hotel housekeeper. He had gone only a short distance when he reached a door around which several men were lounging, and from which came the sound of voices and loud laughter. Stopping, he looked with some curiosity into the door, over which there was a faded sign to indicate that it was the office of a Justice of the Peace—a pleasing collocation of words, to those who could divorce it from any technical significance—Justice, Peace—the seed and the flower of civilisation.

An unwashed, dingy-faced young negro, clothed in rags unspeakably vile, which scarcely concealed his nakedness, was standing in the midst of a group of white men, toward whom he threw now and then a shallow and shifty glance. The air was heavy with the odour of stale tobacco, and the floor dotted with discarded portions of the weed. A white man stood beside a desk and was addressing the audience:

"Now, gentlemen, here's Lot Number Three, a likely young nigger who answers to the name of Sam Brown. Not much to look at, but will make a good field hand, if looked after right and kept away from liquor; used to workin', when in the chain gang, where he's been, off and on, since he was ten years old. Amount of fine an' costs thirty-seven dollars an' a half. A musical nigger, too, who plays the banjo, an' sings jus' like a—like a blackbird. What am I bid for this prime lot?"

The negro threw a dull glance around the crowd with an air of detachment which seemed to say that he was not at all interested in the proceedings. The colonel viewed the scene with something more than curious interest. The fellow looked like an habitual criminal, or at least like a confirmed loafer. This must be one of the idle and worthless blacks with so many of whom the South was afflicted. This was doubtless the method provided by law for dealing with them.

"One year," answered a voice.

"Nine months," said a second.

"Six months," came a third bid, from a tall man with a buggy whip under his arm.

"Are you all through, gentlemen? Six months' labour for thirty-seven fifty is mighty cheap, and you know the law allows you to keep the labourer up to the mark. Are you all done? Sold to Mr. Turner, for Mr. Fetters, for six months."

The prisoner's dull face showed some signs of apprehension when the name of his purchaser was pronounced, and he shambled away uneasily under the constable's vigilant eye.

"The case of the State against Bud Johnson is next in order. Bring in the prisoner."

The constable brought in the prisoner, handcuffed, and placed him in front of the Justice's desk, where he remained standing. He was a short, powerfully built negro, seemingly of pure blood, with a well-rounded head, not unduly low in the brow and quite broad between the ears. Under different circumstances his countenance might have been pleasing; at present it was set in an expression of angry defiance. He had walked with a slight limp, there were several contusions upon his face; and upon entering the room he had thrown a defiant glance around him, which had not quailed even before the stern eye of the tall man, Turner, who, as the agent of the absent Fetters, had bid on Sam Brown. His face then hardened into the blank expression of one who stands in a hostile presence.

"Bud Johnson," said the justice, "you are charged with escaping from the service into which you were sold to pay the fine and costs on a charge of vagrancy. What do you plead—guilty or not guilty?"

The prisoner maintained a sullen silence.

"I'll enter a plea of not guilty. The record of this court shows that you were convicted of vagrancy on December 26th, and sold to Mr. Fetters for four months to pay your fine and costs. The four months won't be up for a week. Mr. Turner may be sworn."

Turner swore to Bud's escape and his pursuit. Haines testified to his capture.

"Have you anything to say?" asked the justice.

"What's de use er my sayin' anything," muttered the Negro. "It won't make no diff'ence. I didn' do nothin', in de fus' place, ter be fine' fer, an' run away 'cause dey did n' have no right ter keep me dere."

"Guilty. Twenty-five dollars an' costs. You are also charged with resisting the officer who made the arrest. Guilty or not guilty? Since you don't speak, I'll enter a plea of not guilty. Mr. Haines may be sworn."

Haines swore that the prisoner had resisted arrest, and had only been captured by the display of a loaded revolver. The prisoner was convicted and fined twenty-five dollars and costs for this second offense.

The third charge, for disorderly conduct in prison, was quickly disposed of, and a fine of twenty-five dollars and costs levied.

"You may consider yo'self lucky," said the magistrate, "that Mr. Haines didn't prefer a mo' serious charge against you. Many a nigger has gone to the gallows for less. And now, gentlemen, I want to clean this case up right here. How much time is offered for the fine and costs of the prisoner, Bud Johnson, amounting to seventy-five dollars fine and thirty-three dollars and fifty-fo' cents costs? You've heard the evidence an' you see the nigger. Ef there ain't much competition for his services and the time is a long one, he'll have his own stubbornness an' deviltry to thank for it. He's strong and healthy and able to do good work for any one that can manage him."

There was no immediate response. Turner walked forward and viewed the prisoner from head to foot with a coldly sneering look.

"Well, Bud," he said, "I reckon we'll hafter try it ag'in. I have never yet allowed a nigger to git the better o' me, an', moreover, I never will. I'll bid eighteen months, Squire; an' that's all he's worth, with his keep."

There was no competition, and the prisoner was knocked down to Turner, for Fetters, for eighteen months.

"Lock 'im up till I'm ready to go, Bill," said Turner to the constable, "an' just leave the irons on him. I'll fetch 'em back next time I come to town."

The unconscious brutality of the proceeding grated harshly upon the colonel's nerves. Delinquents of some kind these men must be, who were thus dealt with; but he had lived away from the South so long that so sudden an introduction to some of its customs came with something of a shock. He had remembered the pleasant things, and these but vaguely, since his thoughts and his interests had been elsewhere; and in the sifting process of a healthy memory he had forgotten the disagreeable things altogether. He had found the pleasant things still in existence, faded but still fragrant. Fresh from a land of labour unions, and of struggle for wealth and power, of strivings first for equality with those above, and, this attained, for a point of vantage to look down upon former equals, he had found in old Peter, only the day before, a touching loyalty to a family from which he could no longer expect anything in return. Fresh from a land of women's clubs and women's claims, he had reveled last night in the charming domestic, life of the old South, so perfectly preserved in a quiet household. Things Southern, as he had already reflected, lived long and died hard, and these things which he saw now in the clear light of day, were also of the South, and singularly suggestive of other things Southern which he had supposed outlawed and discarded long ago.

"Now, Mr. Haines, bring in the next lot," said the Squire.

The constable led out an old coloured man, clad in a quaint assortment of tattered garments, whom the colonel did not for a moment recognise, not having, from where he stood, a full view of the prisoner's face.

"Gentlemen, I now call yo'r attention to Lot Number Fo', left over from befo' the wah; not much for looks, but respectful and obedient, and accustomed, for some time past, to eat very little. Can be made useful in many ways—can feed the chickens, take care of the children, or would make a good skeercrow. What I am bid, gentlemen, for ol' Peter French? The amount due the co't is twenty-fo' dollahs and a half."

There was some laughter at the Squire's facetiousness. Turner, who had bid on the young and strong men, turned away unconcernedly.

"You'd 'a' made a good auctioneer, Squire," said the one-armed man.

"Thank you, Mr. Pearsall. How much am I offered for this bargain?"

"He'd be dear at any price," said one.

"It's a great risk," observed a second.

"Ten yeahs," said a third.

"You're takin' big chances, Mr. Bennet," said another. "He'll die in five, and you'll have to bury him."

"I withdraw the bid," said Mr. Bennet promptly.

"Two yeahs," said another.

The colonel was boiling over with indignation. His interest in the fate of the other prisoners had been merely abstract; in old Peter's case it assumed a personal aspect. He forced himself into the room and to the front.

"May I ask the meaning of this proceeding?" he demanded.

"Well, suh," replied the Justice, "I don't know who you are, or what right you have to interfere, but this is the sale of a vagrant nigger, with no visible means of suppo't. Perhaps, since you're interested, you'd like to bid on 'im. Are you from the No'th, likely?"

"Yes."

"I thought, suh, that you looked like a No'the'n man. That bein' so, doubtless you'd like somethin' on the Uncle Tom order. Old Peter's fine is twenty dollars, and the costs fo' dollars and a half. The prisoner's time is sold to whoever pays his fine and allows him the shortest time to work it out. When his time's up, he goes free."

"And what has old Peter done to deserve a fine of twenty dollars—more money than he perhaps has ever had at any one time?"

" 'Deed, it is, Mars Henry, 'deed it is!" exclaimed Peter, fervently.

"Peter has not been able," replied the magistrate, "to show this co't that he has reg'lar employment, or means of suppo't, and he was therefore tried and convicted yesterday evenin' of vagrancy, under our State law. The fine is intended to discourage laziness and to promote industry. Do you want to bid, suh? I'm offered two yeahs, gentlemen, for old Peter French? Does anybody wish to make it less?"

"I'll pay the fine," said the colonel, "let him go."

"I beg yo' pahdon, suh, but that wouldn't fulfil the requi'ments of the law. He'd be subject to arrest again immediately. Somebody must take the responsibility for his keep."

"I'll look after him," said the colonel shortly.

"In order to keep the docket straight," said the justice, "I should want to note yo' bid. How long shall I say?"

"Say what you like," said the colonel, drawing out his pocketbook.

"You don't care to bid, Mr. Turner?" asked the justice.

"Not by a damn sight," replied Turner, with native elegance. "I buy niggers to work, not to bury."

"I withdraw my bid in favour of the gentleman," said the two-year bidder.

"Thank you," said the colonel.

"Remember, suh," said the justice to the colonel, "that you are responsible for his keep as well as entitled to his labour, for the period of your bid. How long shall I make it?"

"As long as you please," said the colonel impatiently.

"Sold," said the justice, bringing down his gavel, "for life, to—what name, suh?"

"French—Henry French."

There was some manifestation of interest in the crowd; and the colonel was stared at with undisguised curiosity as he paid the fine and costs, which included two dollars for two meals in the guardhouse, and walked away with his purchase—a purchase which his father had made, upon terms not very different, fifty years before.

"One of the old Frenches," I reckon, said a bystander, "come back on a visit."

"Yes," said another, "old 'ristocrats roun' here. Well, they ought to take keer of their old niggers. They got all the good out of 'em when they were young. But they're not runnin' things now."

An hour later the colonel, driving leisurely about the outskirts of the town and seeking to connect his memories more closely with the scenes around him, met a buggy in which sat the man Turner. After the buggy, tied behind one another to a rope, like a coffle of slaves, marched the three Negroes whose time he had bought at the constable's sale. Among them, of course, was the young man who had been called Bud Johnson. The colonel observed that this Negro's face, when turned toward the white man in front of him, expressed a fierce hatred, as of some wild thing of the woods, which finding itself trapped and betrayed, would go to any length to injure its captor.

Turner passed the colonel with no sign of recognition or greeting.

Bud Johnson evidently recognised the friendly gentleman who had interfered in Peter's case. He threw toward the colonel a look which resembled an appeal; but it was involuntary, and lasted but a moment, and, when the prisoner became conscious of it, and realised its uselessness, it faded into the former expression.

What the man's story was, the colonel did not know, nor what were his deserts. But the events of the day had furnished food for reflection. Evidently Clarendon needed new light and leading. Men, even black men, with something to live for, and with work at living wages, would scarcely prefer an enforced servitude in ropes and chains. And the punishment had scarcely seemed to fit the crime. He had observed no great zeal for work among the white people since he came to town; such work as he had seen done was mostly performed by Negroes. If idleness were a crime, the Negroes surely had no monopoly of it.

Nine

Furnished with money for his keep, Peter was ordered if again molested to say that he was in the colonel's service. The latter, since his own plans were for the present uncertain, had no very clear idea of what disposition he would ultimately make of the old man, but he meant to provide in some way for his declining years. He also bought Peter a neat suit of clothes at a clothing store, and directed him to present himself at the hotel on the following morning. The interval would give the colonel time to find something for Peter to do, so that he would be able to pay him a wage. To his contract with the county he attached little importance; he had already intended, since their meeting in the cemetery, to provide for Peter in some way, and the legal responsibility was no additional burden. To Peter himself, to whose homeless old age food was more than philosophy, the arrangement seemed entirely satisfactory.

Colonel French's presence in Clarendon had speedily become known to the public. Upon his return to the hotel, after leaving Peter to his own devices for the day, he found several cards in his letter box, left by gentlemen who had called, during his absence, to see him.

The daily mail had also come in, and the colonel sat down in the office to read it. There was a club notice, and several letters that had been readdressed and forwarded, and a long one from Kirby in reference to some detail of the recent transfer. Before he had finished reading these, a gentleman came up and introduced himself. He proved to be one John McLean, an old schoolmate of the colonel, and later a comrade-in-arms, though the colonel would never have recognised a rather natty major in his own regiment in this shabby middle-aged man, whose shoes were run down at the heel, whose linen was doubtful, and spotted with tobacco juice. The major talked about the weather, which was cool for the season; about the Civil War, about politics, and about the Negroes, who were very trifling, the major said. While they were talking upon this latter theme, there was some commotion in the street, in front of the hotel, and looking up they saw that a horse, attached to a loaded wagon, had fallen in the roadway, and having become entangled in the harness, was kicking furiously. Five or six Negroes were trying to quiet the animal, and release him from the shafts, while a dozen white men looked on and made suggestions.

"An illustration," said the major, pointing through the window toward the scene without, "of what we've got to contend with. Six niggers can't get one horse up without twice as many white men to tell them how. That's why the South is behind the No'th. The niggers, in one way or another, take up most of our time and energy. You folks up there have half your work done before we get our'n started."

The horse, pulled this way and that, in obedience to the conflicting advice of the bystanders, only became more and more intricately entangled. He had caught one foot in a manner that threatened, with each frantic jerk, to result in a broken leg, when the colonel, leaving his visitor without ceremony, ran out into the street, leaned down, and with a few well-directed movements, released the threatened limb.

"Now, boys," he said, laying hold of the prostrate animal, "give a hand here."

The Negroes, and, after some slight hesitation, one or two white men, came to the colonel's aid, and in a moment, the horse, trembling and blowing, was raised to its feet. The driver thanked the colonel and the others who had befriended him, and proceeded with his load.

When the flurry of excitement was over, the colonel went back to the hotel and resumed the conversation with his friend. If the new franchise amendment went through, said the major, the Negro would be eliminated from politics, and the people of the South, relieved of the fear of "nigger domination," could give their attention to better things, and their section would move forward along the path of progress by leaps and bounds. Of himself the major said little except that he had been an alternate delegate to the last Democratic National Nominating Convention, and that he expected to run for coroner at the next county election.

"If I can secure the suppo't of Mr. Fetters in the primaries," he said, "my nomination is assured, and a nomination is of co'se equivalent to an election. But I see there are some other gentlemen that would like to talk to you, and I won't take any mo' of yo' time at present.

"Mr. Blake," he said, addressing a gentleman with short side-whiskers who was approaching them, "have you had the pleasure of meeting Colonel French?"

"No, suh," said the stranger, "I shall be glad to have the honour of an introduction at your hands."

"Colonel French, Mr. Blake—Mr. Blake, Colonel French. You gentlemen will probably like to talk to one another, because you both belong to the same party, I reckon. Mr. Blake is a new man roun' heah—come down from the mountains not mo' than ten yeahs ago, an' fetched his politics with him; but since he was born that way we don't entertain any malice against him. Mo'over, he's not a 'Black and Tan Republican,' but a 'Lily White.' "

"Yes, sir," said Mr. Blake, taking the colonel's hand, "I believe in white supremacy, and the elimination of the nigger vote. If the National Republican Party would only ignore the coloured politicians, and give all the offices to white men, we'll soon build up a strong white Republican party. If I had the post-office here at Clarendon, with the encouragement it would give, and the aid of my clerks and subo'dinates, I could double the white Republican vote in this county in six months."

The major had left them together, and the Lily White, ere he in turn made way for another caller, suggested delicately, that he would appreciate any good word that the colonel might be able to say for him in influential quarters—either personally or through friends who might have the ear of the executive or those close to him—in reference to the postmastership. Realising that the present administration was a business one, in which sentiment played small part, he had secured the endorsement of the leading business men of the county, even that of Mr. Fetters himself. Mr. Fetters was of course a Democrat, but preferred, since the office must go to a Republican, that it should go to a Lily White.

"I hope to see mo' of you, sir," he said, "and I take pleasure in introducing the Honourable Henry Clay Appleton, editor of our local newspaper, the *Anglo-Saxon.* He and I may not agree on free silver and the tariff, but we are entirely in harmony on the subject indicated by the title of his newspaper. Mr. Appleton not only furnishes all the news that's fit to read, but he represents this county in the Legislature, along with Mr. Fetters, and he will no doubt be the next candidate for Congress from this district. He can tell you all that's worth knowin' about Clarendon."

The colonel shook hands with the editor, who had come with a twofold intent—to make the visitor's acquaintance and to interview him upon his impressions of the South. Incidentally he gave the colonel a great deal of information about local conditions. These were not, he admitted, ideal. The town was backward. It needed capital to develop its resources, and it needed to be rid of the fear of Negro domination. The suffrage in the hands of the Negroes had proved a ghastly and expensive joke for all concerned, and the public welfare absolutely demanded that it be taken away. Even the white Republicans were coming around to the same point of view. The new franchise amendment to the State constitution was receiving their unqualified support.

"That was a fine, chivalrous deed of yours this morning, sir," he said, "at Squire Reddick's office. It was just what might have been expected from a Southern gentleman; for we claim you, colonel, in spite of your long absence."

"Yes," returned the colonel, "I don't know what I rescued old Peter from. It looked pretty dark for him there for a little while. I shouldn't have envied his fate had he been bought in by the tall fellow who represented your colleague in the Legislature. The law seems harsh."

"Well," admitted the editor, "I suppose it might seem harsh, in comparison with your milder penal systems up North. But you must consider the circumstances, and make allowances for us. We have so many idle, ignorant Negroes that something must be done to make them work, or else they'll steal, and to keep them in their place, or they would run over us. The law has been in operation only a year or two, and is already having its effect. I'll be glad to introduce a bill for its repeal, as soon as it is no longer needed.

"You must bear in mind, too, colonel, that niggers don't look at imprisonment and enforced labour in the same way white people do—they are not conscious of any disgrace attending stripes or the ball and chain. The State is poor; our white children are suffering for lack of education, and yet we have to spend a large amount of money on the Negro schools. These convict labour contracts are a source of considerable revenue to the State; they make up, in fact, for most of the outlay for Negro education—which I approve of, though I'm frank to say that so far I don't see much good that's come from it. This convict labour is humanely treated; Mr. Fetters has the contract for several counties, and anybody who knows Mr. Fetters knows that there's no kinder-hearted man in the South."

The colonel disclaimed any intention of criticising. He had come back to his old home for a brief visit, to rest and to observe. He was willing to learn and anxious to please. The editor took copious notes of the interview, and upon his departure shook hands with the colonel cordially.

The colonel had tactfully let his visitors talk, while he listened, or dropped a word here and there to draw them out. One fact was driven home to him by every one to whom he had spoken. Fetters dominated the county and the town, and apparently the State. His name was on every lip. His influence was indispensable to every political aspirant. His acquaintance was something to boast of, and his good will held a promise of success. And the colonel had once kicked the Honourable Mr. Fetters, then plain Bill, in presence of an admiring audience, all the way down Main Street from the academy to the bank! Bill had been, to all intents and purposes, a poor white boy; who could not have named with certainty his own grandfather. The Honourable William was undoubtedly a man of great ability. Had the colonel remained in his native State, would he have been able, he wondered, to impress himself so deeply upon the community? Would blood have been of any advantage, under the changed conditions, or would it have been a drawback to one who sought political advancement?

When the colonel was left alone, he went to look for Phil, who was playing with the children of the landlord, in the hotel parlour. Commending him to the care of the Negro maid in charge of them, he left the hotel and called on several gentlemen whose cards he had found in his box at the clerk's desk. Their stores and offices were within a short radius of the hotel. They were all glad to see him, and if there was any initial stiffness or shyness in the attitude of any one, it soon became the warmest cordiality under the influence of the colonel's simple and unostentatious bearing. If he compared the cut of their clothes or their beards to his own, to their disadvantage, or if he found their views narrow and provincial, he gave no sign—their hearts were warm and their welcome hearty.

The colonel was not able to gather, from the conversation of his friends, that Clarendon, or any one in the town—always excepting Fetters, who did not live in the town, but merely overshadowed it—was especially prosperous. There were no mills or mines in the neighbourhood, except a few grist mills, and a sawmill. The bulk of the business consisted in supplying the needs of an agricultural population, and trading in their products. The cotton was baled and shipped to the North, and re-imported for domestic use, in the shape of sheeting and other stuffs. The corn was shipped to the North, and came back in the shape of corn meal and salt pork, the staple articles of diet. Beefsteak and butter were brought from the North, at twenty-five and fifty cents a pound respectively. There were cotton merchants, and corn and feed merchants; there were dry-goods and grocery stores, drug stores and saloons—and more saloons—and the usual proportion of professional men. Since Clarendon was the county seat, there were of course a court house and a jail. There were churches enough, if all filled at once, to hold the entire population of the town, and preachers in proportion. The merchants, of whom a number were Jewish, periodically went into bankruptcy; the majority of their customers did likewise, and thus a fellow-feeling was promoted, and the loss thrown back as far as possible. The lands of the large farmers were mostly mortgaged, either to Fetters, or to the bank of which he was the chief stockholder, for all that could be borrowed on them; while the small farmers, many of whom were coloured, were practically tied to the soil by ropes of debt and chains of contract.

Every one the colonel met during the afternoon had heard of Squire

Reddick's good joke of the morning. That he should have sold Peter to the colonel for life was regarded as extremely clever. Some of them knew old Peter, and none of them had ever known any harm of him, and they were unanimous in their recognition and applause of the colonel's goodheartedness. Moreover, it was an index of the colonel's views. He was one of them, by descent and early associations, but he had been away a long time, and they hadn't really known how much of a Yankee he might have become. By his whimsical and kindly purchase of old Peter's time—or of old Peter, as they smilingly put it, he had shown his appreciation of the helplessness of the Negroes, and of their proper relations to the whites.

"What'll you do with him, Colonel?" asked one gentleman. "An ole nigger like Peter couldn't live in the col' No'th. You'll have to buy a place down here to keep 'im. They wouldn' let you own a nigger at the No'th."

The remark, with the genial laugh accompanying it, was sounding in the colonel's ears, as, on the way back to the hotel, he stepped into the barber shop. The barber, who had also heard the story, was bursting with a desire to unbosom himself upon the subject. Knowing from experience that white gentlemen, in their intercourse with coloured people, were apt to be, in the local phrase; "sometimey," or uncertain in their moods, he first tested, with a few remarks about the weather, the colonel's amiability, and finding him approachable, proved quite talkative and confidential.

"You're Colonel French, ain't you, suh?" he asked as he began applying the lather.

"Yes."

"Yes, suh; I had heard you wuz in town, an' I wuz hopin' you would come in to get shaved. An' w'en I heard 'bout yo' noble conduc' this mawnin' at Squire Reddick's I wanted you to come in all de mo', suh. Ole Uncle Peter has had a lot er bad luck in his day, but he has fell on his feet dis time, suh, sho's you bawn. I'm right glad to see you, suh. I feels closer to you, suh, than I does to mos' white folks, because you know, colonel, I'm livin' in the same house you wuz bawn in."

"Oh, you are the Nichols, are you, who bought our old place?"

"Yes, suh, William Nichols, at yo' service, suh. I've own' de ole house fer twenty yeahs or mo' now, suh, an' we've b'en mighty comfo'table in it, suh. They is a spaciousness, an' a air of elegant sufficiency about the environs and the equipments of the ed'fice, suh, that does credit to the tas'e of the old aristocracy an' of you-all's family, an' teches me in a sof' spot. For I loves the aristocracy; an' I've often tol' my ol' lady, 'Liza,' says I, 'ef I'd be'n bawn white I sho' would 'a' be'n a 'ristocrat. I feels it in my bones.' "

While the barber babbled on with his shrewd flattery, which was sincere enough to carry a reasonable amount of conviction, the colonel listened with curiously mingled feelings. He recalled each plank, each pane of glass, every inch of wall, in the old house. No spot was without its associations. How many a brilliant scene of gaiety had taken place in the spacious parlour where bright eyes had sparkled, merry feet had twinkled, and young hearts beat high with love and hope and joy of living! And not only joy had passed that way, but sorrow. In the front upper chamber his mother had died. Vividly he recalled, as with closed eyes he lay back under the barber's skilful hand, their last parting and his own poignant grief; for she had been not only his mother, but a woman of character, who commanded respect and inspired affection; a beautiful woman whom he had loved with a devotion that bordered on reverence.

Romance, too, had waved her magic wand over the old homestead. His memory smiled indulgently as he recalled one scene. In a corner of the broad piazza, he had poured out his youthful heart, one summer evening, in strains of passionate devotion, to his first love, a beautiful woman of thirty who was visiting his mother, and who had told him between smiles and tears, to be a good boy and wait a little longer, until he was sure of his own mind. Even now, he breathed, in memory, the heavy odour of the magnolia blossoms which overhung the long wooden porch bench or "jogging board" on which the lady sat, while he knelt on the hard floor before her. He felt very young indeed after she had spoken, but her caressing touch upon his hair had so stirred his heart that his vanity had suffered no wound. Why, the family had owned the house since they had owned the cemetery lot! It was hallowed by a hundred memories, and now!——

"Will you have oil on yo' hair, suh, or bay rum?"

"Nichols," exclaimed the colonel, "I should like to buy back the old house. What do you want for it?"

"Why, colonel," stammered the barber, somewhat taken aback at the suddenness of the offer, "I hadn' r'ally thought 'bout sellin' it. You see, suh, I've had it now for twenty years, and it suits me, an' my child'en has growed up in it—an' it kind of has associations, suh."

In principle the colonel was an ardent democrat; he believed in the rights of man, and extended the doctrine to include all who bore the human form. But in feeling he was an equally pronounced aristocrat. A servant's rights he would have defended to the last ditch; familiarity he would have resented with equal positiveness. Something of this ancestral feeling stirred within him now. While Nichols's position in reference to the house was, in principle, equally as correct as the colonel's own, and superior in point of time—since impressions, like photographs, are apt to grow dim with age, and Nichols's were of much more recent date—the barber's display of sentiment only jarred the colonel's sensibilities and strengthened his desire.

"I should advise you to speak up, Nichols," said the colonel. "I had no notion of buying the place when I came in, and I may not be of the same mind to-morrow. Name your own price, but now's your time."

The barber caught his breath. Such dispatch was unheard-of in Clarendon. But Nichols, a keen-eyed mulatto, was a man of thrift and good sense. He would have liked to consult his wife and children about the sale, but to lose an opportunity to make a good profit was to fly in the face of Providence. The house was very old. It needed shingling and painting. The floors creaked; the plaster on the walls was loose; the chimneys needed pointing and the insurance was soon renewable. He owned a smaller house in which he could live. He had been told to name his price; it was as much better to make it too high than too low, as it was easier to come down than to go up. The would-be purchaser was a rich man; the diamond on the third finger of his left hand alone would buy a small house.

"I think, suh," he said, at a bold venture, "that fo' thousand dollars would be 'bout right."

"I'll take it," returned the colonel, taking out his pocket-book. "Here's fifty dollars to bind the bargain. I'll write a receipt for you to sign."

The barber brought pen, ink and paper, and restrained his excitement sufficiently to keep silent, while the colonel wrote a receipt embodying the terms of the contract, and signed it with a steady hand.

"Have the deed drawn up as soon as you like," said the colonel, as he left the shop, "and when it is done I'll give you a draft for the money."

"Yes, suh; thank you, suh, thank you, colonel."

The barber had bought the house at a tax sale at a time of great financial distress, twenty years before, for five hundred dollars. He had made a very good sale, and he lost no time in having the deed drawn up.

When the colonel reached the hotel, he found Phil seated on the doorstep with a little bow-legged black boy and a little white dog. Phil, who had a large heart, had fraternised with the boy and fallen in love with the dog.

"Papa," he said, "I want to buy this dog. His name is Rover; he can shake hands, and I like him very much. This little boy wants ten cents for him, and I did not have the money. I asked him to wait until you came. May I buy him?"

"Certainly, Phil. Here, boy!"

The colonel threw the black boy a silver dollar. Phil took the dog under his arm and followed his father into the house, while the other boy, his glistening eyes glued to the coin in his hand, scampered off as fast as his limbs would carry him. He was back next morning with a pretty white kitten, but the colonel discouraged any further purchases for the time being.

"My dear Laura," said the colonel when he saw his friend the same evening, "I have been in Clarendon two days; and I have already bought a dog, a house and a man."

Miss Laura was startled. "I don't understand," she said.

The colonel proceeded to explain the transaction by which he had acquired, for life, the services of old Peter.

"I suppose it is the law," Miss Laura said, "but it seems hardly right. I had thought we were well rid of slavery. White men do not work any too much. Old Peter was not idle. He did odd jobs, when he could get them; he was polite and respectful; and it was an outrage to treat him so. I am glad you—hired him."

"Yes—hired him. Moreover, Laura. I have bought a house."

"A house! Then you are going to stay! I am so glad! we shall all be so glad. What house?"

"The old place. I went into the barber shop. The barber complimented me on the family taste in architecture, and grew sentimental about *his* associations with the house. This awoke *my* associations, and the collocation jarred—I was selfish enough to want a monopoly of the associations. I bought the house from him before I left the shop."

"But what will you do with it?" asked Miss Laura, puzzled. "You could never *live* in it again—after a coloured family?"

"Why not? It is no less the old house because the barber has reared his brood beneath its roof. There were always Negroes in it when we were there—the place swarmed with them. Hammer and plane, soap and water, paper and paint, can make it new again. The barber, I understand, is a worthy man, and has reared a decent family. His daughter plays the piano, and sings:

'I dreamt that I dwelt in marble halls,
With vassals and serfs by my side.'

I heard her as I passed there yesterday."

Miss Laura gave an apprehensive start.

"There were Negroes in the house in the old days," he went on unnoticing, "and surely a good old house, gone farther astray than ours, might still be redeemed to noble ends. I shall renovate it and live in it while I am here, and at such times as I may return; or if I should tire of it, I can give it to the town for a school, or for a hospital—there is none here. I should like to preserve, so far as I may, the old associations—*my* associations. The house might not fall again into hands as good as those of Nichols, and I should like to know that it was devoted to some use that would keep the old name alive in the community."

"I think, Henry," said Miss Laura, "that if your visit is long enough, you will do more for the town than if you had remained here all your life. For you have lived in a wider world, and acquired a broader view; and you have learned new things without losing your love for the old."

Ten

The deed for the house was executed on Friday, Nichols agreeing to give possession within a week. The lavishness of the purchase price was a subject of much remark in the town, and Nichols's good fortune was congratulated or envied, according to the temper of each individual. The colonel's action in old Peter's case had made him a name for generosity. His reputation for wealth was confirmed by this reckless prodigality. There were some small souls, of course, among the lower whites who were heard to express disgust that, so far, only "niggers" had profited by the colonel's visit. The *Anglo-Saxon*, which came out Saturday morning, gave a large amount of space to Colonel French and his doings. Indeed, the two compositors had remained up late the night before, setting up copy, and the pressman had not reached home until three o'clock; the kerosene oil in the office gave out, and it was necessary to rouse a grocer at midnight to replenish the supply—so far had the advent of Colonel French affected the life of the town.

The *Anglo-Saxon* announced that Colonel Henry French, formerly of Clarendon, who had won distinction in the Confederate Army, and since the war achieved fortune at the North, had returned to visit his birthplace and his former friends. The hope was expressed that Colonel French, who had recently sold out to a syndicate his bagging mills in Connecticut, might seek investments in the South, whose vast undeveloped resources needed only the fructifying flow of abundant capital to make it blossom like the rose. The New South, the *Anglo-Saxon* declared, was happy to welcome capital and enterprise, and hoped that Colonel French might find, in Clarendon, an agreeable residence, and an attractive opening for his trained business energies. That something of the kind was not unlikely, might be gathered from the fact that Colonel French had already repurchased, from William Nichols, a worthy negro barber, the old French mansion, and had taken into his service a former servant of the family, thus foreshadowing a renewal of local ties and a prolonged residence.

The conduct of the colonel in the matter of his old servant was warmly commended. The romantic circumstances of their meeting in the cemetery, and the incident in the justice's court, which were matters of public knowledge and interest, showed that in Colonel French, should he decide to resume his residence in Clarendon, his fellow citizens would find an agreeable neighbour, whose sympathies would be with the South in those difficult matters upon which North and South had so often been at variance, but upon which they were now rapidly becoming one in sentiment.

The colonel, whose active mind could not long remain unoccupied, was busily engaged during the next week, partly in making plans for the renovation of the old homestead, partly in correspondence with Kirby concerning the winding up of the loose ends of their former business. Thus compelled to leave Phil to the care of some one else, he had an excellent opportunity to utilise Peter's services. When the old man, proud of his new clothes, and relieved of any responsibility for his own future, first appeared at the hotel, the colonel was ready with a commission.

"Now, Peter," he said, "I'm going to prove my confidence in you, and test your devotion to the family, by giving you charge of Phil. You may come and get him in the morning after breakfast—you can get your meals in the hotel kitchen—and take him to walk in the streets or the cemetery; but you must be very careful, for he is all I have in the world. In other words, Peter, you are to take as good care of Phil as you did of me when I was a little boy."

"I'll look aftuh 'im, Mars Henry, lak he wuz a lump er pyo' gol'. Me an' him will git along fine, won't we, little Mars Phil?"

"Yes, indeed," replied the child. "I like you, Uncle Peter, and I'll be glad to go with you."

Phil and the old man proved excellent friends, and the colonel, satisfied that the boy would be well cared for, gave his attention to the business of the hour. As soon as Nichols moved out of the old house, there was a shaking of the dry bones among the mechanics of the town. A small army of workmen invaded the premises, and repairs and improvements of all descriptions went rapidly forward—much more rapidly than was usual in Clarendon, for the colonel let all his work by contract, and by a system of forfeits and premiums kept it going at high pressure. In two weeks the house was shingled, painted inside and out, the fences were renewed, the outhouses renovated, and the grounds put in order.

The stream of ready money thus put into circulation by the colonel, soon permeated all the channels of local enterprise. The barber, out of his profits, began the erection of a row of small houses for coloured tenants. This gave employment to masons and carpenters, and involved the sale and purchase of considerable building material. General trade felt the influence of the enhanced prosperity. Groceries, dry-goods stores and saloons, did a thriving business. The ease with which the simply organised community responded to so slight an inflow of money and energy, was not without a pronounced influence upon the colonel's future conduct.

When his house was finished, Colonel French hired a housekeeper, a coloured maid, a cook and a coachman, bought several horses and carriages, and, having sent to New York for his books and pictures and several articles of furniture which he had stored there, began housekeeping in his own establishment. Succumbing willingly to the charm of old associations, and entering more fully into the social life of the town, he began insensibly to think of Clarendon as an established residence, where he would look forward to spending a certain portion of each year. The climate was good for Phil, and to bring up the boy safely would be henceforth his chief concern in life. In the atmosphere of the old town the ideas of race and blood attained a new and larger perspective. It would be too bad for an old family, with a fine history, to die out, and Phil was the latest of the line and the sole hope of its continuance.

The colonel was conscious, somewhat guiltily conscious, that he had neglected the South and all that pertained to it—except the market for burlaps and bagging, which several Southern sales agencies had attended to on behalf of his firm. He was aware, too, that he had felt a certain amount of contempt for its poverty, its quixotic devotion to lost causes and vanished ideals, and a certain disgusted impatience with a people who persistently lagged behind in the march of progress, and permitted a handful of upstart, blatant, self-seeking demagogues to misrepresent them, in Congress and before the country, by intemperate language and persistent hostility to a humble but large and important part of their own constituency. But he was glad to find that this was the mere froth upon the surface, and that underneath it, deep down in the hearts of the people, the currents of life flowed, if less swiftly, not less purely than in more favoured places.

The town needed an element, which he could in a measure supply by residing there, if for only a few weeks each year. And that element was some point of contact with the outer world and its more advanced thought. He might induce some of his Northern friends to follow his example; there were many for whom the mild climate in Winter and the restful atmosphere at all seasons of the year, would be a boon which correctly informed people would be eager to enjoy.

Of the extent to which the influence of the Treadwell household had contributed to this frame of mind, the colonel was not conscious. He had received the freedom of the town, and many hospitable doors were open to him. As a single man, with an interesting little motherless child, he did not lack for the smiles of fair ladies, of which the town boasted not a few. But Mrs. Treadwell's home held the first place in his affections. He had been there first, and first impressions are vivid. They had been kind to Phil, who loved them all, and insisted on Peter's taking him there every day. The colonel found pleasure in Miss Laura's sweet simplicity and openness of character; to which Graciella's vivacity and fresh young beauty formed an attractive counterpart; and Mrs. Treadwell's plaintive minor note had soothed and satisfied Colonel French in this emotional Indian Summer which marked his reaction from a long and arduous business career.

Eleven

In addition to a pronounced attractiveness of form and feature, Miss Graciella Treadwell possessed a fine complexion, a clear eye, and an elastic spirit. She was also well endowed with certain other characteristics of youth; among them ingenuousness, which, if it be a fault, experience is sure to correct; and impulsiveness, which even the school of hard knocks is not always able to eradicate, though it may chasten. To the good points of Graciella, could be added an untroubled conscience, at least up to that period when Colonel French dawned upon her horizon, and for some time thereafter. If she had put herself foremost in all her thoughts, it had been the unconscious egotism of youth, with no definite purpose of self-seeking. The things for which she wished most were associated with distant places, and her longing for them had never taken the form of envy of those around her. Indeed envy is scarcely a vice of youth; it is a weed that flourishes best after the flower of hope has begun to wither. Graciella's views of life, even her youthful romanticism were sane and healthful; but since she had not been tried in the furnace of experience, it could only be said of her that she belonged to the class, always large, but shifting like the sands of the sea, who have never been tempted, and therefore do not know whether they would sin or not.

It was inevitable, with such a nature as Graciella's, in such an embodiment, that the time should come, at some important crisis of her life, when she must choose between different courses; nor was it likely that she could avoid what comes sometime to all of us, the necessity of choosing between good and evil. Her liking for Colonel French had grown since their first meeting. He knew so many things that Graciella wished to know, that when he came to the house she spent a great deal of time in conversation with him. Her aunt Laura was often busy with household duties, and Graciella, as the least employed member of the family, was able to devote herself to his entertainment. Colonel French, a comparatively idle man at this period, found her prattle very amusing.

It was not unnatural for Graciella to think that this acquaintance might be of future value; she could scarcely have thought otherwise. If she should ever go to New York, a rich and powerful friend would be well worth having. Should her going there be delayed very long, she would nevertheless have a tie of friendship in the great city, and a source to which she might at any time apply for information. Her fondness for Colonel French's society was, however, up to a certain time, entirely spontaneous, and coloured by no ulterior purpose. Her hope that his friendship might prove valuable was an afterthought.

It was during this happy period that she was standing, one day, by the garden gate, when Colonel French passed by in his fine new trap, driving a spirited horse; and it was with perfect candour that she waved her hand to him familiarly.

"Would you like a drive?" he called.

"Wouldn't I?" she replied. "Wait till I tell the folks."

She was back in a moment, and ran out of the gate and down the steps. The colonel gave her his hand and she sprang up beside him.

They drove through the cemetery, and into the outlying part of the town, where there were some shaded woodland stretches. It was a pleasant afternoon; cloudy enough to hide the sun. Graciella's eyes sparkled and her cheek glowed with pleasure, while her light brown hair blown about her face by the breeze of their rapid motion was like an aureole.

"Colonel French," she said as they were walking the horse up a hill, "are you going to give a house warming?"

"Why," he said, "I hadn't thought of it. Ought I to give a house warming?"

"You surely ought. Everybody will want to see your house while it is new and bright. You certainly ought to have a house warming."

"Very well," said the colonel. "I make it a rule to shirk no plain duty. If I *ought* to have a house warming, I *will* have it. And you shall be my social mentor. What sort of a party shall it be?"

"Why not make it," she said brightly, "just such a party as your father would have had. You have the old house, and the old furniture. Give an old-time party."

In fitting up his house the colonel had been animated by the same feeling that had moved him to its purchase. He had endeavoured to restore, as far as possible, the interior as he remembered it in his childhood. At his father's death the furniture had been sold and scattered. He had been able, through the kindly interest of his friends, to recover several of the pieces. Others that were lost past hope, had been reproduced from their description. Among those recovered was a fine pair of brass andirons, and his father's mahogany desk, which had been purchased by Major Treadwell at the sale of the elder French's effects.

Miss Laura had been the first to speak of the desk.

"Henry," she had said, "the house would not be complete without your father's desk. It was my father's too, but yours is the prior claim. Take it as a gift from me."

He protested, and would have paid for it liberally, and, when she would take nothing, declared he would not accept it on such terms.

"You are selfish, Henry," she replied, with a smile. "You have brought a new interest into our lives, and into the town, and you will not let us make you any return."

"But I am taking from you something you need," he replied, "and for which you paid. When Major Treadwell bought it, it was merely second-hand furniture, sold under the hammer. Now it has the value of an antique—it is a fine piece and could be sold in New York for a large sum."

"You must take it for nothing, or not at all," she replied firmly.

"It is highway robbery," he said, and could not make up his mind to yield.

Next day, when the colonel went home, after having been down town an hour, he found the desk in his library. The Treadwell ladies had corrupted Peter, who had told them when the colonel would be out of the house and had brought a cart to take the desk away.

When the house was finished, the interior was simple but beautiful. It was furnished in the style that had been prevalent fifty years before. There were some modern additions in the line of comfort and luxury—soft chairs, fine rugs, and a few choice books and pictures—for the colonel had not attempted to conform his own tastes and habits to those of his father. He had some visitors, mostly gentlemen, and there was, as Graciella knew, a lively curiosity among the ladies to see the house and its contents.

The suggestion of a house warming had come originally from Mrs. Treadwell; but Graciella had promptly made it her own and conveyed it to the colonel.

"A bright idea," he replied. "By all means let it be an old-time party—say such a party as my father would have given, or my grandfather. And shall we invite the old people?"

"Well," replied Graciella judicially, "don't have them so old that they can't talk or hear, and must be fed with a spoon. If there were too many old, or not enough young people, I shouldn't enjoy myself."

"I suppose I seem awfully old to you," said the colonel, parenthetically.

"Oh, I don't know," replied Graciella, giving him a frankly critical look. "When you first came I thought you *were* rather old—you see, you are older than Aunt Laura; but you seem to have grown younger—it's curious, but it's true—and now I hardly think of you as old at all."

The colonel was secretly flattered. The wisest man over forty likes to be thought young.

"Very well," he said, "you shall select the guests."

"At an old-time party," continued Graciella, thoughtfully, "the guests should wear old-time clothes. In grandmother's time the ladies wore long flowing sleeves——"

"And hoopskirts," said the colonel.

"And their hair down over their ears."

"Or in ringlets."

"Yes, it is all in grandmother's bound volume of *The Ladies' Book*," said Graciella. "I was reading it only last week."

"My mother took it," returned the colonel.

"Then you must have read 'Letters from a Pastry Cook,' by N. P. Willis when they came out?"

"No," said the colonel with a sigh, "I missed that. I—I wasn't able to read then."

Graciella indulged in a brief mental calculation.

"Why, of course not," she laughed, "you weren't even born when they came out! But they're fine; I'll lend you our copy. You must ask all the girls to dress as their mothers and grandmothers used to dress. Make the requirement elastic, because some of them may not have just the things for one particular period. I'm all right. We have a cedar chest in the attic, full of old things. Won't I look funny in a hoop skirt?"

"You'll look charming in anything," said the colonel.

It was a pleasure to pay Graciella compliments, she so frankly enjoyed them; and the colonel loved to make others happy. In his New York firm Mr. French was always ready to consider a request for an advance of salary; Kirby had often been obliged to play the wicked partner in order to keep expenses down to a normal level. At parties débutantes had always expected Mr. French to say something pleasant to them, and had rarely been disappointed.

The subject of the party was resumed next day at Mrs. Treadwell's, where the colonel went in the afternoon to call.

"An old-time party," declared the colonel, "should have old-time amusements. We must have a fiddler, a black fiddler, to play quadrilles and the Virginia Reel."

"I don't know where you'll find one," said Miss Laura.

"I'll ask Peter," replied the colonel. "He ought to know."

Peter was in the yard with Phil

"Lawd, Mars Henry!" said Peter, "fiddlers is mighty sca'ce dese days, but I reckon ole 'Poleon Campbell kin make you shake yo' feet yit, ef Ole Man Rheumatiz ain' ketched holt er 'im too tight."

"And I will play a minuet on your new piano," said Miss Laura, "and teach the girls beforehand how to dance it. There should be cards for those who do not dance."

So the party was arranged. Miss Laura, Graciella and the colonel made out the list of guests. The invitations were duly sent out for an old-time party, with old-time costumes—any period between 1830 and 1860 permissible—and old-time entertainment.

The announcement created some excitement in social circles, and, like all of Colonel French's enterprises at that happy period of his home-coming, brought prosperity in its train. Dressmakers were kept busy making and altering costumes for the ladies. Old Archie Christmas, the mulatto tailor, sole survivor of a once flourishing craft—Mr. Cohen's Universal Emporium supplied the general public with ready-made clothing, and, twice a year, the travelling salesman of a New York tailoring firm visited Clarendon with samples of suitings, and took orders and measurements—old Archie Christmas, who had not made a full suit of clothes for years, was able, by making and altering men's garments for the colonel's party, to earn enough to keep himself alive for another twelve months. Old Peter was at Archie's shop one day, and they were talking about old times—good old times—for to old men old times are always good times, though history may tell another tale.

"Yo' boss is a godsen' ter dis town," declared old Archie, "he sho' is. De w'ite folks says de young niggers is triflin' 'cause dey don' larn how to do nothin'. But what is dere fer 'em to do? I kin 'member when dis town was full er black an' yaller carpenters an' 'j'iners, black-smiths, wagon makers, shoemakers, tinners, saddlers an' cab'net mak-ers. Now all de fu'nicher, de shoes, de wagons, de buggies, de tinware, de hoss shoes, de nails to fasten 'em on wid—yas, an' fo' de Lawd! even de clothes dat folks wears on dere backs, is made at de Norf, an' dere ain' nothin' lef' fer de ole niggers ter do, let 'lone de young ones. Yo' boss is de right kin'; I hopes he'll stay 'roun' here till you an' me dies."

"I hopes wid you," said Peter fervently, "I sho' does! Yas indeed I does."

Peter was entirely sincere. Never in his life had he worn such good clothes, eaten such good food, or led so easy a life as in the colonel's service. Even the old times paled by comparison with this new golden age; and the long years of poverty and hard luck that stretched behind him seemed to the old man like a distant and unpleasant dream.

The party came off at the appointed time, and was a distinct success. Graciella had made a raid on the cedar chest, and shone resplendent in crinoline, curls, and a patterned muslin. Together with Miss Laura and Ben Dudley, who had come in from Mink Run for the party, she was among the first to arrive. Miss Laura's costume, which belonged to an earlier date, was in keeping with her quiet dignity. Ben wore a suit of his uncle's, which the care of old Aunt Viney had preserved wonderfully well from moth and dust through the years. The men wore stocks and neckcloths, bell-bottomed trousers with straps under their shoes, and frock coats very full at the top and buttoned tightly at the waist. Old Peter, in a long blue coat with brass buttons, acted as butler, helped by a young Negro who did the heavy work. Miss Laura's servant Catherine had rallied from her usual gloom and begged the privilege of acting as lady's maid. 'Poleon Campbell, an old-time Negro fiddler, whom Peter had resurrected from some obscure cabin, oiled his rheumatic joints, tuned his fiddle and rosined his bow, and under the inspiration of good food and drink and liberal wage, played through his whole repertory, which included such ancient favourites as, "Fishers' Hornpipe," "Soldiers' Joy," "Chicken in the Bread-tray," and the "Campbells are Coming." Miss Laura played a minuet, which the young people danced. Major McLean danced the highland fling, and some of the ladies sang old-time songs, and war lyrics, which stirred the heart and moistened the eyes.

Little Phil, in a child's costume of 1840, copied from *The Ladies'*

Book, was petted and made much of for several hours, until he became sleepy and was put to bed.

"Graciella," said the colonel to his young friend, during the evening, "our party is a great success. It was your idea. When it is all over, I want to make you a present in token of my gratitude. You shall select it yourself; it shall be whatever you say."

Graciella was very much elated at this mark of the colonel's friendship. She did not dream of declining the proffered token, and during the next dance her mind was busily occupied with the question of what it should be—a ring, a bracelet, a bicycle, a set of books? She needed a dozen things, and would have liked to possess a dozen others.

She had not yet decided, when Ben came up to claim her for a dance. On his appearance, she was struck by a sudden idea. Colonel French was a man of affairs. In New York he must have a wide circle of influential acquaintances. Old Mr. Dudley was in failing health; he might die at any time, and Ben would then be free to seek employment away from Clarendon. What better place for him than New York? With a position there, he would be able to marry her, and take her there to live.

This, she decided, should be her request of the colonel—that he should help her lover to a place in New York.

Her conclusion was really magnanimous. She might profit by it in the end, but Ben would be the first beneficiary. It was an act of self-denial, for she was giving up a definite and certain good for a future contingency.

She was therefore in a pleasant glow of self-congratulatory mood when she accidentally overheard a conversation not intended for her ears. She had run out to the dining-room to speak to the housekeeper about the refreshments, and was returning through the hall, when she stopped for a moment to look into the library, where those who did not care to dance were playing cards.

Beyond the door, with their backs turned toward her, sat two ladies engaged in conversation. One was a widow, a well-known gossip, and the other a wife known to be unhappily married. They were no longer young, and their views were marked by the cynicism of seasoned experience.

"Oh, there's no doubt about it," said the widow. "He came down here to find a wife. He tried a Yankee wife, and didn't like the breed; and when he was ready for number two, he came back South."

"He showed good taste," said the other.

"That depends," said the widow, "upon whom he chooses. He can probably have his pick."

"No doubt," rejoined the married lady, with a touch of sarcasm, which the widow, who was still under forty, chose to ignore.

"I wonder which is it?" said the widow. "I suppose it's Laura; he spends a great deal of time there, and she's devoted to his little boy, or pretends to be."

"Don't fool yourself," replied the other earnestly, and not without a subdued pleasure in disabusing the widow's mind. "Don't fool yourself, my dear. A man of his age doesn't marry a woman of Laura Treadwell's. Believe me, it's the little one."

"But she has a beau. There's that tall nephew of old Mr. Dudley's. He's been hanging around her for a year or two. He looks very handsome to-night."

"Ah, well, she'll dispose of him fast enough when the time comes. He's only a poor stick, the last of a good stock run to seed. Why, she's been pointedly setting her cap at the colonel all the evening. He's perfectly infatuated; he has danced with her three times to once with Laura."

"It's sad to see a man make a fool of himself," sighed the widow, who was not without some remnants of beauty and a heart still warm and willing. "Children are very forward nowadays."

"There's no fool like an old fool, my dear," replied the other with the cheerful philosophy of the miserable who love company. "These fair women are always selfish and calculating; and she's a bold piece. My husband says Colonel French is worth at least a million. A young wife, who understands her business, could get anything from him that money can buy."

"What a pity, my dear," said the widow, with a spice of malice, seeing her own opportunity, "what a pity that you were older than your husband! Well, it will be fortunate for the child if she marries an old man, for beauty of her type fades early."

Old 'Poleon's fiddle, to which one of the guests was improvising an accompaniment on the colonel's new piano, had struck up "Camptown Races," and the rollicking lilt of the chorus was resounding through the house.

"Gwine ter run all night,
Gwine ter run all day,
I'll bet my money on de bobtail nag,
Oh, who's gwine ter bet on de bay?"

Ben ran out into the hall. Graciella had changed her position and was sitting alone, perturbed in mind.

"Come on, Graciella, let's get into the Virginia reel; it's the last one."

Graciella obeyed mechanically. Ben, on the contrary, was unusually animated. He had enjoyed the party better than any he had ever attended. He had not been at many.

Colonel French, who had entered with zest into the spirit of the occasion, participated in the reel. Every time Graciella touched his hand, it was with the consciousness of a new element in their relations. Until then her friendship for Colonel French had been perfectly ingenuous. She had liked him because he was interesting, and good to her in a friendly way. Now she realised that he was a millionaire, eligible for marriage, from whom a young wife, if she understood her business, might secure the gratification of every wish.

The serpent had entered Eden. Graciella had been tendered the apple. She must choose now whether she would eat.

When the party broke up, the colonel was congratulated on every hand. He had not only given his guests a delightful evening. He had restored an ancient landmark; had recalled, to a people whose life lay mostly in the past, the glory of days gone by, and proved his loyalty to their cherished traditions.

Ben Dudley walked home with Graciella. Miss Laura went ahead of them with Catherine, who was cheerful in the possession of a substantial reward for her services.

"You're not sayin' much to-night," said Ben to his sweetheart, as they walked along under the trees.

Graciella did not respond.

"You're not sayin' much to-night," he repeated.

"Yes," returned Graciella abstractedly, "it was a lovely party!"

Ben said no more. The house warming had also given him food for thought. He had noticed the colonel's attentions to Graciella, and had heard them remarked upon. Colonel French was more than old enough to be Graciella's father; but he was rich. Graciella was poor and ambitious. Ben's only assets were youth and hope, and priority in the field his only claim.

Miss Laura and Catherine had gone in, and when the young people came to the gate, the light still shone through the open door.

"Graciella," he said, taking her hand in his as they stood a moment, "will you marry me?"

"Still harping on the same old string," she said, withdrawing her hand. "I'm tired now, Ben, too tired to talk foolishness."

"Very well, I'll save it for next time. Good night, sweetheart."

She had closed the gate between them. He leaned over it to kiss her, but she evaded his caress and ran lightly up the steps.

"Good night, Ben," she called.

"Good night, sweetheart," he replied, with a pang of foreboding.

In after years, when the colonel looked back upon his residence in Clarendon, this seemed to him the golden moment. There were other times that stirred deeper emotions—the lust of battle, the joy of victory, the chagrin of defeat—moments that tried his soul with tests almost too hard. But, thus far, his new career in Clarendon had been one of pleasant experiences only, and this unclouded hour was its fitting crown.

Twelve

Whenever the colonel visited the cemetery, or took a walk in that pleasant quarter of the town, he had to cross the bridge from which was visible the site of the old Eureka cotton mill of his boyhood, and it was not difficult to recall that it had been, before the War, a busy hive of industry. On a narrow and obscure street, little more than an alley, behind the cemetery, there were still several crumbling tenements, built for the mill operatives, but now occupied by a handful of abjectly poor whites, who kept body and soul together through the doubtful mercy of God and a small weekly dole from the poormaster. The mill pond, while not wide-spreading, had extended back some distance between the sloping banks, and had furnished swimming holes, fishing holes, and what was more to the point at present, a very fine head of water, which, as it struck the colonel more forcibly each time he saw it, offered an opportunity that the town could ill afford to waste. Shrewd minds in the cotton industry had long ago conceived the idea that the South, by reason of its nearness to the source of raw material, its abundant water power, and its cheaper labour, partly due to the smaller cost of living in a mild climate, and the absence of labour agitation, was destined in time to rival and perhaps displace New England in cotton manufacturing. Many Southern mills were already in successful operation. But from lack of capital, or lack of enterprise, nothing of the kind had ever been undertaken in Clarendon although the town was the centre of a cotton-raising district, and there was a mill in an adjoining county. Men who owned land mortgaged it for money to raise cotton; men who rented land from others mortgaged their crops for the same purpose.

It was easy to borrow money in Clarendon—on adequate security—at ten per cent., and Mr. Fetters, the magnate of the county, was always ready, the colonel had learned, to accommodate the needy who could give such security. He had also discovered that Fetters was acquiring the greater part of the land. Many a farmer imagined that he owned a farm, when he was, actually, merely a tenant of Fetters. Occasionally Fetters foreclosed a mortgage, when there was plainly no more to be had from it, and bought in the land, which he added to his own holdings in fee. But as a rule, he found it more profitable to let the borrower retain possession and pay the interest as nearly as he could; the estate would ultimately be good for the debt, if the debtor did not live too long—worry might be counted upon to shorten his days—and the loan, with interest, could be more conveniently collected at his death. To bankrupt an estate was less personal than to break an individual; and widows, and orphans still in their minority, did not vote and knew little about business methods.

To a man of action, like the colonel, the frequent contemplation of the unused water power, which might so easily be harnessed to the car of progress, gave birth, in time, to a wish to see it thus utilised, and the further wish to stir to labour the idle inhabitants of the neighbourhood. In all work the shiftless methods of an older generation still survived. No one could do anything in a quarter of an hour. Nearly all tasks were done by Negroes who had forgotten how to work, or by white people who had never learned. But the colonel had already seen the reviving effect of a little money, directed by a little energy. And so he planned to build a new and larger cotton mill where the old had stood; to shake up this lethargic community; to put its people to work, and to teach them habits of industry, efficiency and thrift. This, he imagined, would be pleasant occupation for his vacation, as well as a true missionary enterprise—a contribution to human progress. Such a cotton mill would require only an inconsiderable portion of his capital, the body of which would be left intact for investment elsewhere; it would not interfere at all with his freedom of movement; for, once built, equipped and put in operation under a competent manager, it would no more require his personal oversight than had the New England bagging mills which his firm had conducted for so many years.

From impulse to action was, for the colonel's temperament, an easy step, and he had scarcely moved into his house, before he quietly set about investigating the title to the old mill site. It had been forfeited many years before, he found, to the State, for non-payment of taxes. There having been no demand for the property at any time since, it had never been sold, but held as a sort of lapsed asset, subject to sale, but open also, so long as it remained unsold, to redemption upon the payment of back taxes and certain fees. The amount of these was ascertained; it was considerably less than the fair value of the property, which was therefore redeemable at a profit.

The owners, however, were widely scattered, for the mill had belonged to a joint-stock company composed of a dozen or more members. Colonel French was pleasantly surprised, upon looking up certain musty public records in the court house, to find that he himself was the owner, by inheritance, of several shares of stock which had been overlooked in the sale of his father's property. Retaining the services of Judge Bullard, the leading member of the Clarendon bar, he set out quietly to secure options upon the other shares. This involved an extensive correspondence, which occupied several weeks. For it was necessary first to find, and then to deal with the scattered representatives of the former owners.

Thirteen

In engaging Judge Bullard, the colonel had merely stated to the lawyer that he thought of building a cotton-mill, but had said nothing about his broader plan. It was very likely, he recognised, that the people of Clarendon might not relish the thought that they were regarded as fit subjects for reform. He knew that they were sensitive, and quick to resent criticism. If some of them might admit, now and then, among themselves, that the town was unprogressive, or declining, there was always some extraneous reason given—the War, the carpetbaggers, the Fifteenth Amendment, the Negroes. Perhaps not one of them had ever quite realised the awful handicap of excuses under which they laboured. Effort was paralysed where failure was so easily explained.

That the condition of the town might be due to causes within itself—to the general ignorance, self-satisfaction and lack of enterprise, had occurred to only a favoured few; the younger of these had moved away, seeking a broader outlook elsewhere; while those who remained were not yet strong enough nor brave enough to break with the past and urge new standards of thought and feeling.

So the colonel kept his larger purpose to himself until a time when greater openness would serve to advance it. Thus Judge Bullard, not being able to read his client's mind, assumed very naturally that the contemplated enterprise was to be of a purely commercial nature, directed to making the most money in the shortest time.

"Some day, Colonel," he said, with this thought in mind, "you might get a few pointers by running over to Carthage and looking through the Excelsior Mills. They get more work there for less money than anywhere else in the South. Last year they declared a forty per cent. dividend. I know the superintendent, and will give you a letter of introduction, whenever you like."

The colonel bore the matter in mind, and one morning, a day or two after his party, set out by train, about eight o'clock in the morning, for Carthage, armed with a letter from the lawyer to the superintendent of the mills.

The town was only forty miles away; but a cow had been caught in a trestle across a ditch, and some time was required for the train crew to release her. Another stop was made in the middle of a swamp, to put off a light mulatto who had presumed on his complexion to ride in the white people's car. He had been successfully spotted, but had impudently refused to go into the stuffy little closet provided at the end of the car for people of his class. He was therefore given an opportunity to reflect, during a walk along the ties, upon his true relation to society. Another stop was made for a gentleman who had sent a Negro boy ahead to flag the train and notify the conductor that he would be along in fifteen or twenty minutes with a couple of lady passengers. A hot journal caused a further delay. These interruptions made it eleven o'clock, a three-hours' run, before the train reached Carthage.

The town was much smaller than Clarendon. It comprised a public square of several acres in extent, on one side of which was the railroad station, and on another the court house. One of the remaining sides was occupied by a row of shops; the fourth straggled off in various directions. The whole wore a neglected air. Bales of cotton goods were piled on the platform, apparently just unloaded from wagons standing near. Several white men and Negroes stood around and stared listlessly at the train and the few who alighted from it.

Inquiring its whereabouts from one of the bystanders, the colonel found the nearest hotel—a two-story frame structure, with a piazza across the front, extending to the street line. There was a buggy standing in front, its horse hitched to one of the piazza posts. Steps led up from the street, but one might step from the buggy to the floor of the piazza, which was without a railing.

The colonel mounted the steps and passed through the door into a small room, which he took for the hotel office, since there were chairs standing against the walls, and at one side a table on which a register lay open. The only person in the room, beside himself, was a young man seated near the door, with his feet elevated to the back of another chair, reading a newspaper from which he did not look up.

The colonel, who wished to make some inquiries and to register for the dinner which he might return to take, looked around him for the clerk, or some one in authority, but no one was visible. While waiting, he walked over to the desk and turned over the leaves of the dog-eared register. He recognised only one name—that of Mr. William Fetters, who had registered there only a day or two before.

No one had yet appeared. The young man in the chair was evidently not connected with the establishment. His expression was so forbidding, not to say arrogant, and his absorption in the newspaper so complete, that the colonel, not caring to address him, turned to the right and crossed a narrow hall to a room beyond, evidently a parlour, since it was fitted up with a faded ingrain carpet, a centre table with a red plush photograph album, and several enlarged crayon portraits hung near the ceiling—of the kind made free of charge in Chicago from photographs, provided the owner orders a frame from the company. No one was in the room, and the colonel had turned to leave it, when he came face to face with a lady passing through the hall.

"Are you looking for some one?" she asked amiably, having noted his air of inquiry.

"Why, yes, madam," replied the colonel, removing his hat, "I was looking for the proprietor—or the clerk."

"Why," she replied, smiling, "that's the proprietor sitting there in the office. I'm going in to speak to him, and you can get his attention at the same time."

Their entrance did not disturb the young man's resposeful attitude, which remained as unchanged as that of a graven image; nor did he exhibit any consciousness at their presence.

"I want a clean towel, Mr. Dickson," said the lady sharply.

The proprietor looked up with an annoyed expression.

"Huh?" he demanded, in a tone of resentment mingled with surprise.

"A clean towel, if you please."

The proprietor said nothing more to the lady, nor deigned to notice the colonel at all, but lifted his legs down from the back of the chair, rose with a sigh, left the room and returned in a few minutes with a towel, which he handed ungraciously to the lady. Then, still paying no attention to the colonel, he resumed his former attitude, and returned to the perusal of his newspaper—certainly the most unconcerned of hotel keepers, thought the colonel, as a vision of spacious lobbies, liveried porters, and obsequious clerks rose before his vision. He made no audible comment, however, but merely stared at the young man curiously, left the hotel, and inquired of a passing Negro the whereabouts of the livery stable. A few minutes later he found the place without difficulty, and hired a horse and buggy.

While the stable boy was putting the harness on the horse, the colonel related to the liveryman, whose manner was energetic and business-like, and who possessed an open countenance and a sympathetic eye, his experience at the hotel.

"Oh, yes," was the reply, "that's Lee Dickson all over. That hotel used to be kep' by his mother. She was a widow woman, an' ever since she died, a couple of months ago, Lee's been playin' the big man, spendin' the old lady's money, and enjoyin' himself. Did you see that hoss'n'-buggy hitched in front of the ho-tel?"

"Yes."

"Well, that's Lee's buggy. He hires it from us. We send it up every mornin' at nine o'clock, when Lee gits up. When he's had his breakfas' he comes out an' gits in the buggy, an' drives to the barber-shop nex' door, gits out, goes in an' gits shaved, comes out, climbs in the buggy, an' drives back to the ho-tel. Then he talks to the cook, comes out an' gits in the buggy, an' drives half-way 'long that side of the square, about two hund'ed feet, to the grocery sto', and orders half a pound of coffee or a pound of lard, or whatever the ho-tel needs for the day, then comes out, climbs in the buggy and drives back. When the mail comes in, if he's expectin' any mail, he drives 'cross the square to the post-office, an' then drives back to the ho-tel. There's other lazy men roun' here, but Lee Dickson takes the cake. However, it's money in our pocket, as long as it keeps up."

"I shouldn't think it would keep up long," returned the colonel. "How can such a hotel prosper?"

"It don't!" replied the liveryman, "but it's the best in town."

"I don't see how there could be a worse," said the colonel.

"There couldn't—it's reached bed rock."

The buggy was ready by this time, and the colonel set out, with a black driver, to find the Excelsior Cotton Mills. They proved to be situated in a desolate sandhill region several miles out of town. The day was hot; the weather had been dry, and the road was deep with a yielding white sand into which the buggy tires sank. The horse soon panted with the heat and the exertion, and the colonel, dressed in brown linen, took off his hat and mopped his brow with his handkerchief. The driver, a taciturn Negro—most of the loquacious, fun-loving Negroes of the colonel's youth seemed to have disappeared—flicked a horsefly now and then, with his whip, from the horse's sweating back.

The first sign of the mill was a straggling group of small frame houses, built of unpainted pine lumber. The barren soil, which would not have supported a firm lawn, was dotted with scraggy bunches of wiregrass. In the open doorways, through which the flies swarmed in and out, grown men, some old, some still in the prime of life, were lounging, pipe in mouth, while old women pottered about the yards, or pushed back their sunbonnets to stare vacantly at the advancing buggy. Dirty babies were tumbling about the cabins. There was a lean and listless yellow dog or two for every baby; and several slatternly black women were washing clothes on the shady sides of the houses. A general air of shiftlessness and squalor pervaded the settlement. There was no sign of joyous childhood or of happy youth.

A turn in the road brought them to the mill, the distant hum of which had already been audible. It was a two-story brick structure with many windows, altogether of the cheapest construction, but situated on the bank of a stream and backed by a noble water power.

They drew up before an open door at one corner of the building. The colonel alighted, entered, and presented his letter of introduction. The superintendent glanced at him keenly, but, after reading the letter, greeted him with a show of cordiality, and called a young man to conduct the visitor through the mill.

The guide seemed in somewhat of a hurry, and reticent of speech; nor was the noise of the machinery conducive to conversation. Some of the colonel's questions seemed unheard, and others were imperfectly answered. Yet the conditions disclosed by even such an inspection were, to the colonel, a revelation. Through air thick with flying particles of cotton, pale, anæmic young women glanced at him curiously, with lack-luster eyes, or eyes in which the gleam was not that of health, or hope, or holiness. Wizened children, who had never known the joys of childhood, worked side by side at long rows of spools to which they must give unremitting attention. Most of the women were using snuff, the odour of which was mingled with the flying particles of cotton, while the floor was thickly covered with unsightly brown splotches.

When they had completed the tour of the mills and returned to the office, the colonel asked some questions of the manager about the equipment, the output, and the market, which were very promptly and courteously answered. To those concerning hours and wages the replies were less definite, and the colonel went away impressed as much by what he had not learned as by what he had seen.

While settling his bill at the livery stable, he made further inquiries.

"Lord, yes," said the liveryman in answer to one of them, "I can tell you all you want to know about that mill. Talk about nigger slavery—the niggers never were worked like white women and children are in them mills. They work 'em from twelve to sixteen hours a day for from fifteen to fifty cents. Them triflin' old pinelanders out there jus' lay aroun' and raise children for the mills, and then set down and chaw tobacco an' live on their children's wages. It's a sin an' a shame, an' there ought to be a law ag'inst it."

The conversation brought out the further fact that vice was rampant among the millhands.

"An' it ain't surprisin'," said the liveryman, with indignation tempered by the easy philosophy of hot climates. "Shut up in jail all day, an' half the night, never breathin' the pyo' air, or baskin' in God's bright sunshine; with no books to read an' no chance to learn, who can blame the po'r things if they have a little joy in the only way they know?"

"Who owns the mill?" asked the colonel.

"It belongs to a company," was the reply, "but Old Bill Fetters owns a majority of the stock—durn, him!"

The colonel felt a thrill of pleasure—he had met a man after his own heart.

"You are not one of Fetters's admirers then?" he asked.

"Not by a durn sight," returned the liveryman promptly. "When I look at them white gals, that ought to be rosy-cheeked an' bright-eyed an' plump an' hearty an' happy, an' them po' little child'en that never get a chance to go fishin' or swimmin' or to learn anything, I allow I wouldn' mind if the durned old mill would catch fire an' burn down. They work children there from six years old up, an' half of 'em die of consumption before they're grown. It's a durned outrage, an' if I ever go to the Legislatur', for which I mean to run, I'll try to have it stopped."

"I hope you will be elected," said the colonel. "What time does the train go back to Clarendon?"

"Four o'clock, if she's on time—but it may be five."

"Do you suppose I can get dinner at the hotel?"

"Oh, yes! I sent word up that I 'lowed you might be back, so they'll be expectin' you."

The proprietor was at the desk when the colonel went in. He wrote his name on the book, and was served with an execrable dinner. He paid his bill of half a dollar to the taciturn proprietor, and sat down on the shady porch to smoke a cigar. The proprietor, having put the money in his pocket, came out and stepped into his buggy, which was still standing alongside the piazza. The colonel watched him drive a stone's throw to a barroom down the street, get down, go in, come out a few minutes later, wiping his mouth with the back of his hand, climb into the buggy, drive back, step out and re-enter the hotel.

It was yet an hour to train time, and the colonel, to satisfy an impulse of curiosity, strolled over to the court house, which could be seen across the square, through the trees. Requesting leave of the

Clerk in the county recorder's office to look at the records of mortgages, he turned the leaves over and found that a large proportion of the mortgages recently recorded—among them one on the hotel property—had been given to Fetters.

The whistle of the train was heard in the distance as the colonel recrossed the square. Glancing toward the hotel, he saw the landlord come out, drive across the square to the station, and sit there until the passengers had alighted. To a drummer with a sample case, he pointed carelessly across the square to the hotel, but made no movement to take the baggage; and as the train moved off, the colonel, looking back, saw him driving back to the hotel.

Fetters had begun to worry the colonel. He had never seen the man, and yet his influence was everywhere. He seemed to brood over the country round about like a great vampire bat, sucking the life-blood of the people. His touch meant blight. As soon as a Fetters mortgage rested on a place, the property began to run down; for why should the nominal owner keep up a place which was destined in the end to go to Fetters? The colonel had heard grewsome tales of Fetters's convict labour plantation; he had seen the operation of Fetters's cotton-mill, where white humanity, in its fairest and tenderest form, was stunted and blighted and destroyed; and he had not forgotten the scene in the justice's office.

The fighting blood of the old Frenches was stirred. The colonel's means were abundant; he did not lack the sinews of war. Clarendon offered a field for profitable investment. He would like to do something for humanity, something to offset Fetters and his kind, who were preying upon the weaknesses of the people, enslaving white and black alike. In a great city, what he could give away would have been but a slender stream, scarcely felt in the rivers of charity poured into the ocean of want; and even his considerable wealth would have made him only a small stockholder in some great aggregation of capital. In this backward old town, away from the great centres of commerce, and scarcely feeling their distant pulsebeat, except when some daring speculator tried for a brief period to corner the cotton market, he could mark with his own eyes the good he might accomplish. It required no great stretch of imagination to see the town, a few years hence, a busy hive of industry, where no man, and no woman obliged to work, need be without employment at fair wages; where the trinity of peace, prosperity and progress would reign supreme; where men like Fetters and methods like his would no longer be tolerated. The forces of enlightenment, set in motion by his aid, and supported by just laws, should engage the retrogade forces represented by Fetters. Communities, like men, must either grow or decay, advance or decline; they could not stand still. Clarendon was decaying. Fetters was the parasite which, by sending out its roots toward rich and poor alike, struck at both extremes of society, and was choking the life of the town like a rank and deadly vine.

The colonel could, if need be, spare the year or two of continuous residence needed to rescue Clarendon from the grasp of Fetters. The climate agreed with Phil, who was growing like a weed; and the colonel could easily defer for a little while his scheme of travel, and the further disposition of his future.

So, when he reached home that night, he wrote an answer to a long and gossipy letter received from Kirby about that time, in which the latter gave a detailed account of what was going on in the colonel's favourite club and among their mutual friends, and reported progress in the search for some venture worthy of their mettle. The colonel replied that Phil and he were well, that he was interesting himself in a local enterprise which would certainly occupy him for some months, and that he would not visit New York during the summer, unless it were to drop in for a day or two on business and return immediately.

A letter from Mrs. Jerviss, received about the same time, was less easily disposed of. She had learned, from Kirby, of the chivalrous manner in which Mr. French had protected her interests and spared her feelings in the fight with Consolidated Bagging. She had not been able, she said, to thank him adequately before he went away, because she had not known how much she owed him; nor could she fittingly express herself on paper. She could only renew her invitation to him to join her house party at Newport in July. The guests would be friends of his—she would be glad to invite any others that he might suggest. She would then have the opportunity to thank him in person.

The colonel was not unmoved by this frank and grateful letter, and he knew perfectly well what reward he might claim from her gratitude. Had the letter come a few weeks sooner, it might have had a different answer. But, now, after the first pang of regret, his only problem was how to refuse gracefully her offered hospitality. He was sorry, he replied, not to be able to join her house party that summer, but during the greater part of it he would be detained in the South by certain matters into which he had been insensibly drawn. As for her thanks, she owed him none; he had only done his duty, and had already been thanked too much.

So thoroughly had Colonel French entered into the spirit of his yet undefined contest with Fetters, that his life in New York, save when these friendly communications recalled it, seemed far away, and of slight retrospective interest. Every one knows of the "blind spot" in the field of vision. New York was for the time being the colonel's blind spot. That it might reassert its influence was always possible, but for the present New York was of no more interest to him than Canton or Bogota. Having revelled for a few pleasant weeks in memories of a remoter past, the reaction had projected his thoughts forward into the future. His life in New York, and in the Clarendon of the present—these were mere transitory embodiments; he lived in the Clarendon yet to be, a Clarendon rescued from Fetters, purified, rehabilitated; and no compassionate angel warned him how tenacious of life that which Fetters stood for might be—that survival of the spirit of slavery, under which the land still groaned and travailed—the growth of generations, which it would take more than one generation to destroy.

In describing to Judge Bullard his visit to the cotton mill, the colonel was not sparing of his indignation.

"The men," he declared with emphasis, "who are responsible for that sort of thing, are enemies of mankind. I've been in business for twenty years, but I have never sought to make money by trading on the souls and bodies of women and children. I saw the little darkies running about the streets down there at Carthage; they were poor and ragged and dirty, but they were out in the air and the sunshine; they have a chance to get their growth; to go to school and learn something. The white children are worked worse than slaves, and are growing up dulled and stunted, physically and mentally. Our folks down here are mighty short-sighted, judge. We'll wake them up. We'll build a model cotton mill, and run it with decent hours and decent wages, and treat the operatives like human beings with bodies to nourish, minds to develop; and souls to save. Fetters and his crowd will have to come up to our standard, or else we'll take their hands away."

Judge Bullard had looked surprised when the colonel began his denunciation; and though he said little, his expression, when the colonel had finished, was very thoughtful and not altogether happy.

Fourteen

It was the week after the colonel's house warming.

Graciella was not happy. She was sitting, erect and graceful, as she always sat, on the top step of the piazza. Ben Dudley occupied the other end of the step. His model stood neglected beside him, and he was looking straight at Graciella, whose eyes, avoiding his, were bent upon a copy of "Jane Eyre," held open in her hand. There was an unwonted silence between them, which Ben was the first to break.

"Will you go for a walk with me?" he asked.

"I'm sorry, Ben," she replied, "but I have an engagement to go driving with Colonel French."

Ben's dark cheek grew darker, and he damned Colonel French softly beneath his breath. He could not ask Graciella to drive, for their old buggy was not fit to be seen, and he had no money to hire a better one. The only reason why he ever had wanted money was because of her. If she must have money, or the things that money alone would buy, he must get money, or lose her. As long as he had no rival there was hope. But could he expect to hold his own against a millionaire, who had the garments and the manners of the great outside world?

"I suppose the colonel's here every night, as well as every day," he said, "and that you talk to him all the time."

"No, Ben, he isn't here every night, nor every day. His old darky, Peter, brings Phil over every day; but when the colonel comes he talks to grandmother and Aunt Laura, as well as to me."

Graciella had risen from the step, and was now enthroned in a splint-bottomed armchair, an attitude more in keeping with the air of dignity which she felt constrained to assume as a cloak for an uneasy conscience.

Graciella was not happy. She had reached the parting of the ways, and realised that she must choose between them. And yet she hesitated. Every consideration of prudence dictated that she choose Colonel French rather than Ben. The colonel was rich and could gratify all her ambitions. There could be no reasonable doubt that he was fond of her; and she had heard it said, by those more experienced than she and therefore better qualified to judge, that he was infatuated with her. Certainly he had shown her a great deal of attention. He had taken her driving; he had lent her books and music; he had brought or sent the New York paper every day for her to read.

He had been kind to her Aunt Laura, too, probably for her niece's sake; for the colonel was kind by nature, and wished to make everyone about him happy. It was fortunate that her Aunt Laura was fond of Philip. If she should decide to marry the colonel, she would have her Aunt Laura come and make her home with them: she could give Philip the attention with which his stepmother's social duties might interfere. It was hardly likely that her aunt entertained any hope of marriage; indeed, Miss Laura had long since professed herself resigned to old maidenhood.

But in spite of these rosy dreams, Graciella was not happy. To marry the colonel she must give up Ben; and Ben, discarded, loomed up larger than Ben, accepted. She liked Ben; she was accustomed to Ben. Ben was young, and youth attracted youth. Other things being equal, she would have preferred him to the colonel. But Ben was poor; he had nothing and his prospects for the future were not alluring. He would inherit little, and that little not until his uncle's death. He had no profession. He was not even a good farmer, and trifled away, with his useless models and mechanical toys, the time he might have spent in making his uncle's plantation productive. Graciella did not know that Fetters had a mortgage on the plantation, or Ben's prospects would have seemed even more hopeless.

She felt sorry not only for herself, but for Ben as well—sorry that he should lose her—for she knew that he loved her sincerely. But her first duty was to herself. Conscious that she possessed talents, social and otherwise, it was not her view of creative wisdom that it should implant in the mind tastes and in the heart longings destined never to be realised. She must discourage Ben—gently and gradually, for of course he would suffer; and humanity, as well as friendship, counselled kindness. A gradual breaking off, too, would be less harrowing to her own feelings.

"I suppose you admire Colonel French immensely," said Ben, with assumed impartiality.

"Oh, I like him reasonably well," she said with an equal lack of candour. "His conversation is improving. He has lived in the metropolis, and has seen so much of the world that he can scarcely speak without saying something interesting. It's a liberal education to converse with people who have had opportunities. It helps to prepare my mind for life at the North."

"You set a great deal of store by the North, Graciella. Anybody would allow, to listen to you, that you didn't love your own country."

"I love the South, Ben, as I loved Aunt Lou, my old black mammy. I've laid in her arms many a day, and I 'most cried my eyes out when she died. But that didn't mean that I never wanted to see any one else. Nor am I going to live in the South a minute longer than I can help, because it's too slow. And New York isn't all—I want to travel and see the world. The South is away behind."

She had said much the same thing weeks before; but then it had been spontaneous. Now she was purposely trying to make Ben see how unreasonable was his hope.

Ben stood, as he obscurely felt, upon delicate ground. Graciella had not been the only person to overhear remarks about the probability of the colonel's seeking a wife in Clarendon, and jealousy had sharpened Ben's perceptions while it increased his fears. He had little to offer Graciella. He was not well educated; he had nothing to recommend him but his youth and his love for her. He could not take her to Europe, or even to New York—at least not yet.

"And at home," Graciella went on seriously, "at home I should want several houses—a town house, a country place, a seaside cottage. When we were tired of one we could go to another, or live in hotels—in the winter in Florida, at Atlantic City in the spring, at Newport in the summer. They say Long Branch has gone out entirely."

Ben had a vague idea that Long Branch was by the seaside, and exposed to storms. "Gone out to sea?" he asked absently. He was sick for love of her, and she was dreaming of watering places.

"No, Ben," said Graciella, compassionately. Poor Ben had so little opportunity for schooling! He was not to blame for his want of knowledge; but could she throw herself away upon an ignoramus? "It's still there, but has gone out of fashion."

"Oh, excuse me! I'm not posted on these fashionable things."

Ben relapsed into gloom. The model remained untouched. He could not give Graciella a house; he would not have a house until his uncle died. Graciella had never seemed so beautiful as to-day, as she sat, dressed in the cool white gown which Miss Laura's slender fingers had done up, and with her hair dressed after the daintiest and latest fashion chronicled in the *Ladies' Fireside Journal*. No wonder, he thought, that a jaded old man of the world like Colonel French should delight in her fresh young beauty!

But he would not give her up without a struggle. She had loved him; she must love him still; and she would yet be his, if he could keep her true to him or free from any promise to another, until her deeper feelings could resume their sway. It could not be possible, after all that had passed between them, that she meant to throw him over, nor was he a man that she could afford to treat in such a fashion. There was more in him than Graciella imagined; he was conscious of latent power of some kind, though he knew not what, and something would surely happen, sometime, somehow, to improve his fortunes. And there was always the hope, the possibility of finding the lost money.

He had brought his great-uncle Ralph's letter with him, as he had promised Graciella. When she read it, she would see the reasonableness of his hope, and might be willing to wait, at least a little while. Any delay would be a point gained. He shuddered to think that he might lose her, and then, the day after the irrevocable vows had been taken, the treasure might come to light, and all their life be spent in vain regrets. Graciella was skeptical about the lost money. Even Mrs. Treadwell, whose faith had been firm for years, had ceased to encourage his hope; while Miss Laura, who at one time had smiled at any mention of the matter, now looked grave if by any chance he let slip a word in reference to it. But he had in his pocket the outward and visible sign of his inward belief, and he would try its effect on Graciella. He would risk ridicule or anything else for her sake.

"Graciella," he said, "I have brought my uncle Malcolm's letter along, to convince you that uncle is not as crazy as he seems, and that there's some foundation for the hope that I may yet be able to give you all you want. I don't want to relinquish the hope, and I want you to share it with me."

He produced an envelope, once white, now yellow with time, on which was endorsed in ink once black but faded to a pale brown, and hardly legible, the name of "Malcolm Dudley, Esq., Mink Run," and in the lower left-hand corner, "By hand of Viney."

The sheet which Ben drew from this wrapper was worn at the folds, and required careful handling. Graciella, moved by curiosity, had come down from her throne to a seat beside Ben upon the porch. She had never had any faith in the mythical gold of old Ralph Dudley. The people of an earlier generation—her Aunt Laura perhaps—may once have believed in it, but they had long since ceased to do more than smile pityingly and shake their heads at the mention of old Malcolm's delusion. But there was in it the element of romance. Strange things had happened, and why might they not happen again? And if they should happen, why not to Ben, dear old, shiftless Ben! She moved a porch pillow close beside him, and, as they bent their heads over the paper her hair mingled with his, and soon her hand rested, unconsciously, upon his shoulder.

"It was a voice from the grave," said Ben, "for my great-uncle Ralph was dead when the letter reached Uncle Malcolm. I'll read it aloud—the writing is sometimes hard to make out, and I know it by heart:

My Dear Malcolm:

I have in my hands fifty thousand dollars of government money, in gold, which I am leaving here at the house for a few days. Since you are not at home, and I cannot wait, I have confided in our girl Viney, whom I can trust. She will tell you, when she gives you this, where I have put the money—I do not write it, lest the letter should fall into the wrong hands; there are many to whom it would be a great temptation. I shall return in a few days, and relieve you of the responsibility. Should anything happen to me, write to the Secretary of State at Richmond for instructions what to do with the money. In great haste,

Your affectionate uncle,
RALPH DUDLEY

Graciella was momentarily impressed by the letter; of its reality there could be no doubt—it was there in black and white, or rather brown and yellow.

"It sounds like a letter in a novel," she said, thoughtfully. "There must have been something."

"There must *be* something, Graciella, for Uncle Ralph was killed the next day, and never came back for the money. But Uncle Malcolm, because he don't know where to look, can't find it; and old Aunt Viney, because she can't talk, can't tell him where it is."

"Why has she never shown him?" asked Graciella.

"There is some mystery," he said, "which she seems unable to explain without speech. And then, she is queer—as queer, in her own way, as uncle is in his. Now, if you'd only marry me, Graciella, and go out there to live, with your uncommonly fine mind, *you'd* find it—you couldn't help but find it. It would just come at your call, like my dog when I whistle to him."

Graciella was touched by the compliment, or by the serious feeling which underlay it. And that was very funny, about calling the money and having it come! She had often heard of people whistling for their money, but had never heard that it came—that was Ben's idea. There really was a good deal in Ben, and perhaps, after all——

But at that moment there was a sound of wheels, and whatever Graciella's thought may have been, it was not completed. As Colonel French lifted the latch of the garden gate and came up the walk toward them, any glamour of the past, any rosy hope of the future, vanished in the solid brilliancy of the present moment. Old Ralph was dead, old Malcolm nearly so; the money had never been found, would never come to light. There on the doorstep was a young man shabbily attired, without means or prospects. There at the gate was a fine horse, in a handsome trap, and coming up the walk an agreeable, well-dressed gentleman of wealth and position. No dead romance could, in the heart of a girl of seventeen, hold its own against so vital and brilliant a reality.

"Thank you, Ben," she said, adjusting a stray lock of hair which had escaped from her radiant crop, "I am not clever enough for that. It is a dream. Your great-uncle Ralph had ridden too long and too far in the sun, and imagined the treasure, which has driven your Uncle Malcolm crazy, and his housekeeper dumb, and has benumbed you so that you sit around waiting, waiting, when you ought to be working, working! No, Ben, I like you ever so much, but you will never take me to New York with your Uncle Ralph's money, nor will you ever earn enough to take me with your own. You must excuse me now, for here comes my cavalier. Don't hurry away; Aunt Laura will be out in a minute. You can stay and work on your model; I'll not be here to interrupt you. Good evening, Colonel French! Did you bring me a *Herald?* I want to look at the advertisements."

"Yes, my dear young lady, there is Wednesday's—it is only two days old. How are you, Mr. Dudley?"

"Tol'able, sir, thank you." Ben was a gentleman by instinct, though his heart was heavy and the colonel a favoured rival.

"By the way," said the colonel, "I wish to have an interview with your uncle, about the old mill site. He seems to have been a stockholder in the company, and we should like his signature, if he is in condition to give it. If not, it may be necessary to appoint you his guardian, with power to act in his place."

"He's all right, sir, in the morning, if you come early enough," replied Ben, courteously. "You can tell what is best to do after you've seen him."

"Thank you," replied the colonel, "I'll have my man drive me out to-morrow about ten, say; if you'll be at home? You ought to be there, you know."

"Very well, sir, I'll be there all day, and shall expect you."

Graciella threw back one compassionate glance, as they drove away behind the colonel's high-stepping brown horse, and did not quite escape a pang at the sight of her young lover, still sitting on the steps in a dejected attitude; and for a moment longer his reproachful eyes haunted her. But Graciella prided herself on being, above all things, practical, and, having come out for a good time, resolutely put all unpleasant thoughts aside.

There was good horse-flesh in the neighbourhood of Clarendon, and the colonel's was of the best. Some of the roads about the town were good—not very well kept roads, but the soil was a sandy loam and was self-draining, so that driving was pleasant in good weather. The colonel had several times invited Miss Laura to drive with him, and had taken her once; but she was often obliged to stay with her mother. Graciella could always be had, and the colonel, who did not like to drive alone, found her a vivacious companion, whose naïve comments upon life were very amusing to a seasoned man of the world. She was as pretty, too, as a picture, and the colonel had always admired beauty—with a tempered admiration.

At Graciella's request they drove first down Main Street, past the post-office, where she wished to mail a letter. They attracted much attention as they drove through the street in the colonel's new trap. Graciella's billowy white gown added a needed touch of maturity to her slender youthfulness. A big straw hat shaded her brown hair, and she sat erect, and held her head high, with a vivid consciousness that she was the central feature of a very attractive whole. The colonel shared her thought, and looked at her with frank admiration.

"You are the cynosure of all eyes," he declared. "I suppose I'm an object of envy to every young fellow in town."

Graciella blushed and bridled with pleasure. "I am not interested in the young men of Clarendon," she replied loftily; "they are not worth the trouble."

"Not even—Ben?" asked the colonel slyly.

"Oh," she replied, with studied indifference, "Mr. Dudley is really a cousin, and only a friend. He comes to see the family."

The colonel's attentions could have but one meaning, and it was important to disabuse his mind concerning Ben. Nor was she the only one in the family who entertained that thought. Of late her grandmother had often addressed her in an unusual way, more as a woman than as a child; and, only the night before, had retold the old story of her own sister Mary, who, many years before, had married a man of fifty. He had worshipped her, and had died, after a decent interval, leaving her a large fortune. From which the old lady had deduced that, on the whole, it was better to be an old man's darling than a young man's slave. She had made no application of the story, but Graciella was astute enough to draw her own conclusions.

Her Aunt Laura, too, had been unusually kind; she had done up the white gown twice a week, had trimmed her hat for her, and had worn old gloves that she might buy her niece a new pair. And her aunt had looked at her wistfully and remarked, with a sigh, that youth was a glorious season and beauty a great responsibility. Poor dear, good old Aunt Laura! When the expected happened, she would be very kind to Aunt Laura, and repay her, so far as possible, for all her care and sacrifice.

Fifteen

It was only a short time after his visit to the Excelsior Mills that Colonel French noticed a falling off in the progress made by his lawyer, Judge Bullard, in procuring the signatures of those interested in the old mill site, and after the passing of several weeks he began to suspect that some adverse influence was at work. This suspicion was confirmed when Judge Bullard told him one day, with some embarrassment, that he could no longer act for him in the matter.

"I'm right sorry, Colonel," he said. "I should like to help you put the thing through, but I simply can't afford it. Other clients, whose business I have transacted for years, and to whom I am under heavy obligations, have intimated that they would consider any further activity of mine in your interest unfriendly to theirs."

"I suppose," said the colonel, "your clients wish to secure the mill site for themselves. Nothing imparts so much value to a thing as the notion that somebody else wants it. Of course, I can't ask you to act for me further, and if you'll make out your bill, I'll hand you a check."

"I hope," said Judge Bullard, "there'll be no ill-feeling about our separation."

"Oh, no," responded the colonel, politely, "not at all. Business is business, and a man's own interests are his first concern."

"I'm glad you feel that way," replied the lawyer, much relieved. He had feared that the colonel might view the matter differently.

"Some men, you know," he said, "might have kept on, and worked against you, while accepting your retainer; there are such skunks at the bar."

"There are black sheep in every fold," returned the colonel with a cold smile. "It would be unprofessional, I suppose, to name your client, so I'll not ask you."

The judge did not volunteer the information, but the colonel knew instinctively whence came opposition to his plan, and investigation confirmed his intuition. Judge Bullard was counsel for Fetters in all matters where skill and knowledge were important, and Fetters held his note, secured by mortgage, for money loaned. For dirty work Fetters used tools of baser metal, but, like a wise man, he knew when these were useless, and was shrewd enough to keep the best lawyers under his control.

The colonel, after careful inquiry, engaged to take Judge Bullard's place, one Albert Caxton, a member of a good old family, a young man, and a capable lawyer, who had no ascertainable connection with Fetters, and who, in common with a small fraction of the best people, regarded Fetters with distrust, and ascribed his wealth to usury and to what, in more recent years, has come to be known as "graft."

To a man of Colonel French's business training, opposition was merely a spur to effort. He had not run a race of twenty years in the commercial field, to be worsted in the first heat by the petty boss of a Southern backwoods county. Why Fetters opposed him he did not know. Perhaps he wished to defeat a possible rival, or merely to keep out principles and ideals which would conflict with his own methods and injure his prestige. But if Fetters wanted a fight, Fetters should have a fight.

Colonel French spent much of his time at young Caxton's office, instructing the new lawyer in the details of the mill affair. Caxton proved intelligent, zealous, and singularly sympathetic with his client's views and plans. They had not been together a week before the colonel realised that he had gained immensely by the change.

The colonel took a personal part in the effort to procure signatures, among others that of old Malcolm Dudley and on the morning following the drive with Graciella, he drove out to Mink Run to see the old gentleman in person and discover whether or not he was in a condition to transact business.

Before setting out, he went to his desk—his father's desk, which Miss Laura had sent to him—to get certain papers for old Mr. Dudley's signature, if the latter should prove capable of a legal act. He had laid the papers on top of some others which had nearly filled one of the numerous small drawers in the desk. Upon opening the drawer he found that one of the papers was missing.

The colonel knew quite well that he had placed the paper in the drawer the night before; he remembered the circumstance very distinctly, for the event was so near that it scarcely required an exercise, not to say an effort, of memory. An examination of the drawer disclosed that the piece forming the back of it was a little lower than the sides. Possibly, thought the colonel, the paper had slipped off and fallen behind the drawer.

He drew the drawer entirely out, and slipped his hand into the cavity. At the back of it he felt the corner of a piece of paper projecting upward from below. The paper had evidently slipped off the top of the others and fallen into a crevice, due to the shrinkage of the wood or some defect of construction.

The opening for the drawer was so shallow that though he could feel the end of the paper, he was unable to get such a grasp of it as would permit him to secure it easily. But it was imperative that he have the paper; and since it bore already several signatures obtained with some difficulty, he did not wish to run the risk of tearing it.

He examined the compartment below to see if perchance the paper could be reached from there, but found that it could not. There was evidently a lining to the desk, and the paper had doubtless slipped down between this and the finished panels forming the back of the desk. To reach it, the colonel procured a screw driver, and turning the desk around, loosened, with some difficulty, the screws that fastened the proper panel, and soon recovered the paper. With it, however, he found a couple of yellow, time-stained envelopes, addressed on the outside to Major John Treadwell.

The envelopes were unsealed. He glanced into one of them, and seeing that it contained a sheet, folded small, presumably a letter, he thrust the two of them into the breast pocket of his coat, intending to hand them to Miss Laura at their next meeting. They were probably old letters and of no consequence, but they should of course be returned to the owners.

In putting the desk back in its place, after returning the panel and closing the crevice against future accidents, the colonel caught his coat on a projecting point and tore a long rent in the sleeve. It was an old coat, and worn only about the house; and when he changed it before leaving to pay his call upon old Malcolm Dudley, he hung it in a back corner in his clothes closet, and did not put it on again for a long time. Since he was very busily occupied in the meantime, the two old letters to which he had attached no importance, escaped his memory altogether.

The colonel's coachman, a young coloured man by the name of Tom, had complained of illness early in the morning, and the colonel took Peter along to drive him to Mink Run, as well as to keep him company. On their way through the town they stopped at Mrs. Tread-well's, where they left Phil, who had, he declared, some important engagement with Graciella.

The distance was not long, scarcely more than five miles. Ben Dudley was in the habit of traversing it on horseback, twice a day. When they had passed the last straggling cabin of the town, their way lay along a sandy road, flanked by fields green with corn and cotton, broken by stretches of scraggy pine and oak, growing upon land once under cultivation, but impoverished by the wasteful methods of slavery; land that had never been regenerated, and was now no longer tilled. Negroes were working in the fields, birds were singing in the trees. Buzzards circled lazily against the distant sky. Although it was only early summer, a languor in the air possessed the colonel's senses, and suggested a certain charity toward those of his neighbours—and they were most of them—who showed no marked zeal for labour.

"Work," he murmured, "is best for happiness, but in this climate idleness has its compensations. What, in the end, do we get for all our labour?"

"Fifty cents a day, an' fin' yo'se'f, suh," said Peter, supposing the soliloquy addressed to himself. "Dat's w'at dey pays roun' hyuh."

When they reached a large clearing, which Peter pointed out as their destination, the old man dismounted with considerable agility, and opened a rickety gate that was held in place by loops of rope. Evidently the entrance had once possessed some pretensions to elegance, for the huge hewn posts had originally been faced with dressed lumber and finished with ornamental capitals, some fragments of which remained; and the one massive hinge, hanging by a slender rust-eaten nail, had been wrought into a fantastic shape. As they drove through the gateway, a green lizard scampered down from the top of one of the posts, where he had been sunning himself, and a rattlesnake lying in the path lazily uncoiled his motley brown length, and sounding his rattle, wriggled slowly off into the rank grass and weeds that bordered the carriage track.

The house stood well back from the road, amid great oaks and elms and unpruned evergreens. The lane by which it was approached was partly overgrown with weeds and grass, from which the mare's fetlocks swept the dew, yet undried by the morning sun.

The old Dudley "mansion," as it was called, was a large two-story frame house, built in the colonial style, with a low-pitched roof, and a broad piazza along the front, running the full length of both stories and supported by thick round columns, each a solid piece of pine timber, gray with age and lack of paint, seamed with fissures by the sun and rain of many years. The roof swayed downward on one side; the shingles were old and cracked and moss-grown; several of the second story windows were boarded up, and others filled with sashes from which most of the glass had disappeared.

About the house, for a space of several rods on each side of it, the ground was bare of grass and shrubbery, rough and uneven, lying in little hillocks and hollows, as though recently dug over at haphazard, or explored by some vagrant drove of hogs. At one side, beyond this barren area, lay a kitchen garden, enclosed by a paling fence. The colonel had never thought of young Dudley as being at all energetic, but so ill-kept a place argued shiftlessness in a marked degree.

When the carriage had drawn up in front of the house, the colonel became aware of two figures on the long piazza. At one end, in a massive oaken armchair, sat an old man—seemingly a very old man, for he was bent and wrinkled, with thin white hair hanging down upon his shoulders. His face, of a highbred and strongly marked type, emphasised by age, had the hawk-like contour, that is supposed to betoken extreme acquisitiveness. His faded eyes were turned toward a woman, dressed in a homespun frock and a muslin cap, who sat bolt upright, in a straight-backed chair, at the other end of the piazza, with her hands folded on her lap, looking fixedly toward her *vis-à-vis*. Neither of them paid the slightest attention to the colonel, and when the old man rose, it was not to step forward and welcome his visitor, but to approach and halt in front of the woman.

"Viney," he said, sharply, "I am tired of this nonsense. I insist upon knowing, immediately, where my uncle left the money."

The woman made no reply, but her faded eyes glowed for a moment, like the ashes of a dying fire, and her figure stiffened perceptibly as she leaned slightly toward him.

"Show me at once, you hussy," he said, shaking his fist, "or you'll have reason to regret it. I'll have you whipped." His cracked voice rose to a shrill shriek as he uttered the threat.

The slumbrous fire in the woman's eyes flamed up for a moment. She rose, and drawing herself up to her full height, which was greater than the old man's, made some incoherent sounds, and bent upon him a look beneath which he quailed.

"Yes, Viney, good Viney," he said, soothingly, "I know it was wrong, and I've always regretted it, always, from the very moment. But you shouldn't bear malice. Servants, the Bible says, should obey their masters, and you should bless them that curse you, and do good to them that despitefully use you. But I was good to you before, Viney, and I was kind to you afterwards, and I know you've forgiven me, good Viney, noble-hearted Viney, and you're going to tell me, aren't you?" he pleaded, laying his hand caressingly upon her arm.

She drew herself away, but, seemingly mollified, moved her lips as though in speech. The old man put his hand to his ear and listened with an air of strained eagerness, well-nigh breathless in its intensity.

"Try again, Viney," he said, "that's a good girl. Your old master thinks a great deal of you, Viney. He is your best friend!"

Again she made an inarticulate response, which he nevertheless seemed to comprehend, for, brightening up immediately, he turned from her, came down the steps with tremulous haste, muttering to himself meanwhile, seized a spade that stood leaning against the steps, passed by the carriage without a glance, and began digging furiously at one side of the yard. The old woman watched him for a while, with a self-absorption that was entirely oblivious of the visitors, and then entered the house.

The colonel had been completely absorbed in this curious drama. There was an air of weirdness and unreality about it all. Old Peter was as silent as if he had been turned into stone. Something in the atmosphere conduced to somnolence, for even the horses stood still, with no signs of restlessness. The colonel was the first to break the spell.

"What's the matter with them, Peter? Do you know?"

"Dey's bofe plumb 'stracted, suh—clean out'n dey min's—dey be'n dat way fer yeahs an' yeahs an' yeahs."

"That's Mr. Dudley, I suppose?"

"Yas, suh, dat's ole Mars Ma'com Dudley, de uncle er young Mistah Ben Dudley w'at hangs 'roun Miss Grac'ella so much."

"And who is the woman?"

"She's a bright mulattah 'oman, suh, w'at use' ter b'long ter de family befo' de wah, an' has kep' house fer ole Mars' Ma'com ever sense. He 'lows dat she knows whar old Mars' Rafe Dudley, *his* uncle, hid a million dollahs endyoin' de wah, an' huh tongue's paralyse' so she can't tell 'im—an' he's be'n tryin' ter fin' out fer de las' twenty-five years. I wo'ked out hyuh one summer on plantation, an' I seen 'em gwine on like dat many 'n' many a time. Dey don' nobody roun' hyuh pay no 'tention to 'em no mo', ev'ybody's so use' ter seein' 'em."

The conversation was interrupted by the appearance of Ben Dudley, who came around the house, and, advancing to the carriage, nodded to Peter, and greeted the colonel respectfully.

"Won't you 'light and come in?" he asked.

The colonel followed him into the house, to a plainly furnished parlour. There was a wide fireplace, with a fine old pair of brass andirons, and a few pieces of old mahogany furniture, incongruously assorted with half a dozen splint-bottomed chairs. The floor was bare, and on the walls half a dozen of the old Dudleys looked out from as many oil paintings, with the smooth glaze that marked the touch of the travelling artist, in the days before portrait painting was superseded by photography and crayon enlargements.

Ben returned in a few minutes with his uncle. Old Malcolm seemed to have shaken off his aberration, and greeted the colonel with grave politeness.

"I am glad, sir," he said, giving the visitor his hand, "to make your acquaintance. I have been working in the garden—the flower-garden—for the sake of the exercise. We have negroes enough, though they are very trifling nowadays, but the exercise is good for my health. I have trouble, at times, with my rheumatism, and with my—my memory." He passed his hand over his brow as though brushing away an imaginary cobweb.

"Ben tells me you have a business matter to present to me?"

The colonel, somewhat mystified, after what he had witnessed, by this sudden change of manner, but glad to find the old man seemingly rational, stated the situation in regard to the mill site. Old Malcolm seemed to understand perfectly, and accepted with willingness the colonel's proposition to give him a certain amount of stock in the new company for the release of such rights as he might possess under the old incorporation. The colonel had brought with him a contract, properly drawn, which was executed by old Malcolm, and witnessed by the colonel and Ben.

"I trust, sir," said Mr. Dudley, "that you will not ascribe it to any discourtesy that I have not called to see you. I knew your father and your grandfather. But the cares of my estate absorb me so completely that I never leave home. I shall send my regards to you now and then by my nephew. I expect, in a very short time, when certain matters are adjusted, to be able to give up, to a great extent, my arduous cares, and lead a life of greater leisure, which will enable me to travel and cultivate a wider acquaintance. When that time comes, sir, I shall hope to see more of you."

The old gentleman stood courteously on the steps while Ben accompanied the colonel to the carriage. It had scarcely turned into the lane when the colonel, looking back, saw the old man digging furiously. The condition of the yard was explained; he had been unjust in ascribing it to Ben's neglect.

"I reckon, suh," remarked Peter, "dat w'en he fin' dat million dollahs, Mistah Ben'll marry Miss Grac'ella an' take huh ter New Yo'k."

"Perhaps—and perhaps not," said the colonel. To himself he added, musingly, "Old Malcolm will start on a long journey before he finds the—million dollars. The watched pot never boils. Buried treasure is never found by those who seek it, but always accidentally, if at all."

On the way back they stopped at the Treadwells' for Phil. Phil was not ready to go home. He was intensely interested in a long-eared mechanical mule, constructed by Ben Dudley out of bits of wood and leather and controlled by certain springs made of rubber bands, by manipulating which the mule could be made to kick furiously. Since the colonel had affairs to engage his attention, and Phil seemed perfectly contented, he was allowed to remain, with the understanding that Peter should come for him in the afternoon.

Sixteen

Little Phil had grown very fond of old Peter, who seemed to lavish upon the child all of his love and devotion for the dead generations of the French family. The colonel had taught Phil to call the old man "Uncle Peter," after the kindly Southern fashion of slavery days, which, denying to negroes the forms of address applied to white people, found in the affectionate terms of relationship—Mammy, Auntie and Uncle—designations that recognised the respect due to age, and yet lost, when applied to slaves, their conventional significance. There was a strong sympathy between the intelligent child and the undeveloped old negro; they were more nearly on a mental level, leaving out, of course, the factor of Peter's experience, than could have been the case with one more generously endowed than Peter, who, though by nature faithful, had never been unduly bright. Little Phil became so attached to his old attendant that, between Peter and the Treadwell ladies, the colonel's housekeeper had to give him very little care.

On Sunday afternoons the colonel and Phil and Peter would sometimes walk over to the cemetery. The family lot was now kept in perfect order. The low fence around it had been repaired, and several leaning headstones straightened up. But, guided by a sense of fitness, and having before him the awful example for which Fetters was responsible, the colonel had added no gaudy monument nor made any alterations which would disturb the quiet beauty of the spot or its harmony with the surroundings. In the Northern cemetery where his young wife was buried, he had erected to her memory a stately mausoleum, in keeping with similar memorials on every hand. But here, in this quiet graveyard, where his ancestors slept their last sleep under the elms and the willows, display would have been out of place. He had, however, placed a wrought-iron bench underneath the trees, where he would sit and read his paper, while little Phil questioned old Peter about his grandfather and his great-grandfather, their prowess on the hunting field, and the wars they fought in; and the old man would delight in detailing, in his rambling and disconnected manner, the past glories of the French family. It was always a new story to Phil, and never grew stale to the old man. If Peter could be believed, there were never white folks so brave, so learned, so wise, so handsome, so kind to their servants, so just to all with whom they had dealings. Phil developed a very great fondness for these dead ancestors, whose graves and histories he soon knew as well as Peter himself. With his lively imagination he found pleasure, as children often do, in looking into the future. The unoccupied space in the large cemetery lot furnished him food for much speculation.

"Papa," he said, upon one of these peaceful afternoons, "there's room enough here for all of us, isn't there—you, and me and Uncle Peter?"

"Yes, Phil," said his father, "there's room for several generations of Frenches yet to sleep with their fathers."

Little Phil then proceeded to greater detail. "Here," he said, "next to grandfather, will be your place, and here next to that, will be mine, and here, next to me will be—but no," he said, pausing reflectively, "that ought to be saved for my little boy when he grows up and dies, that is, when I grow up and have a little boy and he grows up and grows old and dies and leaves a little boy and—but where will Uncle Peter be?"

"Nem mine me, honey," said the old man, "dey can put me somewhar e'se. Hit doan' mattuh 'bout me."

"No, Uncle Peter, you must be here with the rest of us. For you know, Uncle Peter, I'm so used to you now, that I should want you to be near me then."

Old Peter thought to humour the lad. "Put me down hyuh at de foot er de lot, little Mars' Phil, unner dis ellum tree."

"Oh, papa," exclaimed Phil, demanding the colonel's attention, "Uncle Peter and I have arranged everything. You know Uncle Peter is to stay with me as long as I live, and when he dies, he is to be buried here at the foot of the lot, under the elm tree, where he'll be near me all the time, and near the folks that he knows and that know him."

"All right, Phil. You see to it; you'll live longer."

"But, papa, if I should die first, and then Uncle Peter, and you last of all, you'll put Uncle Peter near me, won't you, papa?"

"Why, bless your little heart, Phil, of course your daddy will do whatever you want, if he's here to do it. But you'll live, Phil, please God, until I am old and bent and white-haired, and you are a grown man, with a beard, and a little boy of your own."

"Yas, suh," echoed the old servant, "an' till ole Peter's bones is long sence crumble' inter dus'. None er de Frenches' ain' never died till dey was done growed up."

On the afternoon following the colonel's visit to Mink Run, old Peter, when he came for Phil, was obliged to stay long enough to see the antics of the mechanical mule; and had not that artificial animal suddenly refused to kick, and lapsed into a characteristic balkiness for which there was no apparent remedy, it might have proved difficult to get Phil away.

"There, Philip dear, never mind," said Miss Laura, "we'll have Ben mend it for you when he comes, next time, and then you can play with it again."

Peter had brought with him some hooks and lines, and, he and Phil, after leaving the house, followed the bank of the creek, climbing a fence now and then, until they reached the old mill site, upon which work had not yet begun. They found a shady spot, and seating themselves upon the bank, baited their lines, and dropped them into a quiet pool. For quite a while their patience was unrewarded by anything more than a nibble. By and by a black cat came down from the ruined mill, and sat down upon the bank at a short distance from them.

"I reckon we'll haf ter move, honey," said the old man. "We ain't gwine ter have no luck fishin' 'g'ins' no ole black cat."

"But cats don't fish, Uncle Peter, do they?"

"Law', chile, you'll never know w'at dem critters *kin* do, 'tel you's watched 'em long ez I has! Keep yo' eye on dat one now."

The cat stood by the stream, in a watchful attitude. Suddenly she darted her paw into the shallow water and with a lightning-like movement drew out a small fish, which she took in her mouth, and retired with it a few yards up the bank.

"Jes' look at dat ole devil," said Peter, "playin' wid dat fish jes' lack it wuz a mouse! She'll be comin' down heah terreckly tellin' us ter go 'way fum her fishin' groun's."

"Why, Uncle Peter," said Phil incredulously, "cats can't talk!"

"Can't dey? Hoo said dey couldn'? Ain't Miss Grac'ella an' me be'n tellin' you right along 'bout Bre'r Rabbit and Bre'r Fox an de yuther creturs talkin' an' gwine on jes' lak folks?"

"Yes, Uncle Peter, but those were just stories; they didn't really talk, did they?"

"Law', honey," said the old man, with a sly twinkle in his rheumy eye, "you is de sma'tes' little white boy I ever knowed, but you is got a monst'us heap ter l'arn yit, chile. Nobody ain' done tol' you 'bout de Black Cat an' de Ha'nted House, is dey?"

"No, Uncle Peter—you tell me."

"I didn' knowed but Miss Grac'ella mought a tole you—she knows mos' all de tales."

"No, she hasn't. You tell me about it, Uncle Peter."

"Well," said Peter, "does you 'member dat coal-black man dat drives de lumber wagon?"

"Yes, he goes by our house every day, on the way to the sawmill."

"Well, it all happen' 'long er him. He 'uz gwine long de street one day, w'en he heared two gent'emen—one of 'em was ole Mars' Tom Sellers an' I fuhgot de yuther—but dey 'uz talkin' 'bout dat ole h'anted house down by de creek, 'bout a mile from hyuh, on de yuther side er town, whar we went fishin' las' week. Does you 'member de place?"

"Yes, I remember the house."

"Well, as dis yer Jeff—dat's de lumber-wagon driver's name—as dis yer Jeff come up ter dese yer two gentlemen, one of 'em was sayin, 'I'll bet five dollahs dey ain' narry a man in his town would stay in dat ha'nted house all night.' Dis yer Jeff, he up 'n sez, sezee, 'Scuse me, suh, but ef you'll 'low me ter speak, suh, I knows a man wat'll stay in dat ole ha'nted house all night.' "

"What is a ha'nted house, Uncle Peter?" asked Phil.

"W'y, Law,' chile, a ha'nted house is a house whar dey's ha'nts!"

"And what are ha'nts, Uncle Peter?"

"Ha'nts, honey, is sperrits er dead folks, dat comes back an' hangs roun' whar dey use' ter lib."

"Do all spirits come back, Uncle Peter?"

"No, chile, bress de Lawd, no. Only de bad ones, w'at has be'n so wicked dey can't rest in dey graves. Folks lack yo' gran'daddy and yo' gran'mammy—an' all de Frenches—dey don' none er *dem* come back, fer dey wuz all good people an' is all gone ter hebben. But I'm fergittin' de tale.

" 'Well, hoo's de man—hoo's de man?' ax Mistah Sellers, w'en Jeff tol' 'im dey wuz somebody wat 'ud stay in de ole ha'nted house all night.

" 'I'm de man,' sez Jeff. 'I ain't skeered er no ha'nt dat evuh walked, an' I sleeps in graveya'ds by pref'ence; fac', I jes nach'ly lacks ter talk ter ha'nts. You pay me de five dollahs, an' I'll 'gree ter stay in de ole house f'm nine er clock 'tel daybreak.'

"Dey talk' ter Jeff a w'ile, an' dey made a bahgin wid 'im; dey give 'im one dollah down, an' promus' 'im fo' mo' in de mawnin' ef he stayed 'tel den.

"So w'en he got de dollah he went uptown an' spent it, an' 'long 'bout nine er clock he tuk a lamp, an' went down ter de ole house, an' went inside an' shet de do'.

"Dey wuz a rickety ole table settin' in de middle er de flo'. He sot de lamp on de table. Den he look 'roun' de room, in all de cawners an' up de chimbly, ter see dat dey wan't nobody ner nuthin' hid in de room. Den he tried all de winders an' fastened de do', so dey couldn' nobody ner nuthin' git in. Den he fotch a' ole rickety chair f'm one cawner, and set it by de table, and sot down. He wuz settin' dere, noddin' his head, studyin' 'bout dem other fo' dollahs, an' w'at he wuz gwine buy wid 'em, w'en bimeby he kinder dozed off, an' befo' he knowed it he wuz settin' dere fast asleep."

"W'en he woke up, 'long 'bout 'leven erclock, de lamp had bu'n' down kinder low. He heared a little noise behind him an' look 'roun', an' dere settin' in de middle er de flo' wuz a big black tomcat, wid his tail quirled up over his back, lookin' up at Jeff wid bofe his two big yaller eyes.

"Jeff rub' 'is eyes, ter see ef he wuz 'wake, an w'iles he sot dere wond'rin' whar de hole wuz dat dat ole cat come in at, fus' thing he knowed, de ole cat wuz settin' right up 'side of 'im, on de table, wid his tail quirled up roun' de lamp chimbly.

"Jeff look' at de black cat, an' de black cat look' at Jeff. Den de black cat open his mouf an' showed 'is teef, an' sezee——"

" 'Good evenin'!'

" 'Good evenin' suh,' 'spon' Jeff, trimblin' in de knees, an' kind'er edgin' 'way fum de table.

" 'Dey ain' nobody hyuh but you an' me, is dey?' sez de black cat, winkin' one eye.

" 'No, suh,' sez Jeff, as he made fer de do', *'an' quick ez I kin git out er hyuh, dey ain' gwine ter be nobody hyuh but you!'* "

"Is that all, Uncle Peter?" asked Phil, when the old man came to a halt with a prolonged chuckle.

"Huh?"

"Is that all?"

"No, dey's mo' er de tale, but dat's ernuff ter prove dat black cats kin do mo' dan little w'ite boys 'low dey kin."

"Did Jeff go away?"

"Did he go 'way! Why, chile, he jes' flew away! Befo' he got ter de do', howsomevuh, he 'membered he had locked it, so he didn' stop ter try ter open it, but went straight out'n a winder, quicker'n lightnin', an' kyared de sash 'long wid 'im. An' he'd be'n in sech pow'ful has'e dat he knock' de lamp over an' lack ter sot de house afire. He nevuh got de yuther fo' dollahs of co'se, 'ca'se he didn't stay in de ole ha'nted house all night, but he 'lowed he'd sho'ly 'arned de one dollah he'd had a'ready."

"Why didn't he want to talk to the black cat, Uncle Peter?"

"Why didn' he wan' ter talk ter de black cat? Whoever heared er sich a queshtun! He didn' wan' ter talk wid no black cat, 'ca'se he wuz skeered. Black cats brings 'nuff bad luck w'en dey doan' talk, let 'lone w'en dey does."

"I should like," said Phil, reflectively, "to talk to a black cat. I think it would be great fun."

"Keep away f'm 'em, chile, keep away f'm 'em. Dey is some things too deep fer little boys ter projec' wid, an' black cats is one of 'em."

They moved down the stream and were soon having better luck.

"Uncle Peter," said Phil, while they were on their way home, "there couldn't be any ha'nts at all in the graveyard where my grandfather is buried, could there? Graciella read a lot of the tombstones to me one day, and they all said that all the people were good, and were resting in peace, and had gone to heaven. Tombstones always tell the truth, don't they, Uncle Peter?"

"Happen so, honey, happen so! De French tombstones does; an' as ter de res', I ain' gwine to 'spute 'em, nohow, fer ef I did, de folks under 'em mought come back an' ha'nt me, jes' fer spite."

Seventeen

By considerable effort, and a moderate outlay, the colonel at length secured a majority of interest in the Eureka mill site and made application to the State, through Caxton, for the redemption of the title. The opposition had either ceased or had proved ineffective. There would be some little further delay, but the outcome seemed practically certain, and the colonel did not wait longer to set in motion his plans for the benefit of Clarendon.

"I'm told that Fetters says he'll get the mill anyway," said Caxton, "and make more money buying it under foreclosure than by building a new one. He's ready to lend on it now."

"Oh, damn Fetters!" exclaimed the colonel, elated with his victory. He had never been a profane man, but strong language came so easy in Clarendon that one dropped into it unconsciously. "The mill will be running on full time when Fetters has been put out of business. We've won our first fight, and I've never really seen the fellow yet."

As soon as the title was reasonably secure, the colonel began his preparations for building the cotton mill. The first step was to send for a New England architect who made a specialty of mills, to come down and look the site over, and make plans for the dam, the mill buildings and a number of model cottages for the operatives. As soon as the estimates were prepared, he looked the ground over to see how far he could draw upon local resources for material.

There was good brick clay on the outskirts of the town, where bricks had once been made; but for most of the period since the war such as were used in the town had been procured from the ruins of old buildings—it was cheaper to clean bricks than to make them. Since the construction of the railroad branch to Clarendon the few that were needed from time to time were brought in by train. Not since the building of the Opera House block had there been a kiln of brick made in the town. Inquiry brought out the fact that in case of a demand for bricks there were brickmakers thereabouts; and in accordance with his general plan to employ local labour, the colonel looked up the owner of the brickyard, and asked if he were prepared to take a large contract.

The gentleman was palpably troubled by the question.

"Well, colonel," he said, "I don't know. I'd s'posed you were goin' to impo't yo' bricks from Philadelphia."

"No, Mr. Barnes," returned the colonel, "I want to spend the money here in Clarendon. There seems to be plenty of unemployed labour."

"Yes, there does, till you want somethin' done; then there ain't so much. I s'pose I might find half a dozen niggers round here that know how to make brick; and there's several more that have moved away that I can get back if I send for them. If you r'al'y think you want yo'r brick made here, I'll try to get them out for you. They'll cost you, though, as much, if not more than, you'd have to pay for machine-made bricks from the No'th."

The colonel declared that he preferred the local product.

"Well, I'm shore I don't see why," said the brickmaker. "They'll not be as smooth or as uniform in colour."

"They'll be Clarendon brick," returned the colonel, "and I want this to be a Clarendon enterprise, from the ground up."

"Well," said Barnes resignedly, "if you must have home-made brick, I suppose I'll have to make 'em. I'll see what I can do."

Colonel French then turned the brick matter over to Caxton, who, in the course of a week, worried Barnes into a contract to supply so many thousand brick within a given time.

"I don't like that there time limit," said the brickmaker, "but I reckon I can make them brick as fast as you can get anybody roun' here to lay 'em."

When in the course of another week the colonel saw signs of activity about the old brickyard, he proceeded with the next step, which was to have the ruins of the old factory cleared away.

"Well, colonel," said Major McLean one day when the colonel dropped into the hotel, where the Major hung out a good part of the time, "I s'pose you're goin' to hire white folks to do the work over there."

"Why," replied the colonel, "I hadn't thought about the colour of the workmen. There'll be plenty, I guess, for all who apply, so long as it lasts."

"You'll have trouble if you hire niggers," said the major. "You'll find that they won't work when you want 'em to. They're not reliable, they have no sense of responsibility. As soon as they get a dollar they'll lay off to spend it, and leave yo' work at the mos' critical point."

"Well, now, major," replied the colonel, "I haven't noticed any unnatural activity among the white men of the town. The Negroes have to live, or seem to think they have, and I'll give 'em a chance to turn an honest penny. By the way, major, I need a superintendent to look after the work. It don't require an expert, but merely a good man—gentleman preferred—whom I can trust to see that my ideas are carried out. Perhaps you can recommend such a person?"

The major turned the matter over in his mind before answering. He might, of course, offer his own services. The pay would doubtless be good. But he had not done any real work for years. His wife owned their home. His daughter taught in the academy. He was drawn on jury nearly every term; was tax assessor now and then, and a judge or clerk of elections upon occasion. Nor did he think that steady employment would agree with his health, while it would certainly interfere with his pleasant visits with the drummers at the hotel.

"I'd be glad to take the position myself, colonel," he said, "but I r'aly won't have the time. The campaign will be hummin' in a month or so, an' my political duties will occupy all my leisure. But I'll bear the matter in mind, an' see if I can think of any suitable person."

The colonel thanked him. He had hardly expected the major to offer his services, but had merely wished, for the fun of the thing, to try the experiment. What the colonel really needed was a good foreman—he had used the word "superintendent" merely on the major's account, as less suggestive of work. He found a poor white man, however, Green by name, who seemed capable and energetic, and a gang of labourers under his charge was soon busily engaged in clearing the mill site and preparing for the foundations of a new dam. When it was learned that the colonel was paying his labourers a dollar and a half a day, there was considerable criticism, on the ground that such lavishness would demoralise the labour market, the usual daily wage of the Negro labourer being from fifty to seventy-five cents. But since most of the colonel's money soon found its way, through the channels of trade, into the pockets of the white people, the criticism soon died a natural death.

Eighteen

Once started in his career of active benevolence, the colonel's natural love of thoroughness, combined with a philanthropic zeal as pleasant as it was novel, sought out new reforms. They were easily found. He had begun, with wise foresight, at the foundations of prosperity, by planning an industry in which the people could find employment. But there were subtler needs, mental and spiritual, to be met. Education, for instance, so important to real development, languished in Clarendon. There was a select private school for young ladies, attended by the daughters of those who could not send their children away to school. A few of the town boys went away to military schools. The remainder of the white youth attended the academy, which was a thoroughly democratic institution, deriving its support partly from the public school fund and partly from private subscriptions. There was a coloured public school taught by a Negro teacher.

Neither school had, so far as the colonel could learn, attained any very high degree of efficiency. At one time the colonel had contemplated building a schoolhouse for the children of the mill hands, but upon second thought decided that the expenditure would be more widely useful if made through the channels already established. If the old academy building were repaired, and a wing constructed, for which there was ample room upon the grounds, it would furnish any needed additional accommodation for the children of the operatives, and avoid the drawing of any line that might seem to put these in a class apart. There were already lines enough in the town—the deep and distinct colour line, theoretically all-pervasive, but with occasional curious exceptions; the old line between the "rich white folks" or aristocrats—no longer rich, most of them, but retaining some of their former wealth and clinging tenaciously to a waning prestige—and the "poor whites," still at a social disadvantage, but gradually evolving a solid middle class, with reinforcements from the decaying aristocracy, and producing now and then some ambitious and successful man like Fetters. To emphasise these distinctions was no part of the colonel's plan. To eradicate them entirely in any stated time was of course impossible, human nature being what it was, but he would do nothing to accentuate them. His mill hands should become, like the mill hands in New England towns, an intelligent, self-respecting and therefore respected element of an enlightened population; and the whole town should share equally in anything he might spend for their benefit.

He found much pleasure in talking over these fine plans of his with Laura Treadwell. Caxton had entered into them with the enthusiasm of an impressionable young man, brought into close contact with a forceful personality. But in Miss Laura the colonel found a sympathy that was more than intellectual—that reached down to sources of spiritual strength and inspiration which the colonel could not touch but of which he was conscious and of which he did not hesitate to avail himself at second hand. Little Phil had made the house almost a second home; and the frequent visits of his father had only strengthened the colonel's admiration of Laura's character. He had learned, not from the lady herself, how active in good works she was. A Lady Bountiful in any large sense she could not be, for her means, as she had so frankly said upon his first visit, were small. But a little went a long way among the poor of Clarendon, and the life after all is more than meat, and the body more than raiment, and advice and sympathy were as often needed as other kinds of help. He had offered to assist her charities in a substantial way, and she had permitted it now and then, but had felt obliged at last to cease mentioning them altogether. He was able to circumvent this delicacy now and then through the agency of Graciella, whose theory was that money was made to spend.

"Laura," he said one evening when at the house, "will you go with me to-morrow to visit the academy? I wish to see with your eyes as well as with mine what it needs and what can be done with it. It shall be our secret until we are ready to surprise the town."

They went next morning, without notice to the principal. The school was well ordered, but the equipment poor. The building was old and sadly in need of repair. The teacher was an ex-Confederate officer, past middle life, well taught by the methods in vogue fifty years before, but scarcely in harmony with modern ideals of education. In spite of his perfect manners and unimpeachable character, the Professor, as he was called, was generally understood to hold his position more by virtue of his need and his influence than of his fitness to instruct. He had several young lady assistants who found in teaching the only career open, in Clarendon, to white women of good family.

The recess hour arrived while they were still at school. When the pupils marched out, in orderly array, the colonel, seizing a moment when Miss Treadwell and the professor were speaking about some of the children whom the colonel did not know, went to the rear of one of the schoolrooms and found, without much difficulty, high up on one of the walls, the faint but still distinguishable outline of a pencil caricature he had made there thirty years before. If the wall had been whitewashed in the meantime, the lime had scaled down to the original plaster. Only the name, which had been written underneath, was illegible, though he could reconstruct with his mind's eye and the aid of a few shadowy strokes—"Bill Fetters, Sneak"—in angular letters in the printed form.

The colonel smiled at this survival of youthful bigotry. Yet even then his instinct had been a healthy one; his boyish characterisation of Fetters, schoolboy, was not an inapt description of Fetters, man—mortgage shark, labour contractor and political boss. Bill, seeking official favour, had reported to the Professor of that date some boyish escapade in which his schoolfellows had taken part, and it was in revenge for this meanness that the colonel had chased him ignominiously down Main Street and pilloried him upon the schoolhouse wall. Fetters the man, a Goliath whom no David had yet opposed, had fastened himself upon a weak and disorganised community, during a period of great distress and had succeeded by devious ways in making himself its master. And as the colonel stood looking at the picture he was conscious of a faint echo of his boyish indignation and sense of outraged honour. Already Fetters and he had clashed upon the subject of the cotton mill, and Fetters had retired from the field. If it were written that they should meet in a life-and-death struggle for the soul of Clarendon, he would not shirk the conflict.

"Laura," he said, when they went away, "I should like to visit the coloured school. Will you come with me?"

She hesitated, and he could see with half an eye that her answer was dictated by a fine courage.

"Why, certainly, I will go. Why not? It is a place where a good work is carried on."

"No, Laura," said the colonel smiling, "you need not go. On second thought, I should prefer to go alone."

She insisted, but he was firm. He had no desire to go counter to her instincts, or induce her to do anything that might provoke adverse comment. Miss Laura had all the fine glow of courage, but was secretly relieved at being excused from a trip so unconventional.

So the colonel found his way alone to the schoolhouse, an unpainted frame structure in a barren, sandy lot upon a street somewhat removed from the centre of the town and given over mainly to the humble homes of Negroes. That his unannounced appearance created some embarrassment was quite evident, but his friendliness toward the Negroes had already been noised abroad, and he was welcomed with warmth, not to say effusion, by the principal of the school, a tall, stalwart and dark man with an intelligent expression, a deferential manner, and shrewd but guarded eyes—the eyes of the jungle, the colonel had heard them called; and the thought came to him, was it some ancestral jungle on the distant coast of savage Africa, or the wilderness of another sort in which the black people had wandered and were wandering still in free America? The attendance was not large; at a glance the colonel saw that there were but twenty-five pupils present.

"What is your total enrolment?" he asked the teacher.

"Well, sir," was the reply, "we have seventy-five or eighty on the roll, but it threatened rain this morning, and as a great many of them haven't got good shoes, they stayed at home for fear of getting their feet wet."

The colonel had often noticed the black children paddling around barefoot in the puddles on rainy days, but there was evidently some point of etiquette connected with attending school barefoot. He had passed more than twenty-five children on the streets, on his way to the schoolhouse.

The building was even worse than that of the academy, and the equipment poorer still. Upon the colonel asking to hear a recitation, the teacher made some excuse and shrewdly requested him to make a few remarks. They could recite, he said, at any time, but an opportunity to hear Colonel French was a privilege not to be neglected.

The colonel, consenting good-humouredly, was introduced to the school in very flowery language. The pupils were sitting, the teacher informed them, in the shadow of a great man. A distinguished member of the grand old aristocracy of their grand old native State had gone to the great North and grown rich and famous. He had returned to his old home to scatter his vast wealth where it was most needed, and to give his fellow townsmen an opportunity to add their applause to his world-wide fame. He was present to express his sympathy with their feeble efforts to rise in the world, and he wanted the scholars all to listen with the most respectful attention.

Colonel French made a few simple remarks in which he spoke of the advantages of education as a means of forming character and of fitting boys and girls for the work of men and women. In former years his people had been charged with direct responsibility for the care of many coloured children, and in a larger and indirect way they were still responsible for their descendants. He urged them to make the best of their opportunities and try to fit themselves for useful citizenship. They would meet with the difficulties that all men must, and with some peculiarly their own. But they must look up and not down, forward and not back, seeking always incentives to hope rather than excuses for failure. Before leaving, he arranged with the teacher, whose name was Taylor, to meet several of the leading coloured men, with whom he wished to discuss some method of improving their school and directing their education to more definite ends. The meeting was subsequently held.

"What your people need," said the colonel to the little gathering at the schoolhouse one evening, "is to learn not only how to read and write and think, but to do these things to some definite end. We live in an age of specialists. To make yourselves valuable members of society, you must learn to do well some particular thing, by which you may reasonably expect to earn a comfortable living in your own home, among your neighbours, and save something for old age and the education of your children. Get together. Take advice from some of your own capable leaders in other places. Find out what you can do for yourselves, and I will give you three dollars for every one you can gather, for an industrial school or some similar institution. Take your time, and when you're ready to report, come and see me, or write to me, if I am not here."

The result was the setting in motion of a stagnant pool. Who can measure the force of hope? The town had been neglected by mission boards. No able or ambitious Negro had risen from its midst to found an institution and find a career. The coloured school received a grudging dole from the public funds, and was left entirely to the supervision of the coloured people. It would have been surprising had the money always been expended to the best advantage.

The fact that a white man, in some sense a local man, who had yet come from the far North, the land of plenty, with feelings friendly to their advancement, had taken a personal interest in their welfare and proved it by his presence among them, gave them hope and inspiration for the future. They had long been familiar with the friendship that curbed, restricted and restrained, and concerned itself mainly with their limitations. They were almost hysterically eager to welcome the co-operation of a friend who, in seeking to lift them up, was obsessed by no fear of pulling himself down or of narrowing in some degree the gulf that separated them—who was willing not only to help them, but to help them to a condition in which they might be in less need of help. The colonel touched the reserves of loyalty in the Negro nature, exemplified in old Peter and such as he. Who knows, had these reserves been reached sooner by strict justice and patient kindness, that they might not long since have helped to heal the wounds of slavery?

"And now, Laura," said the colonel, "when we have improved the schools and educated the people, we must give them something to occupy their minds. We must have a library, a public library."

"That will be splendid!" she replied with enthusiasm.

"A public library," continued the colonel, "housed in a beautiful building, in a conspicuous place, and decorated in an artistic manner—a shrine of intellect and taste, at which all the people, rich and poor, black and white, may worship."

Miss Laura was silent for a moment, and thoughtful.

"But, Henry," she said with some hesitation, "do you mean that coloured people should use the library?"

"Why not?" he asked. "Do they not need it most? Perhaps not many of them might wish to use it; but to those who do, should we deny the opportunity? Consider their teachers—if the blind lead the blind, shall they not both fall into the ditch?"

"Yes, Henry, that is the truth; but I am afraid the white people wouldn't wish to handle the same books."

"Very well, then we will give the coloured folks a library of their own, at some place convenient for their use. We need not strain our ideal by going too fast. Where shall I build the library?"

"The vacant lot," she said, "between the post-office and the bank."

"The very place," he replied. "It belonged to our family once, and I shall be acquiring some more ancestral property. The cows will need to find a new pasture."

The announcement of the colonel's plan concerning the academy and the library evoked a hearty response on the part of the public, and the *Anglo-Saxon* hailed it as the dawning of a new era. With regard to the colonel's friendly plans for the Negroes, there was less enthusiasm and some difference of opinion. Some commended the colonel's course. There were others, good men and patriotic, men who would have died for liberty, in the abstract, men who sought to walk uprightly, and to live peaceably with all, but who, by much brooding over the conditions surrounding their life, had grown hopelessly pessimistic concerning the Negro.

The subject came up in a little company of gentlemen who were gathered around the colonel's table one evening, after the coffee had been served, and the Havanas passed around.

"Your zeal for humanity does you infinite credit, Colonel French," said Dr. Mackenzie, minister of the Presbyterian Church, who was one of these prophetic souls, "but I fear your time and money and effort will be wasted. The Negroes are hopelessly degraded. They have degenerated rapidly since the war."

"How do you know, doctor? You came here from the North long after the war. What is your standard of comparison?"

"I voice the unanimous opinion of those who have known them at both periods."

"*I* don't agree with you; and I lived here before the war. There is certainly one smart Negro in town. Nichols, the coloured barber, owns five houses, and overreached me in a bargain. Before the war he was a chattel. And Taylor, the teacher, seems to be a very sensible fellow."

"Yes," said Dr. Price, who was one of the company, "Taylor is a very intelligent Negro. Nichols and he have learned how to live and prosper among the white people."

"They are exceptions," said the preacher, "who only prove the rule. No, Colonel French, for a long time *I* hoped that there was a future for these poor, helpless blacks. But of late I have become profoundly convinced that there is no place in this nation for the Negro, except under the sod. We will not assimilate him, we cannot deport him——"

"And therefore, O man of God, must we exterminate him?"

"It is God's will. We need not stain our hands with innocent blood. If we but sit passive, and leave their fate to time, they will die away in discouragement and despair. Already disease is sapping their vitals. Like other weak races, they will vanish from the pathway of the strong, and there is no place for them to flee. When they go hence, it is to go forever. It is the law of life, which God has given to the earth. To coddle them, to delude them with false hopes of an unnatural equality which not all the power of the Government has been able to maintain, is only to increase their unhappiness. To a doomed race, ignorance is euthanasia, and knowledge is but pain and sorrow. It is His will that the fittest should survive, and that those shall inherit the earth who are best prepared to utilise its forces and gather its fruits."

"My dear doctor, what you say may all be true, but, with all due respect, I don't believe a word of it. I am rather inclined to think that these people have a future; that there is a place for them here; that they have made fair progress under discouraging circumstances; that they will not disappear from our midst for many generations, if ever; and that in the meantime, as we make or mar them, we shall make or mar our civilisation. No society can be greater or wiser or better than the average of all its elements. Our ancestors brought these people here, and lived in luxury, some of them—or went into bankruptcy, more of them—on their labour. After three hundred years of toil they might be fairly said to have earned their liberty. At any rate, they are here. They constitute the bulk of our labouring class. To teach them is to make their labour more effective and therefore more profitable; to increase their needs is to increase our profits in supplying them. I'll take my chances on the Golden Rule. I am no lover of the Negro, *as* Negro—I do not know but I should rather see him elsewhere. I think our land would have been far happier had none but white men ever set foot upon it after the red men were driven back. But they are here, through no fault of theirs, as we are. They were born here. We have given them our language—which they speak more or less corruptly; our religion—which they practise certainly no better than we; and our blood—which our laws make a badge of disgrace. Perhaps we could not do them strict justice, without a great sacrifice upon our own part.

But they are men, and they should have their chance—at least *some* chance."

"I shall pray for your success," sighed the preacher. "With God all things are possible, if He will them. But I can only anticipate your failure."

"The colonel is growing so popular, with his ready money and his cheerful optimism," said old General Thornton, another of the guests, "that we'll have to run him for Congress, as soon as he is reconverted to the faith of his fathers."

Colonel French had more than once smiled at the assumption that a mere change of residence would alter his matured political convictions. His friends seemed to look upon them, so far as they differed from their own, as a mere veneer, which would scale off in time, as had the multiplied coats of whitewash over the pencil drawing made on the school-house wall in his callow youth.

"You see," the old general went on, "it's a social matter down here, rather than a political one. With this ignorant black flood sweeping up against us, the race question assumes an importance which overshadows the tariff and the currency and everything else. For instance, I had fully made up my mind to vote the other ticket in the last election. I didn't like our candidate nor our platform. There was a clean-cut issue between sound money and financial repudiation, and I was tired of the domination of populists and demagogues. All my better instincts led me toward a change of attitude, and I boldly proclaimed the fact. I declared my political and intellectual independence, at the cost of many friends; even my own son-in-law scarcely spoke to me for a month. When I went to the polls, old Sam Brown, the triflingest nigger in town, whom I had seen sentenced to jail more than once for stealing—old Sam Brown was next to me in the line.

" 'Well, Gin'l,' he said, 'I'm glad you is got on de right side at las', an' is gwine to vote *our* ticket.' "

"This was too much! I could stand the other party in the abstract, but not in the concrete. I voted the ticket of my neighbours and my friends. We had to preserve our institutions, if our finances went to smash. Call it prejudice—call it what you like—it's human nature, and you'll come to it, colonel, you'll come to it—and then we'll send you to Congress."

"I might not care to go," returned the colonel, smiling.

"You could not resist, sir, the unanimous demand of a determined constituency. Upon the rare occasions when, in this State, the office has had a chance to seek the man, it has never sought in vain."

Nineteen

Time slipped rapidly by, and the colonel had been in Clarendon a couple of months when he went home one afternoon, and not finding Phil and Peter, went around to the Treadwells' as the most likely place to seek them.

"Henry," said Miss Laura, "Philip does not seem quite well to-day. There are dark circles under his eyes, and he has been coughing a little."

The colonel was startled. Had his growing absorption in other things led him to neglect his child? Phil needed a mother. This dear, thoughtful woman, whom nature had made for motherhood, had seen things about his child, that he, the child's father, had not perceived. To a mind like Colonel French's, this juxtaposition of a motherly heart and a motherless child seemed very pleasing.

He despatched a messenger on horseback immediately for Dr.

Price. The colonel had made the doctor's acquaintance soon after coming to Clarendon, and out of abundant precaution, had engaged him to call once a week to see Phil. A physician of skill and experience, a gentleman by birth and breeding, a thoughtful student of men and manners, and a good story teller, he had proved excellent company and the colonel soon numbered him among his intimate friends. He had seen Phil a few days before, but it was yet several days before his next visit.

Dr. Price owned a place in the country, several miles away, on the road to Mink Run, and thither the messenger went to find him. He was in his town office only at stated hours. The colonel was waiting at home, an hour later, when the doctor drove up to the gate with Ben Dudley, in the shabby old buggy to which Ben sometimes drove his one good horse on his trips to town.

"I broke one of my buggy wheels going out home this morning," explained the doctor, "and had just sent it to the shop when your messenger came. I would have ridden your horse back, and let the man walk in, but Mr. Dudley fortunately came along and gave me a lift."

He looked at Phil, left some tablets, with directions for their use, and said that it was nothing serious and the child would be all right in a day or two.

"What he needs, colonel, at his age, is a woman's care. But for that matter none of us ever get too old to need that."

"I'll have Tom hitch up and take you home," said the colonel, when the doctor had finished with Phil, "unless you'll stay to dinner."

"No, thank you," said the doctor, "I'm much obliged, but I told my wife I'd be back to dinner. I'll just sit here and wait for young Dudley, who's going to call for me in an hour. There's a fine mind, colonel, that's never had a proper opportunity for development. If he'd had half the chance that your boy will, he would make his mark. Did you ever see his uncle Malcolm?"

The colonel described his visit to Mink Run, the scene on the piazza, the interview with Mr. Dudley, and Peter's story about the hidden treasure.

"Is the old man sane?" he asked.

"His mind is warped, undoubtedly," said the doctor, "but I'll leave it to you whether it was the result of an insane delusion or not—if you care to hear his story—or perhaps you've heard it?"

"No, I have not," returned the colonel, "but I should like to hear it."

This was the story that the doctor told:

When the last century had passed the half-way mark, and had started upon its decline, the Dudleys had already owned land on Mink Run for a hundred years or more, and were one of the richest and most conspicuous families in the State. The first great man of the family, General Arthur Dudley, an ardent patriot, had won distinction in the War of Independence, and held high place in the councils of the infant nation. His son became a distinguished jurist, whose name is still a synonym for legal learning and juridical wisdom. In Ralph Dudley, the son of Judge Dudley, and the immediate predecessor of the demented old man in whom now rested the title to the remnant of the estate, the family began to decline from its eminence. Ralph did not marry, but led a life of ease and pleasure, wasting what his friends thought rare gifts, and leaving his property to the management of his nephew Malcolm, the orphan son of a younger brother and his uncle's prospective heir. Malcolm Dudley proved so capable a manager that for year after year the large estate was left almost entirely in his charge, the owner looking to it merely for revenue to lead his own life in other places.

The Civil War gave Ralph Dudley a career, not upon the field, for which he had no taste, but in administrative work, which suited his talents, and imposed more arduous tasks than those of actual warfare. Valour was of small account without arms and ammunition. A commissariat might be improvised, but gunpowder must be manufactured or purchased.

Ralph's nephew Malcolm kept bachelor's hall in the great house. The only women in the household were an old black cook, and the housekeeper, known as "Viney"—a Negro corruption of Lavinia—a tall, comely young light mulattress, with a dash of Cherokee blood, which gave her straighter, blacker and more glossy hair than most women of mixed race have, and perhaps a somewhat different temperamental endowment. Her duties were not onerous; compared with the toiling field hands she led an easy life. The household had been thus constituted for ten years and more, when Malcolm Dudley began paying court to a wealthy widow.

This lady, a Mrs. Todd, was a war widow, who had lost her husband in the early years of the struggle. War, while it took many lives, did not stop the currents of life, and weeping widows sometimes found consolation. Mrs. Todd was of Clarendon extraction, and had returned to the town to pass the period of her mourning. Men were scarce in those days, and Mrs. Todd was no longer young, Malcolm Dudley courted her, proposed marriage, and was accepted.

He broke the news to his housekeeper by telling her to prepare the house for a mistress. It was not a pleasant task, but he was a resolute man. The woman had been in power too long to yield gracefully. Some passionate strain of the mixed blood in her veins broke out in a scene of hysterical violence. Her pleadings, remonstrances, rages, were all in vain. Mrs. Todd was rich, and he was poor; should his uncle see fit to marry—always a possibility—he would have nothing. He would carry out his purpose.

The day after this announcement Viney went to town, sought out the object of Dudley's attentions, and told her something; just what, no one but herself and the lady ever knew. When Dudley called in the evening, the widow refused to see him, and sent instead, a curt note cancelling their engagement.

Dudley went home puzzled and angry. On the way thither a suspicion flashed into his mind. In the morning he made investigations, after which he rode round by the residence of his overseer. Returning to the house at noon, he ate his dinner in an ominous silence, which struck terror to the heart of the woman who waited on him and had already repented of her temerity. When she would have addressed him, with a look he froze the words upon her lips. When he had eaten he looked at his watch, and ordered a boy to bring his horse round to the door. He waited until he saw his overseer coming toward the house, then sprang into the saddle and rode down the lane, passing the overseer with a nod.

Ten minutes later Dudley galloped back up the lane and sprang from his panting horse. As he dashed up the steps he met the overseer coming out of the house.

"You have not——"

"I have, sir, and well! The she-devil bit my hand to the bone, and would have stabbed me if I hadn't got the knife away from her. You'd better have the niggers look after her; she's shamming a fit."

Dudley was remorseful, and finding Viney unconscious, sent hastily for a doctor.

"The woman has had a stroke," said that gentleman curtly, after an examination, "brought on by brutal treatment. By G-d, Dudley, I wouldn't have thought this of you! I own Negroes, but I treat them like human beings. And such a woman! I'm ashamed of my own race, I swear I am! If we are whipped in this war and the slaves are freed, as Lincoln threatens, it will be God's judgment!"

Many a man has been shot by Southern gentlemen for language less offensive; but Dudley's conscience made him meek as Moses.

"It was a mistake," he faltered, "and I shall discharge the overseer who did it."

"You had better shoot him," returned the doctor. "He has no soul—and what is worse, no discrimination."

Dudley gave orders that Viney should receive the best of care. Next day he found, behind the clock, where she had laid it, the letter which Ben Dudley, many years after, had read to Graciella on Mrs. Treadwell's piazza. It was dated the morning of the previous day.

An hour later he learned of the death of his uncle, who had been thrown from a fractious horse, not far from Mink Run, and had broken his neck in the fall. A hasty search of the premises did not disclose the concealed treasure. The secret lay in the mind of the stricken woman. As soon as Dudley learned that Viney had eaten and drunk and was apparently conscious, he went to her bedside and took her limp hand in his own.

"I'm sorry, Viney, mighty sorry, I assure you. Martin went further than I intended, and I have discharged him for his brutality. You'll be sorry, Viney, to learn that your old Master Ralph is dead; he was killed by an accident within ten miles of here. His body will be brought home to-day and buried to-morrow."

Dudley thought he detected in her expressionless face a shade of sorrow. Old Ralph, high liver and genial soul, had been so indulgent a master, that his nephew suffered by the comparison.

"I found the letter he left with you," he continued softly, "and must take charge of the money immediately. Can you tell me where it is?"

One side of Viney's face was perfectly inert, as the result of her disorder, and any movement of the other produced a slight distortion that spoiled the face as the index of the mind. But her eyes were not dimmed, and into their sombre depths there leaped a sudden fire—only a momentary flash, for almost instantly she closed her lids, and when she opened them a moment later, they exhibited no trace of emotion.

"You will tell me where it is?" he repeated. A request came awkwardly to his lips; he was accustomed to command.

Viney pointed to her mouth with her right hand, which was not affected.

"To be sure," he said hastily, "you cannot speak—not yet."

He reflected for a moment. The times were unsettled. Should a wave of conflict sweep over Clarendon, the money might be found by the enemy. Should Viney take a turn for the worse and die, it would be impossible to learn anything from her at all. There was another thought, which had rapidly taken shape in his mind. No one but Viney knew that his uncle had been at Mink Run. The estate had been seriously embarrassed by Roger's extravagant patriotism, following upon the heels of other and earlier extravagances. The fifty thousand dollars would in part make good the loss; as his uncle's heir, he had at least a moral claim upon it, and possession was nine points of the law.

"Is it in the house?" he asked.

She made a negative sign.

"In the barn?"

The same answer.

"In the yard? the garden? the spring house? the quarters?"

No question he could put brought a different answer. Dudley was puzzled. The woman was in her right mind; she was no liar—of this servile vice at least she was free. Surely there was some mystery.

"You saw my uncle?" he asked thoughtfully.

She nodded affirmatively.

"And he had the money, in gold?"

Yes.

"He left it here?"

Yes, positively.

"Do you know where he hid it?"

She indicated that she did, and pointed again to her silent tongue.

"You mean that you must regain your speech before you can explain?"

She nodded yes, and then, as if in pain, turned her face away from him.

Viney was carefully nursed. The doctor came to see her regularly.

She was fed with dainty food, and no expense was spared to effect her cure. In due time she recovered from the paralytic stroke, in all except the power of speech, which did not seem to return. All of Dudley's attempts to learn from her the whereabouts of the money were equally futile. She seemed willing enough, but, though she made the effort, was never able to articulate; and there was plainly some mystery about the hidden gold which only words could unravel.

If she could but write, a few strokes of the pen would give him his heart's desire! But, alas! Viney may as well have been without hands, for any use she could make of a pen. Slaves were not taught to read or write, nor was Viney one of the rare exceptions. But Dudley was a man of resource—he would have her taught. He employed a teacher for her, a free coloured man who knew the rudiments. But Viney, handicapped by her loss of speech, made wretched progress. From whatever cause, she manifested a remarkable stupidity, while seemingly anxious to learn. Dudley himself took a hand in her instruction, but with no better results, and, in the end, the attempt to teach her was abandoned as hopeless.

Years rolled by. The fall of the Confederacy left the slaves free and completed the ruin of the Dudley estate. Part of the land went, at ruinous prices, to meet mortgages at ruinous rates; part lay fallow, given up to scrub oak and short-leaf pine; merely enough was cultivated, or let out on shares to Negro tenants, to provide a living for old Malcolm and a few servants. Absorbed in dreams of the hidden gold and in the search for it, he neglected his business and fell yet deeper into debt. He worried himself into a lingering fever, through which Viney nursed him with every sign of devotion, and from which he rose with his mind visibly weakened.

When the slaves were freed, Viney had manifested no desire to leave her old place. After the tragic episode which had led to their mutual undoing, there had been no relation between them but that of master and servant. But some gloomy attraction, or it may have been habit, held her to the scene of her power and of her fall. She had no kith nor kin, and her affliction separated her from the rest of mankind. Nor would Dudley have been willing to let her go, for in her lay the secret of the treasure; and, since all other traces of her ailment had disappeared, so her speech might return. The fruitless search was never relinquished, and in time absorbed all of Malcolm Dudley's interest. The crops were left to the servants, who neglected them. The yard had been dug over many times. Every foot of ground for rods around had been sounded with a pointed iron bar. The house had suffered in the search. No crack or cranny had been left unexplored. The spaces between the walls, beneath the floors, under the hearths—every possible hiding place had been searched, with little care for any resulting injury.

Into this household Ben Dudley, left alone in the world, had come when a boy of fifteen. He had no special turn for farming, but such work as was done upon the old plantation was conducted under his supervision. In the decaying old house, on the neglected farm, he had grown up in harmony with his surroundings. The example of his old uncle, wrecked in mind by a hopeless quest, had never been brought home to him as a warning; use had dulled its force. He had never joined in the search, except casually, but the legend was in his mind. Unconsciously his standards of life grew around it. Some day he would be rich, and in order to be sure of it, he must remain with his uncle, whose heir he was. For the money was there, without a doubt. His great-uncle had hid the gold and left the letter—Ben had read it.

The neighbours knew the story, or at least some vague version of it, and for a time joined in the search—surreptitiously, as occasion offered, and each on his own account. It was the common understanding that old Malcolm was mentally unbalanced. The neighbouring Negroes, with generous imagination, fixed his mythical and elusive treasure at a million dollars. Not one of them had the faintest conception of the bulk or purchasing power of one million dollars in gold; but when one builds a castle in the air, why not make it lofty and spacious?

From this unwholesome atmosphere Ben Dudley found relief, as he grew older, in frequent visits to Clarendon, which invariably ended at the Treadwells', who were, indeed, distant relatives. He had one good horse, and in an hour or less could leave behind him the shabby old house, falling into ruin, the demented old man, digging in the disordered yard, the dumb old woman watching him from her inscrutable eyes; and by a change as abrupt as that of coming from a dark room into the brightness of midday, find himself in a lovely garden, beside a beautiful girl, whom he loved devotedly, but who kept him on the ragged edge of an uncertainty that was stimulating enough, but very wearing.

Twenty

The summer following Colonel French's return to Clarendon was unusually cool, so cool that the colonel, pleasantly occupied with his various plans and projects, scarcely found the heat less bearable than that of New York at the same season. During a brief torrid spell he took Phil to a Southern mountain resort for a couple of weeks, and upon another occasion ran up to New York for a day or two on business in reference to the machinery for the cotton mill, which was to be ready for installation some time during the fall. But these were brief interludes, and did not interrupt the current of his life, which was flowing very smoothly and pleasantly in its new channel, if not very swiftly, for even the colonel was not able to make things move swiftly in Clarendon during the summer time, and he was well enough pleased to see them move at all.

Kirby was out of town when the colonel was in New York, and

therefore he did not see him. His mail was being sent from his club to Denver, where he was presumably looking into some mining proposition. Mrs. Jerviss, the colonel supposed, was at the seaside, but he had almost come face to face with her one day on Broadway. She had run down to the city on business of some sort. Moved by the instinct of defense, the colonel, by a quick movement, avoided the meeting, and felt safer when the lady was well out of sight. He did not wish, at this time, to be diverted from his Southern interests, and the image of another woman was uppermost in his mind.

One moonlight evening, a day or two after his return from this brief Northern trip, the colonel called at Mrs. Treadwells'. Caroline opened the door. Mrs. Treadwell, she said, was lying down. Miss Graciella had gone over to a neighbour's, but would soon return. Miss Laura was paying a call, but would not be long. Would the colonel wait? No, he said, he would take a walk, and come back later.

The streets were shady, and the moonlight bathed with a silvery glow that part of the town which the shadows did not cover. Strolling aimlessly along the quiet, unpaved streets, the colonel, upon turning a corner, saw a lady walking a short distance ahead of him. He thought he recognised the figure, and hurried forward; but ere he caught up with her, she turned and went into one of a row of small houses which he knew belonged to Nichols, the coloured barber, and were occupied by coloured people. Thinking he had been mistaken in the woman's identity, he slackened his pace, and ere he had passed out of hearing, caught the tones of a piano, accompanying the words,

"I dreamt that I dwelt in marble halls,
With vassals and serfs at my s-i-i-de."

It was doubtless the barber's daughter. The barber's was the only coloured family in town that owned a piano. In the moonlight, and at a distance of some rods, the song sounded well enough, and the colonel lingered until it ceased, and the player began to practise scales, when he continued his walk. He had smoked a couple of cigars, and was returning toward Mrs. Treadwells', when he met, face to face, Miss Laura Treadwell coming out of the barber's house. He lifted his hat and put out his hand.

"I called at the house a while ago, and you were all out. I was just going back. I'll walk along with you."

Miss Laura was visibly embarrassed at the meeting. The colonel gave no sign that he noticed her emotion, but went on talking.

"It is a delightful evening," he said.

"Yes," she replied, and then went on, "you must wonder what I was doing there."

"I suppose," he said, "that you were looking for a servant, or on some mission of kindness and good will."

Miss Laura was silent for a moment and he could feel her hand tremble on the arm he offered her.

"No, Henry," she said, "why should I deceive you? I did not go to find a servant, but to serve. I have told you we were poor, but not how poor. I can tell you what I could not say to others, for you have lived away from here, and I know how differently from most of us you look at things. I went to the barber's house to give the barber's daughter music lessons—for money."

The colonel laughed contagiously.

"You taught her to sing—

'I dreamt that I dwelt in marble halls?' "

"Yes, but you must not judge my work too soon," she replied. "It is not finished yet."

"You shall let me know when it is done," he said, "and I will walk by and hear the finished product. Your pupil has improved wonderfully. I heard her singing the song the day I came back—the first time

I walked by the old house. She sings it much better now. You are a good teacher, as well as a good woman."

Miss Laura laughed somewhat excitedly, but was bent upon her explanation.

"The girl used to come to the house," she said. "Her mother belonged to us before the war, and we have been such friends as white and black can be. And she wanted to learn to play, and offered to pay me well for lessons, and I gave them to her. We never speak about the money at the house; mother knows it, but feigns that I do it out of mere kindness, and tells me that I am spoiling the coloured people. Our friends are not supposed to know it, and if any of them do, they are kind and never speak of it. Since you have been coming to the house, it has not been convenient to teach her there, and I have been going to her home in the evening."

"My dear Laura," said the colonel, remorsefully, "I have driven you away from your own home, and all unwittingly. I applaud your enterprise and your public spirit. It is a long way from the banjo to the piano—it marks the progress of a family and foreshadows the evolution of a race. And what higher work than to elevate humanity?"

They had reached the house. Mrs. Treadwell had not come down, nor had Graciella returned. They went into the parlour. Miss Laura turned up the lamp.

Graciella had run over to a neighbour's to meet a young lady who was visiting a young lady who was a friend of Graciella's. She had remained a little longer than she had meant to, for among those who had called to see her friend's friend was young Mr. Fetters, the son of the magnate, lately returned home from college. Barclay Fetters was handsome, well-dressed and well-mannered. He had started at one college, and had already changed to two others. Stories of his dissipated habits and reckless extravagance had been bruited about. Graciella knew his family history, and had imbibed the old-fashioned notions of her grandmother's household, so that her acknowledgment of the introduction was somewhat cold, not to say distant. But as she felt the charm of his manner, and saw that the other girls were vieing with one another for his notice, she felt a certain triumph that he exhibited a marked preference for her conversation. Her reserve gradually broke down, and she was talking with animation and listening with pleasure, when she suddenly recollected that Colonel French would probably call, and that she ought to be there to entertain him, for which purpose she had dressed herself very carefully. He had not spoken yet, but might be expected to speak at any time; such marked attentions as his could have but one meaning; and for several days she had had a premonition that before the week was out he would seek to know his fate; and Graciella meant to be kind.

Anticipating this event, she had politely but pointedly discouraged Ben Dudley's attentions, until Ben's pride, of which he had plenty in reserve, had awaked to activity. At their last meeting he had demanded a definite answer to his oft-repeated question.

"Graciella," he had said, "are you going to marry me? Yes or no. I'll not be played with any longer. You must marry me for myself, or not at all. Yes or no."

"Then no, Mr. Dudley," she had replied with spirit, and without a moment's hesitation, "I will not marry you. I will never marry you, not if I should die an old maid."

She was sorry they had not parted friends, but she was not to blame. After her marriage, she would avoid the embarrassment of meeting him, by making the colonel take her away. Sometime she might, through her husband, be of service to Ben, and thus make up, in part at least, for his disappointment.

As she ran up through the garden and stepped upon the porch—her slippers were thin and made no sound—she heard Colonel French's voice in the darkened parlour. Some unusual intonation struck her, and she moved lightly and almost mechanically forward, in the shadow, toward a point where she could see through the window and remain screened from observation. So intense was her interest in what she heard, that she stood with her hand on her heart, not even conscious that she was doing a shameful thing.

Her aunt was seated and Colonel French was standing near her. An open Bible lay upon the table. The colonel had taken it up and was reading:

" 'Who can find a virtuous woman? For her price is far above rubies. The heart of her husband doth safely trust in her. She will do him good and not evil all the days of her life. Strength and honour are her clothing, and she shall rejoice in time to come.'

"Laura," he said, "the proverb maker was a prophet as well. In these words, written four thousand years ago, he has described you, line for line."

The glow which warmed her cheek, still smooth, the light which came into her clear eyes, the joy that filled her heart at these kind words, put the years to flight, and for the moment Laura was young again.

"You have been good to Phil," the colonel went on, "and I should like him to be always near you and have your care. And you have been kind to me, and made me welcome and at home in what might otherwise have seemed, after so long an absence, a strange land. You bring back to me the best of my youth, and in you I find the inspiration for good deeds. Be my wife, dear Laura, and a mother to my boy, and we will try to make you happy."

"Oh, Henry," she cried with fluttering heart, "I am not worthy to be your wife. I know nothing of the world where you have lived, nor whether I would fit into it."

"You are worthy of any place," he declared, "and if one please you more than another, I shall make your wishes mine."

"But, Henry, how could I leave my mother? And Graciella needs my care."

"You need not leave your mother—she shall be mine as well as yours. Graciella is a dear, bright child; she has in her the making of a noble woman; she should be sent away to a good school, and I will see to it. No, dear Laura, there are no difficulties, no giants in the pathway that will not fly or fall when we confront them."

He had put his arm around her and lifted her face to his. He read his answer in her swimming eyes, and when he had reached down and kissed her cheek, she buried her head on his shoulder and shed some tears of happiness. For this was her secret: she was sweet and good; she would have made any man happy, who had been worthy of her, but no man had ever before asked her to be his wife. She had lived upon a plane so simple, yet so high, that men not equally high-minded had never ventured to address her, and there were few such men, and chance had not led them her way. As to the others—perhaps there were women more beautiful, and certainly more enterprising. She had not repined; she had been busy and contented. Now this great happiness was vouchsafed her, to find in the love of the man whom she admired above all others a woman's true career.

"Henry," she said, when they had sat down on the old hair-cloth sofa, side by side, "you have made me very happy; so happy that I wish to keep my happiness all to myself—for a little while. Will you let me keep our engagement secret until I—am accustomed to it? It may be silly or childish, but it seems like a happy dream, and I wish to assure myself of its reality before I tell it to anyone else."

"To me," said the colonel, smiling tenderly into her eyes, "it is the realisation of an ideal. Since we met that day in the cemetery you have seemed to me the embodiment of all that is best of my memories of the old South; and your gentleness, your kindness, your tender grace, your self-sacrifice and devotion to duty, mark you a queen among women, and my heart shall be your throne. As to the announcement, have it as you will—it is the lady's privilege."

"You are very good," she said tremulously. "This hour repays me for all I have ever tried to do for others."

Graciella felt very young indeed—somewhere in the neighbourhood of ten, she put it afterward, when she reviewed the situation in a calmer frame of mind—as she crept softly away from the window and around the house to the back door, and up the stairs and into her own chamber, where, all oblivious of danger to her clothes or her complexion, she threw herself down upon her own bed and burst into a passion of tears. She had been cruelly humiliated. Colonel French, whom she had imagined in love with her, had regarded her merely as a child, who ought to be sent to school—to acquire what, she asked herself, good sense or deportment? Perhaps she might acquire more good sense—she had certainly made a fool of herself in this case—but she had prided herself upon her manners. Colonel French had been merely playing with her, like one would with a pet monkey; and he had been in love, all the time, with her Aunt Laura, whom the girls had referred to compassionately, only that same evening, as a hopeless old maid.

It is fortunate that youth and hope go generally hand in hand. Graciella possessed a buoyant spirit to breast the waves of disappointment. She had her cry out, a good, long cry; and when much weeping had dulled the edge of her discomfiture she began to reflect that all was not yet lost. The colonel would not marry her, but he would still marry in the family. When her Aunt Laura became Mrs. French, she would doubtless go often to New York, if she would not live there always. She would invite Graciella to go with her, perhaps to live with her there.

As for going to school, that was a matter which her own views should control; at present she had no wish to return to school. She might take lessons in music, or art; her aunt would hardly care for her to learn stenography now, or go into magazine work. Her aunt would surely not go to Europe without inviting her, and Colonel French was very liberal with his money, and would deny his wife nothing, though Graciella could hardly imagine that any man would be infatuated with her Aunt Laura.

But this was not the end of Graciella's troubles. Graciella had a heart, although she had suppressed its promptings, under the influence of a selfish ambition. She had thrown Ben Dudley over for the colonel; the colonel did not want her, and now she would have neither. Ben had been very angry, unreasonably angry, she had thought at the time, and objectionably rude in his manner. He had sworn never to speak to her again. If he should keep his word, she might be very unhappy. These reflections brought on another rush of tears, and a very penitent, contrite, humble-minded young woman cried herself to sleep before Miss Laura, with a heart bursting with happiness, bade the colonel good-night at the gate, and went upstairs to lie awake in her bed in a turmoil of pleasant emotions.

Miss Laura's happiness lay not alone in the prospect that Colonel French would marry her, nor in any sordid thought of what she would gain by becoming the wife of a rich man. It rested in the fact that this man, whom she admired, and who had come back from the outer world to bring fresh ideas, new and larger ideals to lift and broaden and revivify the town, had passed by youth and beauty and vivacity, and had chosen her to share this task, to form the heart and mind and manners of his child, and to be the tie which would bind him most strongly to her dear South. For she was a true child of the soil; the people about her, white and black, were her people, and this marriage, with its larger opportunities for usefulness, would help her to do that for which hitherto she had only been able to pray and to hope. To the boy she would be a mother indeed; to lead him in the paths of truth and loyalty and manliness and the fear of God—it was a priceless privilege, and already her mother-heart yearned to begin the task.

And then after the flow came the ebb. Why had he chosen her? Was it *merely* as an abstraction—the embodiment of an ideal, a survival from a host of pleasant memories, and as a mother for his child, who needed care which no one else could give, and as a helpmate in carrying out his schemes of benevolence? Were these his only motives; and, if so, were they sufficient to ensure her happiness? Was he marrying her through a mere sentimental impulse, or for calculated convenience, or from both? She must be certain; for his views might change. He was yet in the full flow of philanthropic enthusiasm. She shared his faith in human nature and the triumph of right ideas; but once or twice she had feared he was underrating the power of conservative forces; that he had been away from Clarendon so long as to lose the perspective of actual conditions, and that he was cherishing expectations which might be disappointed. Should this ever prove true, his disillusion might be as far-reaching and as sudden as his enthusiasm. Then, if he had not loved her for herself, she might be very unhappy. She would have rejoiced to bring him youth and beauty, and the things for which other women were preferred; she would have loved to be the perfect mate, one in heart, mind, soul and body, with the man with whom she was to share the journey of life.

But this was a passing thought, born of weakness and self-distrust, and she brushed it away with the tear that had come with it, and smiled at its absurdity. Her youth was past; with nothing to expect but an old age filled with the small expedients of genteel poverty, there had opened up to her, suddenly and unexpectedly, a great avenue for happiness and usefulness. It was foolish, with so much to be grateful for, to sigh for the unattainable. His love must be all the stronger since it took no thought of things which others would have found of controlling importance. In choosing her to share his intellectual life he had paid her a higher compliment than had he praised the glow of her cheek or the contour of her throat. In confiding Phil to her care he had given her a sacred trust and confidence, for she knew how much he loved the child.

Twenty-one

The colonel's schemes for the improvement of Clarendon went forward, with occasional setbacks. Several kilns of brick turned out badly, so that the brickyard fell behind with its orders, thus delaying the work a few weeks. The foundations of the old cotton mill had been substantially laid, and could be used, so far as their position permitted for the new walls. When the bricks were ready, a gang of masons was put to work. White men and coloured were employed, under a white foreman. So great was the demand for labour and so stimulating the colonel's liberal wage, that even the drowsy Negroes around the market house were all at work, and the pigs who had slept near them were obliged to bestir themselves to keep from being run over by the wagons that were hauling brick and lime and lumber through the streets. Even the cows in the vacant lot between the post-office and the bank occasionally lifted up their gentle eyes as though wondering what strange fever possessed the two-legged creatures around them, urging them to such unnatural activity.

The work went on smoothly for a week or two, when the colonel had some words with Jim Green, the white foreman of the masons. The cause of the dispute was not important, but the colonel, as the master, insisted that certain work should be done in a certain way. Green wished to argue the point. The colonel brought the discussion to a close with a peremptory command. The foreman took offense, declared that he was no nigger to be ordered around, and quit. The colonel promoted to the vacancy George Brown, a coloured man, who was the next best workman in the gang.

On the day when Brown took charge of the job the white bricklayers, of whom there were two at work, laid down their tools.

"What's the matter?" asked the colonel, when they reported for their pay. "Aren't you satisfied with the wages?"

"Yes, we've got no fault to find with the wages."

"Well?"

"We won't work under George Brown. We don't mind working *with* niggers, but we won't work *under* a nigger."

"I'm sorry, gentlemen, but I must hire my own men. Here is your money."

They would have preferred to argue their grievance, and since the colonel had shut off discussion they went down to Clay Jackson's saloon and argued the case with all comers, with the usual distortion attending one-sided argument. Jim Green had been superseded by a nigger—this was the burden of their grievance.

Thus came the thin entering wedge that was to separate the colonel from a measure of his popularity. There had been no objection to the colonel's employing Negroes, no objection to his helping their school—if he chose to waste his money that way; but there were many who took offense when a Negro was preferred to a white man.

Through Caxton the colonel learned of this criticism. The colonel showed no surprise, and no annoyance, but in his usual good-humoured way replied:

"We'll go right along and pay no attention to him. There were only two white men in the gang, and they have never worked under the Negro; they quit as soon as I promoted him. I have hired many men in my time and have made it an unvarying rule to manage my own business in my own way. If anybody says anything to you about it, you tell them just that. These people have got to learn that we live in an industrial age, and success demands of an employer that he utilise the most available labour. After Green was discharged, George Brown was the best mason left. He gets more work out of the men than Green did—even in the old slave times Negroes made the best of overseers; they knew their own people better than white men could and got more out of them. When the mill is completed it will give employment to five hundred white women and fifty white men. But every dog must have his day, so give the Negro his."

The colonel attached no great importance to the incident; the places of the workmen were filled, and the work went forward. He knew the Southern sensitiveness, and viewed it with a good-natured tolerance, which, however, stopped at injustice to himself or others. The very root of his reform was involved in the proposition to discharge a competent foreman because of an unreasonable prejudice. Matters of feeling were all well enough in some respects—no one valued more highly than the colonel the right to choose his own associates—but the right to work and to do one's best work, was fundamental, as was the right to have one's work done by those who could do it best. Even a healthy social instinct might be perverted into an unhealthy and unjust prejudice; most things evil were the perversion of good.

The feeling with which the colonel thus came for the first time directly in contact, a smouldering fire capable always of being fanned into flame, had been greatly excited by the political campaign which began about the third month after his arrival in Clarendon. An ambitious politician in a neighbouring State had led a successful campaign on the issue of Negro disfranchisement. Plainly unconstitutional, it was declared to be as plainly necessary for the preservation of the white race and white civilisation. The example had proved contagious, and Fetters and his crowd, who dominated their State, had raised the issue there. At first the pronouncement met with slight response. The sister State had possessed a Negro majority, which, in view of reconstruction history was theoretically capable of injuring the State. Such was not the case here. The State had survived reconstruction with small injury. White supremacy existed, in the main, by virtue of white efficiency as compared with efficiency of a lower grade; there had been places, and instances, where other methods had been occasionally employed to suppress the Negro vote, but, taken as a whole, the supremacy of the white man was secure. No Negro had held a State office for twenty years. In Clarendon they had even ceased to be summoned as jurors, and when a Negro met a white man, he gave him the wall, even if it were necessary to take the gutter to do so. But this was not enough; this supremacy must be made permanent. Negroes must be taught that they need never look for any different state of things. New definitions were given to old words, new pictures set in old frames, new wine poured into old bottles.

"So long," said the candidate for governor, when he spoke at Clarendon during the canvas, at a meeting presided over by the editor of the *Anglo-Saxon*, "so long as one Negro votes in the State, so long are we face to face with the nightmare of Negro domination. For example, suppose a difference of opinion among white men so radical as to divide their vote equally, the ballot of one Negro would determine the issue. Can such a possibility be contemplated without a shudder? Our duty to ourselves, to our children, and their unborn descendants, and to our great and favoured race, impels us to protest, by word, by vote, by arms if need be, against the enforced equality of an inferior race. Equality anywhere, means ultimately, equality everywhere. Equality at the polls means social equality; social equality means intermarriage and corruption of blood, and degeneration and decay. What gentleman here would want his daughter to marry a blubber-lipped, cocoanut-headed, kidney-footed, etc., etc., nigger?"

There could be but one answer to the question, and it came in thunders of applause. Colonel French heard the speech, smiled at the old arguments, but felt a sudden gravity at the deep-seated feeling which they evoked. He remembered hearing, when a boy, the same arguments. They had served their purpose once before, with other issues, to plunge the South into war and consequent disaster. Had the lesson been in vain? He did not see the justice nor the expediency of the proposed anti-Negro agitation. But he was not in politics, and confined his protests to argument with his friends, who listened but were not convinced.

Behind closed doors, more than one of the prominent citizens admitted that the campaign was all wrong; that the issues were unjust and reactionary, and that the best interests of the State lay in uplifting every element of the people rather than selecting some one class for discouragement and degradation, and that the white race could hold its own, with the Negroes or against them, in any conceivable state of political equality. They listened to the colonel's quiet argument that no State could be freer or greater or more enlightened than the average of its citizenship, and that any restriction of rights that rested upon anything but impartial justice, was bound to re-act, as slavery had done, upon the prosperity and progress of the State. They listened, which the colonel regarded as a great point gained, and they agreed in part, and he could almost understand why they let their feelings govern their reason and their judgment, and said no word to prevent an unfair and unconstitutional scheme from going forward to a successful issue. He knew that for a white man to declare, in such a community, for equal rights or equal justice for the Negro, or to take the Negro's side in any case where the race issue was raised, was to court social ostracism and political death, or, if the feeling provoked were strong enough, an even more complete form of extinction.

So the colonel was patient, and meant to be prudent. His own arguments avoided the stirring up of prejudice, and were directed to the higher motives and deeper principles which underlie society, in the light of which humanity is more than race, and the welfare of the State above that of any man or set of men within it; it being an axiom as true in statesmanship as in mathematics, that the whole is greater than any one of its parts. Content to await the uplifting power of industry and enlightenment, and supremely confident of the result, the colonel went serenely forward in his work of sowing that others might reap.

Twenty-two

The atmosphere of the Treadwell home was charged, for the next few days, with electric currents. Graciella knew that her aunt was engaged to Colonel French. But she had not waited, the night before, to hear her aunt express the wish that the engagement should be kept secret. She was therefore bursting with information of which she could manifest no consciousness without confessing that she had been eavesdropping—a thing which she knew Miss Laura regarded as detestably immoral. She wondered at her aunt's silence. Except a certain subdued air of happiness there was nothing to distinguish Miss Laura's calm demeanor from that of any other day. Graciella had determined upon her own attitude toward her aunt. She would kiss her, and wish her happiness, and give no sign that any thought of Colonel French had ever entered her own mind. But this little drama, rehearsed in the privacy of her own room, went unacted, since the curtain did not rise upon the stage.

The colonel came and went as usual. Some dissimulation was required on Graciella's part to preserve her usual light-hearted manner toward him. She may have been to blame in taking the colonel's attentions as intended for herself; she would not soon forgive his slighting reference to her. In his eyes she had been only a child, who ought to go to school. He had been good enough to say that she had the making of a fine woman. Thanks! She had had a lover for at least two years, and a proposal of marriage before Colonel French's shadow had fallen athwart her life. She wished her Aunt Laura happiness; no one could deserve it more, but was it possible to be happy with a man so lacking in taste and judgment?

Her aunt's secret began to weigh upon her mind, and she effaced herself as much as possible when the colonel came. Her grandmother had begun to notice this and comment upon it, when the happening of a certain social event created a diversion. This was the annual entertainment known as the Assembly Ball. It was usually held later in the year, but owing to the presence of several young lady visitors in the town, it had been decided to give it early in the fall.

The affair was in the hands of a committee, by whom invitations were sent to most people in the county who had any claims to gentility. The gentlemen accepting were expected to subscribe to the funds for hall rent, music and refreshments. These were always the best the town afforded. The ball was held in the Opera House, a rather euphemistic title for the large hall above Barstow's cotton warehouse, where third-class theatrical companies played one-night stands several times during the winter, and where an occasional lecturer or conjurer held forth. An amateur performance of "Pinafore" had once been given there. Henry W. Grady had lectured there upon White Supremacy; the Reverend Sam Small had preached there on Hell. It was also distinguished as having been refused, even at the request of the State Commissioner of Education, as a place for Booker T. Washington to deliver an address, which had been given at the town hall instead. The Assembly Balls had always been held in the Opera House. In former years the music had been furnished by local Negro musicians, but there were no longer any of these, and a band of string music was brought in from another town. So far as mere wealth was concerned, the subscribers touched such extremes as Ben Dudley on the one hand and Colonel French on the other, and included Barclay Fetters, whom Graciella had met on the evening before her disappointment.

The Treadwell ladies were of course invited, and the question of ways and means became paramount. New gowns and other accessories were imperative. Miss Laura's one party dress had done service until it was past redemption, and this was Graciella's first Assembly Ball. Miss Laura took stock of the family's resources, and found that she could afford only one gown. This, of course, must be Graciella's. Her own marriage would entail certain expenses which demanded some present self-denial. She had played wall-flower for several years, but now that she was sure of a partner, it was a real sacrifice not to attend the ball. But Graciella was young, and in such matters youth has a prior right; for she had yet to find her mate.

Graciella magnanimously offered to remain at home, but was easily prevailed upon to go. She was not entirely happy, for the humiliating failure of her hopes had left her for the moment without a recognised admirer, and the fear of old maidenhood had again laid hold of her heart. Her Aunt Laura's case was no consoling example. Not one man in a hundred would choose a wife for Colonel French's reasons. Most men married for beauty, and Graciella had been told that beauty that matured early, like her own, was likely to fade early.

One humiliation she was spared. She had been as silent about her hopes as Miss Laura was about her engagement. Whether this was due to mere prudence or to vanity—the hope of astonishing her little world by the unexpected announcement—did not change the comforting fact that she had nothing to explain and nothing for which to be pitied. If her friends, after the manner of young ladies, had hinted at the subject and sought to find a meaning in Colonel French's friendship, she had smiled enigmatically. For this self-restraint, whatever had been its motive, she now reaped her reward. The announcement of her aunt's engagement would account for the colonel's attentions to Graciella as a mere courtesy to a young relative of his affianced.

With regard to Ben, Graciella was quite uneasy. She had met him only once since their quarrel, and had meant to bow to him politely, but with dignity, to show that she bore no malice; but he had ostentatiously avoided her glance. If he chose to be ill-natured, she had thought, and preferred her enmity to her friendship, her conscience was at least clear. She had been willing to forget his rudeness and be a friend to him. She could have been his true friend, if nothing more; and he would need friends, unless he changed a great deal.

When her mental atmosphere was cleared by the fading of her dream, Ben assumed larger proportions. Perhaps he had had cause for complaint; at least it was only just to admit that he thought so. Nor had he suffered in her estimation by his display of spirit in not waiting to be jilted but in forcing her hand before she was quite ready to play it. She could scarcely expect him to attend her to the ball; but he was among the subscribers, and could hardly avoid meeting her, or dancing with her, without pointed rudeness. If he did not ask her to dance, then either the Virginia reel, or the lancers, or quadrilles, would surely bring them together; and though Graciella sighed, she did not despair. She could, of course, allay his jealousy at once by telling him of her Aunt Laura's engagement, but this was not yet practicable. She must find some other way of placating him.

Ben Dudley also had a problem to face in reference to the ball—a problem which has troubled impecunious youth since balls were invented—the problem of clothes. He was not obliged to go to the ball. Graciella's outrageous conduct relieved him of any obligation to invite her, and there was no other woman with whom he would have cared to go, or who would have cared, so far as he knew, to go with him. For he was not a lady's man, and but for his distant relationship would probably never have gone to the Treadwells'. He was looked upon by young women as slow, and he knew that Graciella had often been impatient at his lack of sprightliness. He could pay his subscription, which was really a sort of gentility tax, the failure to meet which would merely forfeit future invitations, and remain at home. He did not own a dress suit, nor had he the money to spare for one. He, or they, for he and his uncle were one in such matters, were in debt already, up to the limit of their credit, and he had sold the last bale of old cotton to pay the last month's expenses, while the new crop, already partly mortgaged, was not yet picked. He knew that some young fellows in town rented dress suits from Solomon Cohen, who, though he kept only four suits in stock at a time, would send to New York for others to rent out on this occasion, and return them afterwards. But Ben would not wear another man's clothes. He had borne insults from Graciella that he never would have borne from any one else, and that he would never bear again; but there were things at which his soul protested. Nor would Cohen's suits have fitted him. He was so much taller than the average man for whom store clothes were made.

He remained in a state of indecision until the day of the ball. Late in the evening he put on his black cutaway coat, which was getting a little small, trousers to match, and a white waistcoat, and started to town on horseback so as to arrive in time for the ball, in case he should decide, at the last moment, to take part.

Twenty-three

The Opera House was brilliantly lighted on the night of the Assembly Ball. The dancers gathered at an earlier hour than is the rule in the large cities. Many of the guests came in from the country, and returned home after the ball, since the hotel could accommodate only a part of them.

When Ben Dudley, having left his horse at a livery stable, walked up Main Street toward the hall, carriages were arriving and discharging their freight. The ladies were prettily gowned, their faces were bright and animated, and Ben observed that most of the gentlemen wore dress suits; but also, much to his relief, that a number, sufficient to make at least a respectable minority, did not. He was rapidly making up his mind to enter, when Colonel French's carriage, drawn by a pair of dashing bays and driven by a Negro in livery, dashed up to the door and discharged Miss Graciella Treadwell, radiantly beautiful in a new low-cut pink gown, with pink flowers in her hair, a thin gold chain with a gold locket at the end around her slender throat, white slippers on her feet and long white gloves upon her shapely hands and wrists.

Ben shrank back into the shadow. He had never been of an envious disposition; he had always looked upon envy as a mean vice, unworthy of a gentleman; but for a moment something very like envy pulled at his heartstrings. Graciella worshipped the golden calf. *He* worshipped Graciella. But he had no money; he could not have taken her to the ball in a closed carriage, drawn by blooded horses and driven by a darky in livery.

Graciella's cavalier wore, with the ease and grace of long habit, an evening suit of some fine black stuff that almost shone in the light from the open door. At the sight of him the waist of Ben's own coat shrunk up to the arm-pits, and he felt a sinking of the heart as they passed out of his range of vision. He would not appear to advantage by the side of Colonel French, and he would not care to appear otherwise than to advantage in Graciella's eyes. He would not like to make more palpable, by contrast, the difference between Colonel French and himself; nor could he be haughty, distant, reproachful, or anything but painfully self-conscious, in a coat that was not of the proper cut, too short in the sleeves, and too tight under the arms.

While he stood thus communing with his own bitter thoughts, another carriage, drawn by a pair of beautiful black horses, drew up to the curb in front of him. The horses were restive, and not inclined to stand still. Some one from the inside of the carriage called to the coachman through the open window.

"Ransom," said the voice, "stay on the box. Here, you, open this carriage door!"

Ben looked around for the person addressed, but saw no one near but himself.

"You boy there, by the curb, open this door, will you, or hold the horses, so my coachman can!"

"Are you speaking to me?" demanded Ben angrily.

Just then one of the side-lights of the carriage flashed on Ben's face.

"Oh, I beg pardon," said the man in the carriage, carelessly, "I took you for a nigger."

There could be no more deadly insult, though the mistake was not unnatural. Ben was dark, and the shadow made him darker.

Ben was furious. The stranger had uttered words of apology, but his tone had been insolent, and his apology was more offensive than his original blunder. Had it not been for Ben's reluctance to make a disturbance, he would have struck the offender in the mouth. If he had had a pistol, he could have shot him; his great uncle Ralph, for instance, would not have let him live an hour.

While these thoughts were surging through his heated brain, the young man, as immaculately clad as Colonel French had been, left the carriage, from which he helped a lady, and with her upon his arm, entered the hall. In the light that streamed from the doorway, Ben recognised him as Barclay Fetters, who, having finished a checkered scholastic career, had been at home at Sycamore for several months. Much of this time he had spent in Clarendon, where his father's wealth and influence gave him entrance to good society, in spite of an ancestry which mere character would not have offset. He knew young Fetters very well by sight, since the latter had to pass Mink Run whenever he came to town from Sycamore. Fetters may not have known him, since he had been away for much of the time in recent years, but he ought to have been able to distinguish between a white man—a gentleman—and a Negro. It was the insolence of an upstart. Old Josh Fetters had been, in his younger days, his uncle's overseer. An overseer's grandson treated him, Ben Dudley, like dirt under his feet! Perhaps he had judged him by his clothes. He would like to show Barclay

Fetters, if they ever stood face to face, that clothes did not make the man, nor the gentleman.

Ben decided after this encounter that he would not go on the floor of the ballroom; but unable to tear himself away, he waited until everybody seemed to have gone in; then went up the stairs and gained access, by a back way, to a dark gallery in the rear of the hall, which the ushers had deserted for the ballroom, from which he could, without discovery, look down upon the scene below. His eyes flew to Graciella as the needle to the pole. She was dancing with Colonel French.

The music stopped, and a crowd of young fellows surrounded her. When the next dance, which was a waltz, began, she moved out upon the floor in the arms of Barclay Fetters.

Ben swore beneath his breath. He had heard tales of Barclay Fetters which, if true, made him unfit to touch a decent woman. He left the hall, walked a short distance down a street and around the corner to the bar in the rear of the hotel, where he ordered a glass of whiskey. He had never been drunk in his life, and detested the taste of liquor; but he was desperate and had to do something; he would drink till he was drunk, and forget his troubles. Having never been intoxicated, he had no idea whatever of the effect liquor would have upon him.

With each succeeding drink, the sense of his wrongs broadened and deepened. At one stage his intoxication took the form of an intense self-pity. There was something rotten in the whole scheme of things. Why should he be poor, while others were rich, and while fifty thousand dollars in gold were hidden in or around the house where he lived? Why should Colonel French, an old man, who was of no better blood than himself, be rich enough to rob him of the woman whom he loved? And why, above all, should Barclay Fetters have education and money and every kind of opportunity, which he did not appreciate, while he, who would have made good use of them, had nothing? With this sense of wrong, which grew as his brain clouded more and more, there came, side by side, a vague zeal to right these wrongs. As he grew drunker still, his thoughts grew less coherent; he lost sight of his special grievance, and merely retained the combative instinct.

He had reached this dangerous stage, and had, fortunately, passed it one step farther along the road to unconsciousness—fortunately, because had he been sober, the result of that which was to follow might have been more serious—when two young men, who had come down from the ballroom for some refreshment, entered the barroom and asked for cocktails. While the barkeeper was compounding the liquor, the young men spoke of the ball.

"That little Treadwell girl is a peach," said one. "I could tote a bunch of beauty like that around the ballroom all night."

The remark was not exactly respectful, nor yet exactly disrespectful. Ben looked up from his seat. The speaker was Barclay Fetters, and his companion one Tom McRae, another dissolute young man of the town. Ben got up unsteadily and walked over to where they stood.

"I want you to un'erstan'," he said thickly, "that no gen'l'man would mensh'n a lady's name in a place like this, or shpeak dissuspeckerly 'bout a lady 'n any place; an' I want you to unerstan' fu'thermo' that you're no gen'l'man, an' that I'm goin' t' lick you, by G—d!"

"The hell you are!" returned Fetters. A scowl of surprise rose on his handsome face, and he sprang to an attitude of defence.

Ben suited the action to the word, and struck at Fetters. But Ben was drunk and the other two were sober, and in three minutes Ben lay on the floor with a sore head and a black eye. His nose was bleeding copiously, and the crimson stream had run down upon his white shirt and vest. Taken all in all, his appearance was most disreputable. By this time the liquor he had drunk had its full effect, and complete unconsciousness supervened to save him, for a little while, from the realisation of his disgrace.

"Who is the mucker, anyway?" asked Barclay Fetters, readjusting his cuffs, which had slipped down in the melee.

"He's a chap by the name of Dudley," answered McRae; "lives at Mink Run, between here and Sycamore, you know."

"Oh, yes, I've seen him—the 'po' white' chap that lives with the old lunatic that's always digging for buried treasure——

'For my name was Captain Kidd,
As I sailed, as I sailed.'

But let's hurry back, Tom, or we'll lose the next dance."

Fetters and his companion returned to the ball. The barkeeper called a servant of the hotel, with whose aid, Ben was carried upstairs and put to bed, bruised in body and damaged in reputation.

Twenty-four

Ben's fight with young Fetters became a matter of public comment the next day after the ball. His conduct was cited as sad proof of the degeneracy of a once fine old family. He had been considered shiftless and not well educated, but no one had suspected that he was a drunkard and a rowdy. Other young men in the town, high-spirited young fellows with plenty of money, sometimes drank a little too much, and occasionally, for a point of honour, gentlemen were obliged to attack or defend themselves, but when they did, they used pistols, a gentleman's weapon. Here, however, was an unprovoked and brutal attack with fists, upon two gentlemen in evening dress and without weapons to defend themselves, "one of them," said the *Anglo-Saxon*, "the son of our distinguished fellow citizen and colleague in the legislature, the Honourable William Fetters."

When Colonel French called to see Miss Laura, the afternoon of next day after the ball, the ladies were much concerned about the affair.

"Oh, Henry," exclaimed Miss Laura, "what is this dreadful story about Ben Dudley? They say he was drinking at the hotel, and became intoxicated, and that when Barclay Fetters and Tom McRae went into the hotel, he said something insulting about Graciella, and when they rebuked him for his freedom he attacked them violently, and that when finally subdued he was put to bed unconscious and disgracefully intoxicated. Graciella is very angry, and we all feel ashamed enough to sink into the ground. What can be the matter with Ben? He hasn't been around lately, and he has quarrelled with Graciella. I never would have expected anything like this from Ben."

"It came from his great-uncle Ralph," said Mrs. Treadwell. "Ralph was very wild when he was young, but settled down into a very polished gentleman. I danced with him once when he was drunk, and I never knew it—it was my first ball, and I was intoxicated myself, with excitement. Mother was scandalised, but father laughed and said boys would be boys. But poor Ben hasn't had his uncle's chances, and while he has always behaved well here, he could hardly be expected to carry his liquor like a gentleman of the old school."

"My dear ladies," said the colonel, "we have heard only one side of the story. I guess there's no doubt Ben was intoxicated, but we know he isn't a drinking man, and one drink—or even one drunk—doesn't make a drunkard, nor one fight a rowdy. Barclay Fetters and Tom McRae are not immaculate, and perhaps Ben can exonerate himself."

"I certainly hope so," said Miss Laura earnestly. "I am sorry for Ben, but I could not permit a drunken rowdy to come to the house, or let my niece be seen upon the street with him."

"It would only be fair," said the colonel, "to give him a chance to explain, when he comes in again. I rather like Ben. He has some fine mechanical ideas, and the making of a man in him, unless I am mistaken. I have been hoping to find a place for him in the new cotton mill, when it is ready to run."

They were still speaking of Ben, when there was an irresolute knock at the rear door of the parlour, in which they were seated.

"Miss Laura, O Miss Laura," came a muffled voice. "Kin I speak to you a minute. It's mighty pertickler, Miss Laura, fo' God it is!"

"Laura," said the colonel, "bring Catharine in. I saw that you were troubled once before when you were compelled to refuse her something. Henceforth your burdens shall be mine. Come in, Catharine," he called, "and tell us what's the matter. What's your trouble? What's it all about?"

The woman, red-eyed from weeping, came in, wringing her apron.

"Miss Laura," she sobbed, "an' Colonel French, my husban' Bud is done gone and got inter mo' trouble. He's run away f'm Mistah Fettuhs, w'at he wuz sol' back to in de spring, an' he's done be'n fine' fifty dollahs mo', an' he's gwine ter be sol' back ter Mistah Fettuhs in de mawnin', fer ter finish out de ole fine and wo'k out de new one. I's be'n ter see 'im in de gyard house, an' he say Mistah Haines, w'at use' ter be de constable and is a gyard fer Mistah Fettuhs now, beat an' 'bused him so he couldn' stan' it; an' 'ceptin' I could pay all dem fines, he'll be tuck back dere; an'he say ef dey evah beats him ag'in, dey'll eithuh haf ter kill him, er he'll kill some er dem. An' Bud is a rash man, Miss Laura, an' I'm feared dat he'll do w'at he say, an' ef dey kills him er he kills any er dem, it'll be all de same ter me—I'll never see 'm no mo' in dis worl'. Ef I could borry de money, Miss Laura—Mars' Colonel—I'd wuk my fingers ter de bone 'tel I paid back de las' cent. Er ef you'd buy Bud, suh, lack you did Unc' Peter, he would n' mind wukkin' fer you, suh, fer Bud is a good wukker we'n folks treats him right; an' he had n' never had no trouble nowhar befo' he come hyuh, suh."

"How did he come to be arrested the first time?" asked the colonel.

"He didn't live hyuh, suh; I used ter live hyuh, an' I ma'ied him down ter Madison, where I wuz wukkin'. We fell out one day, an' I got mad and lef' 'im—it wuz all my fault an' I be'n payin' fer it evuh since—an' I come back home an' went ter wuk hyuh, an' he come aftuh me, an de fus' day he come, befo' I knowed he wuz hyuh, dis yer Mistah Haines tuck 'im up, an' lock 'im up in de gyard house, like a hog in de poun', an' he didn' know nobody, an' dey didn' give 'im no chanst ter see nobody, an' dey tuck 'im roun' ter Squi' Reddick nex' mawnin', an' fined 'im an' sol' 'im ter dis yer Mistuh Fettuhs fer ter wo'k out de fine; an' I be'n wantin' all dis time ter hyuh fum 'im, an' I'd done be'n an' gone back ter Madison to look fer 'im, an' foun' he wuz gone. An' God knows I didn' know what had become er 'im, 'tel he run away de yuther time an' dey tuck 'im an' sent 'im back again. An' he hadn' done nothin' de fus' time, suh, but de Lawd know w'at he won' do ef dey sen's 'im back any mo'."

Catharine had put her apron to her eyes and was sobbing bitterly. The story was probably true. The colonel had heard underground rumours about the Fetters plantation and the manner in which it was supplied with labourers, and his own experience in old Peter's case had made them seem not unlikely. He had seen Catharine's husband, in the justice's court, and the next day, in the convict gang behind Turner's buggy. The man had not looked like a criminal; that he was surly and desperate may as well have been due to a sense of rank injustice as to an evil nature. That a wrong had been done, under cover of law, was at least more than likely; but a deed of mercy could be made to right it. The love of money might be the root of all evil, but its control was certainly a means of great good. The colonel glowed with the consciousness of this beneficent power to scatter happiness.

"Laura," he said, "I will attend to this; it is a matter about which you should not be troubled. Don't be alarmed, Catharine. Just be a good girl and help Miss Laura all you can, and I'll look after your husband, and pay his fine and let him work it out as a free man."

"Thank'y, suh, thank'y, Mars' Colonel, an' Miss Laura! An' de

Lawd is gwine bless you, suh, you an' my sweet young lady, fuh bein' good to po' folks w'at can't do nuthin' to he'p deyse'ves out er trouble," said Catharine backing out with her apron to her eyes.

On leaving Miss Laura, the colonel went round to the office of Squire Reddick, the justice of the peace, to inquire into the matter of Bud Johnson. The justice was out of town, his clerk said, but would be in his office at nine in the morning, at which time the colonel could speak to him about Johnson's fine.

The next morning was bright and clear, and cool enough to be bracing. The colonel, alive with pleasant thoughts, rose early and after a cold bath, and a leisurely breakfast, walked over to the mill site, where the men were already at work. Having looked the work over and given certain directions, he glanced at his watch, and finding it near nine, set out for the justice's office in time to reach it by the appointed hour. Squire Reddick was at his desk, upon which his feet rested, while he read a newspaper. He looked up with an air of surprise as the colonel entered.

"Why, good mornin', Colonel French," he said genially. "I kind of expected you a while ago; the clerk said you might be around. But you didn' come, so I supposed you'd changed yo' mind."

"The clerk said that you would be here at nine," replied the colonel; "it is only just nine."

"Did he? Well, now, that's too bad! I do generally git around about nine, but I was earlier this mornin' and as everybody was here, we started in a little sooner than usual. You wanted to see me about Bud Johnson?"

"Yes, I wish to pay his fine and give him work."

"Well, that's too bad; but you weren't here, and Mr. Turner was, and he bought his time again for Mr. Fetters. I'm sorry, you know, but first come, first served."

The colonel was seriously annoyed. He did not like to believe there was a conspiracy to frustrate his good intention; but that result had been accomplished, whether by accident or design. He had failed in the first thing he had undertaken for the woman he loved and was to marry. He would see Fetters's man, however, and come to some arrangement with him. With Fetters the hiring of the Negro was purely a commercial transaction, conditioned upon a probable profit, for the immediate payment of which, and a liberal bonus, he would doubtless relinquish his claim upon Johnson's services.

Learning that Turner, who had acted as Fetters's agent in the matter, had gone over to Clay Johnson's saloon, he went to seek him there. He found him, and asked for a proposition. Turner heard him out.

"Well, Colonel French," he replied with slightly veiled insolence, "I bought this nigger's time for Mr. Fetters, an' unless I'm might'ly mistaken in Mr. Fetters, no amount of money can get the nigger until he's served his time out. He's defied our rules and defied the law, and defied me, and assaulted one of the guards; and he ought to be made an example of. We want to keep 'im; he's a bad nigger, an' we've got to handle a lot of 'em, an' we need 'im for an example—he keeps us in trainin'."

"Have you any power in the matter?" demanded the colonel, restraining his contempt.

"Me? No, not *me!* I couldn't let the nigger go for his weight in gol'—an' wouldn' if I could. I bought 'im in for Mr. Fetters, an' he's the only man that's got any say about 'im."

"Very well," said the colonel as he turned away, "I'll see Fetters."

"I don't know whether you will or not," said Turner to himself, as he shot a vindictive glance at the colonel's retreating figure. "Fetters has got this county where he wants it, an' I'll bet dollars to bird shot he ain't goin' to let no coon-flavoured No'the'n interloper come down here an' mix up with his arrangements, even if he did hail from this town way back yonder. This here nigger problem is a South'en problem, and outsiders might's well keep their han's off. Me and Haines an' Fetters is the kind o' men to settle it."

The colonel was obliged to confess to Miss Laura his temporary set-back, which he went around to the house and did immediately.

"It's the first thing I've undertaken yet for your sake, Laura, and I've got to report failure, so far."

"It's only the first step," she said, consolingly.

"That's all. I'll drive out to Fetters's place to-morrow, and arrange the matter. By starting before day, I can make it and transact my business, and get back by night, without hurting the horses."

Catharine was called in and the situation explained to her. Though clearly disappointed at the delay, and not yet free of apprehension that Bud might do something rash, she seemed serenely confident of the colonel's ultimate success. In her simple creed, God might sometimes seem to neglect his black children, but no harm could come to a Negro who had a rich white gentleman for friend and protector.

Twenty-five

It was not yet sunrise when the colonel set out next day, after an early breakfast, upon his visit to Fetters. There was a crisp freshness in the air, the dew was thick upon the grass, the clear blue sky gave promise of a bright day and a pleasant journey.

The plantation conducted by Fetters lay about twenty miles to the south of Clarendon, and remote from any railroad, a convenient location for such an establishment, for railroads, while they bring in supplies and take out produce, also bring in light and take out information, both of which are fatal to certain fungus growths, social as well as vegetable, which flourish best in the dark.

The road led by Mink Run, and the colonel looked over toward the house as they passed it. Old and weather-beaten it seemed, even in the distance, which lent it no enchantment in the bright morning light. When the colonel had travelled that road in his boyhood, great forests of primeval pine had stretched for miles on either hand, broken at intervals by thriving plantations. Now all was changed. The tall and stately growth of the long-leaf pine had well nigh disappeared; fifteen years before, the turpentine industry, moving southward from Virginia, along the upland counties of the Appalachian slope, had swept through Clarendon County, leaving behind it a trail of blasted trunks and abandoned stills. Ere these had yielded to decay, the sawmill had followed, and after the sawmill the tar kiln, so that the dark green forest was now only a waste of blackened stumps and undergrowth, topped by the vulgar short-leaved pine and an occasional oak or juniper. Here and there they passed an expanse of cultivated land, and there were many smaller clearings in which could be seen, plowing with gaunt mules or stunted steers, some heavy-footed Negro or listless "po' white man;" or women and children, black or white. In reply to a question, the coachman said that Mr. Fetters had worked all that country for turpentine years before, and had only taken up cotton raising after the turpentine had been exhausted from the sand hills.

He had left his mark, thought the colonel. Like the plague of locusts, he had settled and devoured and then moved on, leaving a barren waste behind him.

As the morning advanced, the settlements grew thinner, until suddenly, upon reaching the crest of a hill, a great stretch of cultivated lowland lay spread before them. In the centre of the plantation, near the road which ran through it, stood a square, new, freshly painted frame house, which would not have seemed out of place in some Ohio or Michigan city, but here struck a note alien to its surroundings. Off to one side, like the Negro quarters of another generation, were several rows of low, unpainted cabins, built of sawed lumber, the boards running up and down, and battened with strips where the edges met. The fields were green with cotton and with corn, and there were numerous gangs of men at work, with an apparent zeal quite in contrast with the leisurely movement of those they had passed on the way. It was a very pleasing scene.

"Dis yer, suh," said the coachman in an awed tone, "is Mistah Fetters's plantation. You ain' gwine off nowhere, and leave me alone whils' you are hyuh, is you, suh?"

"No," said the colonel, "I'll keep my eye on you. Nobody'll trouble you while you're with me."

Passing a clump of low trees, the colonel came upon a group at sight of which he paused involuntarily. A gang of Negroes were at work. Upon the ankles of some was riveted an iron band to which was soldered a chain, at the end of which in turn an iron ball was fastened. Accompanying them was a white man, in whose belt was stuck a revolver, and who carried in one hand a stout leather strap, about two inches in width with a handle by which to grasp it. The gang paused momentarily to look at the traveller, but at a meaning glance from the overseer fell again to their work of hoeing cotton. The white man stepped to the fence, and Colonel French addressed him.

"Good morning."

"Mornin', suh."

"Will you tell me where I can find Mr. Fetters?" inquired the colonel.

"No, suh, unless he's at the house. He may have went away this mornin', but I haven't heard of it. But you drive along the road to the house, an' somebody'll tell you."

The colonel seemed to have seen the overseer before, but could not remember where.

"Sam," he asked the coachman, "who is that white man?"

"Dat's Mistah Haines, suh—use' ter be de constable at Cla'endon, suh. I wouldn' lak to be in no gang under him, suh, sho' I wouldn', no, suh!"

After this ejaculation, which seemed sincere as well as fervent, Sam whipped up the horses and soon reached the house. A Negro boy came out to meet them.

"Is Mr. Fetters at home," inquired the colonel?

"I—I don' know, suh—I—I'll ax Mars' Turner. *He's* hyuh."

He disappeared round the house and in a few minutes returned with Turner, with whom the colonel exchanged curt nods.

"I wish to see Mr. Fetters," said the colonel.

"Well, you can't see him."

"Why not?"

"Because he ain't here. He left for the capital this mornin', to be gone a week. You'll be havin' a fine drive, down here and back."

The colonel ignored the taunt.

"When will Mr. Fetters return?" he inquired.

"I'm shore I don't know. He don't tell me his secrets. But I'll tell *you,* Colonel French, that if you're after that nigger, you're wastin' your time. He's in Haines's gang, and Haines loves him so well that Mr. Fetters has to keep Bud in order to keep Haines. There's no accountin' for these vi'lent affections, but they're human natur', and they have to be 'umoured."

"I'll talk to your master," rejoined the colonel, restraining his indignation and turning away.

Turner looked after him vindictively.

"He'll talk to my *master*, like as if I was a nigger! It'll be a long time before he talks to Fetters, if that's who he means—if I can prevent it. Not that it would make any difference, but I'll just keep him on the anxious seat."

It was nearing noon, but the colonel had received no invitation to stop, or eat, or feed his horses. He ordered Sam to turn and drive back the way they had come.

As they neared the group of labourers they had passed before, the colonel saw four Negroes, in response to an imperative gesture from the overseer, seize one of their number, a short, thickset fellow, overpower some small resistance which he seemed to make, throw him down with his face to the ground, and sit upon his extremities while the overseer applied the broad leathern thong vigorously to his bare back.

The colonel reached over and pulled the reins mechanically. His instinct was to interfere; had he been near enough to recognise in the Negro the object of his visit, Bud Johnson, and in the overseer the ex-constable, Haines, he might have yielded to the impulse. But on second thought he realised that he had neither authority nor strength to make good his interference. For aught he knew, the performance might be strictly according to law. So, fighting a feeling of nausea which he could hardly conquer, he ordered Sam to drive on.

The coachman complied with alacrity, as though glad to escape from a mighty dangerous place. He had known friendless coloured folks, who had strayed down in that neighbourhood to be lost for a long time; and he had heard of a spot, far back from the road, in a secluded part of the plantation, where the graves of convicts who had died while in Fetters's service were very numerous.

Twenty-six

During the next month the colonel made several attempts to see Fetters, but some fatality seemed always to prevent their meeting. He finally left the matter of finding Fetters to Caxton, who ascertained that Fetters would be in attendance at court during a certain week, at Carthage, the county seat of the adjoining county, where the colonel had been once before to inspect a cotton mill. Thither the colonel went on the day of the opening of court. His train reached town toward noon and he went over to the hotel. He wondered if he would find the proprietor sitting where he had found him some weeks before. But the buggy was gone from before the piazza, and there was a new face behind the desk. The colonel registered, left word that he would be in to dinner, and then went over to the court house, which lay behind the trees across the square.

The court house was an old, square, hip-roofed brick structure, whose walls, whitewashed the year before, had been splotched and discoloured by the weather. From one side, under the eaves, projected a beam, which supported a bell rung by a rope from the window below. A hall ran through the centre, on either side of which were the county offices, while the court room with a judge's room and jury room, occupied the upper floor.

The colonel made his way across the square, which showed the usual signs of court being in session. There were buggies hitched to trees and posts here and there, a few Negroes sleeping in the sun, and several old coloured women with little stands for the sale of cakes, and fried fish, and cider.

The colonel went upstairs to the court room. It was fairly well filled, and he remained standing for a few minutes near the entrance. The civil docket was evidently on trial, for there was a jury in the box, and a witness was being examined with some prolixity with reference to the use of a few inches of land which lay on one side or on the other of a disputed boundary. From what the colonel could gather, that particular line fence dispute had been in litigation for twenty years, had cost several lives, and had resulted in a feud that involved a whole township.

The testimony was about concluded when the colonel entered, and the lawyers began their arguments. The feeling between the litigants seemed to have affected their attorneys, and the court more than once found it necessary to call counsel to order. The trial was finished, however, without bloodshed; the case went to the jury, and court was adjourned until two o'clock.

The colonel had never met Fetters, nor had he seen anyone in the court room who seemed likely to be the man. But he had seen his name freshly written on the hotel register, and he would doubtless go there for dinner. There would be ample time to get acquainted and transact his business before court reassembled for the afternoon.

Dinner seemed to be a rather solemn function, and except at a table occupied by the judge and the lawyers, in the corner of the room farthest from the colonel, little was said. A glance about the room showed no one whom the colonel could imagine to be Fetters, and he was about to ask the waiter if that gentleman had yet entered the dining room, when a man came in and sat down on the opposite side of the table. The colonel looked up, and met the cheerful countenance of the liveryman from whom he had hired a horse and buggy some weeks before.

"Howdy do?" said the newcomer amiably. "Hope you've been well."

"Quite well," returned the colonel, "how are you?"

"Oh, just tol'able. Tendin' co't?"

"No, I came down here to see a man that's attending court—your friend Fetters. I suppose he'll be in to dinner."

"Oh, yes, but he ain't come in yet. I reckon you find the ho-tel a little different from the time you were here befo'."

"This is a better dinner than I got," replied the colonel, "and I haven't seen the landlord anywhere, nor his buggy."

"No, he ain't here no more. Sad loss to Carthage! You see Bark Fetters—that's Bill's boy that's come home from the No'th from college—Bark Fetters come down here one day, an' went in the ho-tel, an' when Lee Dickson commenced to put on his big airs, Bark cussed 'im out, and Lee, who didn't know Bark from Adam, cussed 'im back, an' then Bark hauled off an' hit 'im. They had it hot an' heavy for a while. Lee had more strength, but Bark had more science, an' laid Lee out col'. Then Bark went home an' tol' the ole man, who had a mortgage on the ho-tel, an' he sol' Lee up. I hear he's barberin' or somethin' er that sort up to Atlanta, an' the hotel's run by another man. There's Fetters comin' in now."

The colonel glanced in the direction indicated, and was surprised at the appearance of the redoubtable Fetters, who walked over and took his seat at the table with the judge and the lawyers. He had expected to meet a tall, long-haired, red-faced, truculent individual, in a slouch hat and a frock coat, with a loud voice and a dictatorial manner, the typical Southerner of melodrama. He saw a keen-eyed, hard-faced, small man, slightly gray, clean-shaven, wearing a well-fitting city-made business suit of light tweed. Except for a few little indications, such as the lack of a crease in his trousers, Fetters looked like any one of a hundred business men whom the colonel might have met on Broadway in any given fifteen minutes during business hours.

The colonel timed his meal so as to leave the dining-room at the same moment with Fetters. He went up to Fetters, who was chewing a toothpick in the office, and made himself known.

"I am Mr. French," he said—he never referred to himself by his military title—"and you, I believe, are Mr. Fetters?"

"Yes, sir, that's my name," replied Fetters without enthusiasm, but eyeing the colonel keenly between narrowed lashes.

"I've been trying to see you for some time, about a matter," continued the colonel, "but never seemed able to catch up with you before."

"Yes, I heard you were at my house, but I was asleep upstairs, and didn't know you'd be'n there till you'd gone."

"Your man told me you had gone to the capital for two weeks."

"My man? Oh, you mean Turner! Well, I reckon you must have riled Turner somehow, and he thought he'd have a joke on you."

"I don't quite see the joke," said the colonel, restraining his displeasure. "But that's ancient history. Can we sit down over here in the shade and talk by ourselves for a moment?"

Fetters followed the colonel out of doors, where they drew a couple of chairs to one side, and the colonel stated the nature of his business. He wished to bargain for the release of a Negro, Bud Johnson by name, held to service by Fetters under a contract with Clarendon County. He was willing to pay whatever expense Fetters had been to on account of Johnson, and an amount sufficient to cover any estimated profits from his services.

Meanwhile Fetters picked his teeth nonchalantly, so nonchalantly as to irritate the colonel. The colonel's impatience was not lessened by the fact that Fetters waited several seconds before replying.

"Well, Mr. Fetters, what say you?"

"Colonel French," said Fetters, "I reckon you can't have the nigger."

"Is it a matter of money?" asked the colonel. "Name your figure. I don't care about the money. I want the man for a personal reason."

"So do I," returned Fetters, coolly, "and money's no object to me. I've more now than I know what to do with."

The colonel mastered his impatience. He had one appeal which no Southerner could resist.

"Mr. Fetters," he said, "I wish to get this man released to please a lady."

"Sorry to disoblige a lady," returned Fetters, "but I'll have to keep the nigger. I run a big place, and I'm obliged to maintain discipline. This nigger has been fractious and contrary, and I've sworn that he shall work out his time. I have never let any nigger get the best of me—or white man either," he added significantly.

The colonel was angry, but controlled himself long enough to make one more effort. "I'll give you five hundred dollars for your contract," he said rising from his chair.

"You couldn't get him for five thousand."

"Very well, sir," returned the colonel, "this is not the end of this. I will see, sir, if a man can be held in slavery in this State, for a debt he is willing and ready to pay. You'll hear more of this before I'm through with it."

"Another thing, Colonel French," said Fetters, his quiet eyes glittering as he spoke, "I wonder if you recollect an incident that occurred years ago, when we went to the academy in Clarendon?"

"If you refer," returned the colonel promptly, "to the time I chased you down Main Street, yes—I recalled it the first time I heard of you when I came back to Clarendon—and I remember why I did it. It is a good omen."

"That's as it may be," returned Fetters quietly. "I didn't have to recall it; I've never forgotten it. Now you want something from me, and you can't have it."

"We shall see," replied the colonel. "I bested you then, and I'll best you now."

"We shall see," said Fetters.

Fetters was not at all alarmed, indeed he smiled rather pityingly. There had been a time when these old aristocrats could speak, and the earth trembled, but that day was over. In this age money talked, and he had known how to get money, and how to use it to get more. There were a dozen civil suits pending against him in the court house there, and he knew in advance that he should win them every one, without directly paying any juryman a dollar. That any nigger should get away while he wished to hold him, was—well, inconceivable. Colonel French might have money, but he, Fetters, had men as well; and if Colonel French became too troublesome about this nigger, this friendship for niggers could be used in such a way as to make Clarendon too hot for Colonel French. He really bore no great malice against Colonel French for the little incident of their school days, but he had not forgotten it, and Colonel French might as well learn a lesson. He, Fetters, had not worked half a lifetime for a commanding position, to yield it to Colonel French or any other man. So Fetters smoked his cigar tranquilly, and waited at the hotel for his anticipated verdicts. For there could not be a jury impanelled in the county which did not have on it a majority of men who were mortgaged to Fetters. He even held the Judge's note for several hundred dollars.

The colonel waited at the station for the train back to Clarendon. When it came, it brought a gang of convicts, consigned to Fetters. They had been brought down in the regular "Jim Crow" car, for the colonel saw coloured women and children come out ahead of them.

The colonel watched the wretches, in coarse striped garments, with chains on their legs and shackles on their hands, unloaded from the train and into the waiting wagons. There were burly Negroes and flat-shanked, scrawny Negroes. Some wore the ashen hue of long confinement. Some were shamefaced, some reckless, some sullen. A few white convicts among them seemed doubly ashamed—both of their condition and of their company; they kept together as much as they were permitted, and looked with contempt at their black companions in misfortune. Fetters's man and Haines, armed with whips, and with pistols in their belts, were present to oversee the unloading, and the colonel could see them point him out to the State officers who had come in charge of the convicts, and see them look at him with curious looks. The scene was not edifying. There were criminals in New York, he knew very well, but he had never seen one. They were not marched down Broadway in stripes and chains. There were certain functions of society, as of the body, which were more decently performed in retirement. There was work in the State for the social reformer, and the colonel, undismayed by his temporary defeat, metaphorically girded up his loins, went home, and, still metaphorically, set out to put a spoke in Fetters's wheel.

Twenty-seven

His first step was to have Caxton look up and abstract for him the criminal laws of the State. They were bad enough, in all conscience. Men could be tried without jury and condemned to infamous punishments, involving stripes and chains, for misdemeanours which in more enlightened States were punished with a small fine or brief detention. There were, for instance, no degrees of larceny, and the heaviest punishment might be inflicted, at the discretion of the judge, for the least offense.

The vagrancy law, of which the colonel had had some experience, was an open bid for injustice and "graft" and clearly designed to profit the strong at the expense of the weak. The crop-lien laws were little more than the instruments of organised robbery. To these laws the colonel called the attention of some of his neighbours with whom he was on terms of intimacy. The enlightened few had scarcely known of their existence, and quite agreed that the laws were harsh and ought to be changed.

But when the colonel, pursuing his inquiry, undertook to investigate the operation of these laws, he found an appalling condition. The statutes were mild and beneficent compared with the results obtained under cover of them. Caxton spent several weeks about the State looking up the criminal records, and following up the sentences inflicted, working not merely for his fee, but sharing the colonel's indignation at the state of things unearthed. Convict labour was contracted out to private parties, with little or no effective State supervision, on terms which, though exceedingly profitable to the State, were disastrous to free competitive labour. More than one lawmaker besides Fetters was numbered among these contractors.

Leaving the realm of crime, they found that on hundreds of farms, ignorant Negroes, and sometimes poor whites, were held in bondage under claims of debt, or under contracts of exclusive employment for long terms of years—contracts extorted from ignorance by craft, aided by State laws which made it a misdemeanour to employ such persons elsewhere. Free men were worked side by side with convicts from the penitentiary, and women and children herded with the most depraved criminals, thus breeding a criminal class to prey upon the State.

In the case of Fetters alone the colonel found a dozen instances where the law, bad as it was, had not been sufficient for Fetters's purpose, but had been plainly violated. Caxton discovered a discharged guard of Fetters, who told him of many things that had taken place at Sycamore; and brought another guard one evening, at that time employed there, who told him, among other things, that Bud Johnson's life, owing to his surliness and rebellious conduct, and some spite which Haines seemed to bear against him, was simply a hell on earth—that even a strong Negro could not stand it indefinitely.

A case was made up and submitted to the grand jury. Witnesses were summoned at the colonel's instance. At the last moment they all weakened, even the discharged guard, and their testimony was not sufficient to justify an indictment.

The colonel then sued out a writ of habeas corpus for the body of Bud Johnson, and it was heard before the common pleas court at Clarendon, with public opinion divided between the colonel and Fetters. The court held that under his contract, for which he had paid the consideration, Fetters was entitled to Johnson's services.

The colonel, defeated but still undismayed, ordered Caxton to prepare a memorial for presentation to the federal authorities, calling their attention to the fact that peonage, a crime under the Federal statutes, was being flagrantly practised in the State. This allegation was supported by a voluminous brief, giving names and dates and particular instances of barbarity. The colonel was not without some quiet support in this movement; there were several public-spirited men in the county, including his able lieutenant Caxton, Dr. Price and old General Thornton, none of whom were under any obligation to Fetters, and who all acknowledged that something ought to be done to purge the State of a great disgrace.

There was another party, of course, which deprecated any scandal which would involve the good name of the State or reflect upon the South, and who insisted that in time these things would pass away and there would be no trace of them in future generations. But the colonel insisted that so also would the victims of the system pass away, who, being already in existence, were certainly entitled to as much consideration as generations yet unborn; it was hardly fair to sacrifice them to a mere punctilio. The colonel had reached the conviction that the regenerative forces of education and enlightenment, in order to have any effect in his generation, must be reinforced by some positive legislative or executive action, or else the untrammelled forces of graft and greed would override them; and he was human enough, at this stage of his career to wish to see the result of his labours, or at least a promise of result.

The colonel's papers were forwarded to the proper place, whence they were referred from official to official, and from department to department. That it might take some time to set in motion the machinery necessary to reach the evil, the colonel knew very well, and hence was not impatient at any reasonable delay. Had he known that his presentation had created a sensation in the highest quarter, but that owing to the exigencies of national politics it was not deemed wise, at that time, to do anything which seemed like an invasion of State rights or savoured of sectionalism, he might not have been so serenely confident of the outcome. Nor had Fetters known as much, would he have done the one thing which encouraged the colonel more than anything else. Caxton received a message one day from Judge Bullard, representing Fetters, in which Fetters made the offer that if Colonel French would stop his agitation on the labour laws, and withdraw any papers he had filed, and promise to drop the whole matter, he would release Bud Johnson.

The colonel did not hesitate a moment. He had gone into this fight for Johnson—or rather to please Miss Laura. He had risen now to higher game; nothing less than the system would satisfy him.

"But, Colonel," said Caxton, "it's pretty hard on the nigger. They'll kill him before his time's up. If you'll give me a free hand, I'll get him anyway."

"How?"

"Perhaps it's just as well you shouldn't know. But I have friends at Sycamore."

"You wouldn't break the law?" asked the colonel.

"Fetters is breaking the law," replied Caxton. "He's holding Johnson for debt—and whether that is lawful or not, he certainly has no right to kill him."

"You're right," replied the colonel. "Get Johnson away, I don't care how. The end justifies the means—that's an argument that goes down here. Get him away, and send him a long way off, and he can write for his wife to join him. His escape need not interfere with our other plans. We have plenty of other cases against Fetters."

Within a week, Johnson, with the connivance of a bribed guard, a poor-white man from Clarendon, had escaped from Fetters and seemingly vanished from Beaver County. Fetters's lieutenants were active in their search for him, but sought in vain.

Twenty-eight

Ben Dudley awoke the morning after the assembly ball, with a violent headache and a sense of extreme depression, which was not relieved by the sight of his reflection in the looking-glass of the bureau in the hotel bedroom where he found himself.

One of his eyes was bloodshot, and surrounded by a wide area of discolouration, and he was conscious of several painful contusions on other portions of his body. His clothing was badly disordered and stained with blood; and, all in all, he was scarcely in a condition to appear in public. He made such a toilet as he could, and, anxious to avoid observation, had his horse brought from the livery around to the rear door of the hotel, and left for Mink Run by the back streets. He did not return to town for a week, and when he made his next appearance there, upon strictly a business visit, did not go near the Treadwells', and wore such a repellent look that no one ventured to speak to him about his encounter with Fetters and McRae. He was humiliated and ashamed, and angry with himself and all the world. He had lost Graciella already; any possibility that might have remained of regaining her affection, was destroyed by his having made her name the excuse for a barroom broil. His uncle was not well, and with the decline of his health, his monomania grew more acute and more absorbing, and he spent most of his time in the search for the treasure and in expostulations with Viney to reveal its whereabouts. The supervision of the plantation work occupied Ben most of the time, and during his intervals of leisure he sought to escape unpleasant thoughts by busying himself with the model of his cotton gin.

His life had run along in this way for about two weeks after the ball, when one night Barclay Fetters, while coming to town from his father's plantation at Sycamore, in company with Turner, his father's foreman, was fired upon from ambush, in the neighbourhood of Mink Run, and seriously wounded. Groaning heavily and in a state of semi-unconsciousness he was driven by Turner, in the same buggy in which he had been shot, to Doctor Price's house, which lay between Mink Run and the town.

The doctor examined the wound, which was serious. A charge of buckshot had been fired at close range, from a clump of bushes by the wayside, and the charge had taken effect in the side of the face. The sight of one eye was destroyed beyond a peradventure, and that of the other endangered by a possible injury to the optic nerve. A sedative was administered, as many as possible of the shot extracted, and the wounds dressed. Meantime a messenger was despatched to Sycamore for Fetters, senior, who came before morning post-haste. To his anxious inquiries the doctor could give no very hopeful answer.

"He's not out of danger," said Doctor Price, "and won't be for several days. I haven't found several of those shot, and until they're located I can't tell what will happen. Your son has a good constitution, but it has been abused somewhat and is not in the best condition to throw off an injury."

"Do the best you can for him, Doc," said Fetters, "and I'll make it worth your while. And as for the double-damned scoundrel that shot him in the dark, I'll rake this county with a fine-toothed comb till he's found. If Bark dies, the murderer shall hang as high as Haman, if it costs me a million dollars, or, if Bark gets well, he shall have the limit of the law. No man in this State shall injure me or mine and go unpunished."

The next day Ben Dudley was arrested at Mink Run, on a warrant sworn out by Fetters, senior, charging Dudley with attempted murder. The accused was brought to Clarendon, and lodged in Beaver County jail.

Ben sent for Caxton, from whom he learned that his offense was not subject to bail until it became certain that Barclay Fetters would recover. For in the event of his death, the charge would be murder; in case of recovery, the offense would be merely attempted murder, or shooting with intent to kill, for which bail was allowable. Meantime he would have to remain in jail.

In a day or two young Fetters was pronounced out of danger, so far as his life was concerned, and Colonel French, through Caxton, offered to sign Ben's bail bond. To Caxton's surprise Dudley refused to accept bail at the colonel's hands.

"I don't want any favours from Colonel French," he said decidedly. "I prefer to stay in jail rather than to be released on his bond."

So he remained in jail.

Graciella was not so much surprised at Ben's refusal to accept bail. She had reasoned out, with a fine instinct, the train of emotions which had brought her lover to grief, and her own share in stirring them up. She could not believe that Ben was capable of shooting a man from ambush; but even if he had, it would have been for love of her; and if he had not, she had nevertheless been the moving cause of the disaster. She would not willingly have done young Mr. Fetters an injury. He had favoured her by his attentions, and, if all stories were true, he had behaved better than Ben, in the difficulty between them, and had suffered more. But she loved Ben, as she grew to realise, more and more. She wanted to go and see Ben in jail but her aunt did not think it proper. Appearances were all against Ben, and he had not purged himself by any explanation. So Graciella sat down and wrote him a long letter. She knew very well that the one thing that would do him most good would be the announcement of her Aunt Laura's engagement to Colonel French. There was no way to bring this about, except by first securing her aunt's permission. This would make necessary a frank confession, to which, after an effort, she nerved herself.

"Aunt Laura," she said, at a moment when they were alone together, "I know why Ben will not accept bail from Colonel French, and why he will not tell his side of the quarrel between himself and Mr. Fetters. He was foolish enough to imagine that Colonel French was coming to the house to see me, and that I preferred the colonel to him. And, Aunt Laura, I have a confession to make; I have done something for which I want to beg your pardon. I listened that night, and overheard the colonel ask you to be his wife. Please, dear Aunt Laura, forgive me, and let me write and tell Ben—just Ben, in confidence. No one else need know it."

Miss Laura was shocked and pained, and frankly said so, but could not refuse the permission, on condition that Ben should be pledged to keep her secret, which, for reasons of her own, she was not yet ready to make public. She, too, was fond of Ben, and hoped that he might clear himself of the accusation. So Graciella wrote the letter. She was no more frank in it, however, on one point, than she had been with her aunt, for she carefully avoided saying that she *had* taken Colonel French's attentions seriously, or built any hopes upon them, but chided Ben for putting such a construction upon her innocent actions, and informed him, as proof of his folly, and in the strictest confidence, that Colonel French was engaged to her Aunt Laura. She expressed her sorrow for his predicament, her profound belief in his innocence, and her unhesitating conviction that he would be acquitted of the pending charge.

To this she expected by way of answer a long letter of apology, explanation, and protestations of undying love.

She received, instead, a brief note containing a cold acknowledgment of her letter, thanking her for her interest in his welfare, and assuring her that he would respect Miss Laura's confidence. There was no note of love or reproachfulness—mere cold courtesy.

Graciella was cut to the quick, so much so that she did not even notice Ben's mistakes in spelling. It would have been better had he overwhelmed her with reproaches—it would have shown at least that he still loved her. She cried bitterly, and lay awake very late that night, wondering what else she could do for Ben that a self-respecting young lady might. For the first time, she was more concerned about Ben than about herself. If by marrying him immediately she could have saved him from danger and disgrace she would have done so without one selfish thought—unless it were selfish to save one whom she loved.

The preliminary hearing in the case of the State *vs.* Benjamin Dudley was held as soon as Doctor Price pronounced Barclay Fetters out of danger. The proceedings took place before Squire Reddick, the same justice from whom the colonel had bought Peter's services, and from whom he had vainly sought to secure Bud Johnson's release.

In spite of Dudley's curt refusal of his assistance, the colonel, to whom Miss Laura had conveyed a hint of the young man's frame of mind, had instructed Caxton to spare no trouble or expense in the prisoner's interest. There was little doubt, considering Fetters's influence and vindictiveness, that Dudley would be remanded, though the evidence against him was purely circumstantial; but it was important that the evidence should be carefully scrutinised, and every legal safeguard put to use.

The case looked bad for the prisoner. Barclay Fetters was not present, nor did the prosecution need him; his testimony could only have been cumulative.

Turner described the circumstances of the shooting from the trees by the roadside near Mink Run, and the driving of the wounded man to Doctor Price's.

Doctor Price swore to the nature of the wound, its present and probable consequences, which involved the loss of one eye and perhaps the other, and produced the shot he had extracted.

McRae testified that he and Barclay Fetters had gone down between dances, from the Opera Ball, to the hotel bar, to get a glass of seltzer. They had no sooner entered the bar than the prisoner, who had evidently been drinking heavily and showed all the signs of intoxication, had picked a quarrel with them and assaulted Mr. Fetters. Fetters, with the aid of the witness, had defended himself. In the course of the altercation, the prisoner had used violent and profane language, threatening, among other things, to kill Fetters. All this testimony was objected to, but was admitted as tending to show a motive for the crime. This closed the State's case.

Caxton held a hurried consultation with his client. Should they put in any evidence, which would be merely to show their hand, since the prisoner would in any event undoubtedly be bound over? Ben was unable to deny what had taken place at the hotel, for he had no distinct recollection of it—merely a blurred impression, like the memory of a bad dream. He could not swear that he had not threatened Fetters. The State's witnesses had refrained from mentioning the lady's name; he could do no less. So far as the shooting was concerned, he had had no weapon with which to shoot. His gun had been stolen that very day, and had not been recovered.

"The defense will offer no testimony," declared Caxton, at the result of the conference.

The justice held the prisoner to the grand jury, and fixed the bond at ten thousand dollars. Graciella's information had not been without its effect, and when Caxton suggested that he could still secure bail, he had little difficulty in inducing Ben to accept Colonel French's friendly offices. The bail bond was made out and signed, and the prisoner released.

Caxton took Ben to his office after the hearing. There Ben met the colonel, thanked him for his aid and friendship, and apologised for his former rudeness.

"I was in a bad way, sir," he said, "and hardly knew what I was doing. But I know I didn't shoot Bark Fetters, and never thought of such a thing."

"I'm sure you didn't, my boy," said the colonel, laying his hand, in familiar fashion, upon the young fellow's shoulder, "and we'll prove it before we quit. There are some ladies who believe the same thing, and would like to hear you say it."

"Thank you, sir," said Ben. "I should like to tell them, but I shouldn't want to enter their house until I am cleared of this charge. I think too much of them to expose them to any remarks about harbouring a man out on bail for a penitentiary offense. I'll write to them, sir, and thank them for their trust and friendship, and you can tell them for me, if you will, that I'll come to see them when not only I, but everybody else, can say that I am fit to go."

"Your feelings do you credit," returned the colonel warmly, "and however much they would like to see you, I'm sure the ladies will appreciate your delicacy. As your friend and theirs, you must permit me to serve you further, whenever the opportunity offers, until this affair is finished."

Ben thanked the colonel from a full heart, and went back to Mink Run, where, in the effort to catch up the plantation work, which had fallen behind in his absence, he sought to forget the prison atmosphere and lose the prison pallor. The disgrace of having been in jail was indelible, and the danger was by no means over. The sympathy of his friends would have been priceless to him, but to remain away from them would be not only the honourable course to pursue, but a just punishment for his own folly. For Graciella, after all, was only a girl—a young girl, and scarcely yet to be judged harshly for her actions; while he was a man grown, who knew better, and had not acted according to his lights.

Three days after Ben Dudley's release on bail, Clarendon was treated to another sensation. Former constable Haines, now employed as an overseer at Fetters's convict farm, while driving in a buggy to Clarendon, where he spent his off-duty spells, was shot from ambush near Mink Run, and his right arm shattered in such a manner as to require amputation.

Twenty-nine

Colonel French's interest in Ben Dudley's affairs had not been permitted to interfere with his various enterprises. Work on the chief of these, the cotton mill, had gone steadily forward, with only occasional delays, incident to the delivery of material, the weather, and the health of the workmen, which was often uncertain for a day or two after pay day. The coloured foreman of the brick-layers had been seriously ill; his place had been filled by a white man, under whom the walls were rising rapidly. Jim Green, the foreman whom the colonel had formerly discharged, and the two white bricklayers who had quit at the same time, applied for reinstatement. The colonel took the two men on again, but declined to restore Green, who had been discharged for insubordination.

Green went away swearing vengeance. At Clay Johnson's saloon he hurled invectives at the colonel, to all who would listen, and with anger and bad whiskey, soon worked himself into a frame of mind that was ripe for any mischief. Some of his utterances were reported to the colonel, who was not without friends—the wealthy seldom are; but he paid no particular attention to them, except to keep a watchman at the mill at night, lest this hostility should seek an outlet in some attempt to injure the property. The precaution was not amiss, for once the watchman shot at a figure prowling about the mill. The lesson was sufficient, apparently, for there was no immediate necessity to repeat it.

The shooting of Haines, while not so sensational as that of Barclay Fetters, had given rise to considerable feeling against Ben Dudley. That two young men should quarrel, and exchange shots, would not ordinarily have been a subject of extended remark. But two attempts at assassination constituted a much graver affair. That Dudley was responsible for this second assault was the generally accepted opinion. Fetters's friends and hirelings were openly hostile to young Dudley, and Haines had been heard to say, in his cups, at Clay Jackson's saloon, that when young Dudley was tried and convicted and sent to the penitentiary, he would be hired out to Fetters, who had the country contract, and that he, Haines, would be delighted to have Dudley in his gang. The feeling against Dudley grew from day to day, and threats and bets were openly made that he would not live to be tried. There was no direct proof against him, but the moral and circumstantial evidence was quite sufficient to convict him in the eyes of Fetter's friends and supporters. The colonel was sometimes mentioned, in connection with the affair as a friend of Ben's, for whom he had given bail, and as an enemy of Fetters, to whom his antagonism in various ways had become a matter of public knowledge and interest.

One day, while the excitement attending the second shooting was thus growing, Colonel French received through the mail a mysteriously worded note, vaguely hinting at some matter of public importance which the writer wished to communicate to him, and requesting a private interview for the purpose, that evening, at the colonel's house. The note, which had every internal evidence of sincerity, was signed by Henry Taylor, the principal of the coloured school, whom the colonel had met several times in reference to the proposed industrial school. From the tenor of the communication, and what he knew about Taylor, the colonel had no doubt that the matter was one of importance, at least not one to be dismissed without examination. He thereupon stepped into Caxton's office and wrote an answer to the letter, fixing eight o'clock that evening as the time, and his own library as the place, of a meeting with the teacher.. This letter he deposited in the post-office personally—it was only a step from Caxton's office. Upon coming out of the post-office he saw the teacher standing on an opposite corner. When the colonel had passed out of sight, Taylor crossed the street, entered the post-office, and soon emerged with the letter. He had given no sign that he saw the colonel, but had looked rather ostentatiously the other way when that gentleman had glanced in his direction.

At the appointed hour there was a light step on the colonel's piazza. The colonel was on watch, and opened the door himself, ushering Taylor into his library, a very handsome and comfortable room, the door of which he carefully closed behind them.

The teacher looked around cautiously.

"Are we alone, sir?"

"Yes, entirely so."

"And can any one hear us?"

"No. What have you got to tell me?"

"Colonel French," replied the other, "I'm in a hard situation, and I want you to promise that you'll never let on to any body that I told you what I'm going to say."

"All right, Mr. Taylor, if it is a proper promise to make. You can trust my discretion."

"Yes, sir, I'm sure I can. We coloured folks, sir, are often accused of trying to shield criminals of our own race, or of not helping the officers of the law to catch them. Maybe we does, suh," he said, lapsing in his earnestness, into bad grammar, "maybe we does sometimes, but not without reason."

"What reason?" asked the colonel.

"Well, sir, fer the reason that we ain't always shore that a coloured man will get a fair trial, or any trial at all, or that he'll get a just sentence after he's been tried. We have no hand in makin' the laws, or in enforcin' 'em; we are not summoned on jury; and yet we're asked to do the work of constables and sheriffs who are paid for arrestin' criminals, an' for protectin' 'em from mobs, which they don't do."

"I have no doubt every word you say is true, Mr. Taylor, and such a state of things is unjust, and will some day be different, if I can help to make it so. But, nevertheless, all good citizens, whatever their colour, ought to help to preserve peace and good order."

"Yes, sir, so they ought; and I want to do just that; I want to co-operate, and a whole heap of us want to co-operate with the good white people to keep down crime and lawlessness. I know there's good white people who want to see justice done—but they ain't always strong enough to run things; an' if any one of us coloured folks tells on another one, he's liable to lose all his frien's. But I believe, sir, that I can trust you to save me harmless, and to see that nothin' mo' than justice is done to the coloured man."

"Yes, Taylor, you can trust me to do all that I can, and I think I have considerable influence, Now, what's on your mind? Do you know who shot Haines and Mr. Fetters?"

"Well, sir, you're a mighty good guesser. It ain't so much Mr. Fetters an' Mr. Haines I'm thinkin' about, for that place down the country is a hell on earth, an' they're the devils that runs it. But there's a friend of yo'rs in trouble, for something he didn' do, an' I wouldn' stan' for an innocent man bein' sent to the penitentiary—though many a po' Negro has been. Yes, sir, I know that Mr. Ben Dudley didn' shoot them two white men."

"So do I," rejoined the colonel. "Who did?"

"It was Bud Johnson, the man you tried to get away from Mr. Fetters—yo'r coachman tol' us about it, sir, an' we know how good a friend of ours you are, from what you've promised us about the school. An' I wanted you to know, sir. You are our friend, and have showed confidence in us, and I wanted to prove to you that we are not ungrateful, an' that we want to be good citizens."

"I had heard," said the colonel, "that Johnson had escaped and left the county."

"So he had, sir, but he came back. They had 'bused him down at that place till he swore he'd kill every one that had anything to do with him. It was Mr. Turner he shot at the first time and he hit young Mr. Fetters by accident. He stole a gun from ole Mr. Dudley's place at Mink Run, shot Mr. Fetters with it, and has kept it ever since, and shot Mr. Haines with it. I suppose they'd 'a' ketched him before, if it hadn't be'n for suspectin' young Mr. Dudley."

"Where is Johnson now," asked the colonel.

"He's hidin' in an old log cabin down by the swamp back of Mink Run. He sleeps in the daytime, and goes out at night to get food and watch for white men from Mr. Fetters's place."

"Does his wife know where he is?"

"No, sir; he ain't never let her know.

"By the way, Taylor," asked the colonel, "how do *you* know all this?"

"Well, sir," replied the teacher, with something which, in an uneducated Negro would have been a very pronounced chuckle, "there's mighty little goin' on roun' here that I *don't* find out, sooner or later."

"Taylor," said the colonel, rising to terminate the interview, "you have rendered a public service, have proved yourself a good citizen, and have relieved Mr. Dudley of serious embarrassment. I will see that steps are taken to apprehend Johnson, and will keep your participation in the matter secret, since you think it would hurt your influence with your people. And I promise you faithfully that every effort shall be made to see that Johnson has a fair trial and no more than a just punishment."

He gave the Negro his hand.

"Thank you, sir, thank you, sir," replied the teacher, returning the colonel's clasp. "If there were more white men like you, the coloured folks would have no more trouble."

The colonel let Taylor out, and watched him as he looked cautiously up and down the street to see that he was not observed. That coloured folks, or any other kind, should ever cease to have trouble, was a vain imagining. But the teacher had made a well-founded complaint of injustice which ought to be capable of correction; and he had performed a public-spirited action, even though he had felt constrained to do it in a clandestine manner.

About his own part in the affair the colonel was troubled. It was becoming clear to him that the task he had undertaken was no light one—not the task of apprehending Johnson and clearing Dudley, but that of leavening the inert mass of Clarendon with the leaven of enlightenment. With the best of intentions, and hoping to save a life, he had connived at turning a murderer loose upon the community. It was true that the community, through unjust laws, had made him a murderer, but it was no part of the colonel's plan to foster or promote evil passions, or to help the victims of the law to make reprisals. His aim was to bring about, by better laws and more liberal ideas, peace, harmony, and universal good will. There was a colossal work for him to do, and for all whom he could enlist with him in this cause. The very standards of right and wrong had been confused by the race issue, and must be set right by the patient appeal to reason and humanity. Primitive passions and private vengeance must be subordinated to law and order and the higher good. A new body of thought must be built up, in which stress must be laid upon the eternal verities, in the light of which difficulties which now seemed unsurmountable would be gradually overcome.

But this halcyon period was yet afar off, and the colonel roused himself to the duty of the hour. With the best intentions he had let loose upon the community, in a questionable way, a desperate character. It was no less than his plain duty to put the man under restraint. To rescue from Fetters a man whose life was threatened, was one thing. To leave a murderer at large now would be to endanger innocent lives, and imperil Ben Dudley's future.

The arrest of Bud Johnson brought an end to the case against Ben Dudley. The prosecuting attorney, who was under political obligations to Fetters, seemed reluctant to dismiss the case, until Johnson's guilt should have been legally proved; but the result of the Negro's preliminary hearing rendered this position no longer tenable; the case against Ben was nolled, and he could now hold up his head as a free man, with no stain upon his character.

Indeed, the reaction in his favour as one unjustly indicted, went far to wipe out from the public mind the impression that he was a drunkard and a rowdy. It was recalled that he was of good family and that his forebears had rendered valuable service to the State, and that he had never been seen to drink before, or known to be in a fight, but that on the contrary he was quiet and harmless to a fault. Indeed, the Clarendon public would have admired a little more spirit in a young man, even to the extent of condoning an occasional lapse into license.

There was sincere rejoicing at the Treadwell house when Ben, now free in mind, went around to see the ladies. Miss Laura was warmly sympathetic and congratulatory; and Graciella, tearfully happy, tried to make up by a sweet humility, through which shone the true womanliness of a hitherto undeveloped character, for the past stings and humiliations to which her selfish caprice had subjected her lover. Ben resumed his visits, if not with quite their former frequency, and it was only a day or two later that the colonel found him and Graciella, with his own boy Phil, grouped in familiar fashion on the steps, where Ben was demonstrating with some pride of success, the operation of his model, into which he was feeding cotton when the colonel came up.

The colonel stood a moment and looked at the machine.

"It's quite ingenious," he said. "Explain the principle."

Ben described the mechanism, in brief, well-chosen words which conveyed the thought clearly and concisely, and revealed a fine mind for mechanics and at the same time an absolute lack of technical knowledge.

"It would never be of any use, sir," he said, at the end, "for everybody has the other kind. But it's another way, and I think a better."

"It is clever," said the colonel thoughtfully, as he went into the house.

The colonel had not changed his mind at all since asking Miss Laura to be his wife. The glow of happiness still warmed her cheek, the spirit of youth still lingered in her eyes and in her smile. He might go a thousand miles before meeting a woman who would please him more, take better care of Phil, or preside with more dignity over his household. Her simple grace would adapt itself to wealth as easily as it had accommodated itself to poverty. It would be a pleasure to travel with her to new scenes and new places, to introduce her into a wider world, to see her expand in the generous sunlight of ease and freedom from responsibility.

True to his promise, the colonel made every effort to see that Bud Johnson should be protected against mob violence and given a fair trial. There was some intemperate talk among the partisans of Fetters, and an ominous gathering upon the streets the day after the arrest, but Judge Miller, of the Beaver County circuit, who was in Clarendon that day, used his influence to discountenance any disorder, and promised a speedy trial of the prisoner. The crime was not the worst of crimes, and there was no excuse for riot or lynch law. The accused could not escape his just punishment.

As a result of the judge's efforts, supplemented by the colonel's and those of Doctor Price and several ministers, any serious fear of disorder was removed, and a handful of Fetters's guards who had come up from his convict farm and foregathered with some choice spirits of the town at Clay Jackson's saloon, went back without attempting to do what they had avowedly come to town to accomplish.

Thirty

One morning the colonel, while overseeing the work at the new mill building, stepped on the rounded handle of a chisel, which had been left lying carelessly on the floor, and slipped and fell, spraining his ankle severely. He went home in his buggy, which was at the mill, and sent for Doctor Price, who put his foot in a plaster bandage and ordered him to keep quiet for a week.

Peter and Phil went around to the Treadwells' to inform the ladies of the accident. On reaching the house after the accident, the colonel had taken off his coat, and sent Peter to bring him one from the closet off his bedroom.

When the colonel put on the coat, he felt some papers in the inside pocket, and taking them out, recognised the two old letters he had taken from the lining of his desk several months before. The housekeeper, in a moment of unusual zeal, had discovered and mended the tear in the sleeve, and Peter had by chance selected this particular coat to bring to his master. When Peter started, with Phil, to go to the Treadwells', the colonel gave him the two letters.

"Give these," he said, "to Miss Laura, and tell her I found them in the old desk."

It was not long before Miss Laura came, with Graciella, to call on the colonel. When they had expressed the proper sympathy, and had been assured that the hurt was not dangerous, Miss Laura spoke of another matter.

"Henry," she said, with an air of suppressed excitement, "I have made a discovery. I don't quite know what it means, or whether it amounts to anything, but in one of the envelopes you sent me just now there was a paper signed by Mr. Fetters. I do not know how it could have been left in the desk; we had searched it, years ago, in every nook and cranny, and found nothing."

The colonel explained the circumstances of his discovery of the papers, but prudently refrained from mentioning how long ago they had taken place.

Miss Laura handed him a thin, oblong, yellowish slip of paper, which had been folded in the middle; it was a printed form, upon which several words had been filled in with a pen.

"It was enclosed in this," she said, handing him another paper.

The colonel took the papers and glanced over them.

"Mother thinks," said Miss Laura anxiously, "that they are the papers we were looking for, that prove that Fetters was in father's debt."

The colonel had been thinking rapidly. The papers were, indeed, a promissory note from Fetters to Mr. Treadwell, and a contract and memorandum of certain joint transactions in turpentine and cotton futures. The note was dated twenty years back. Had it been produced at the time of Mr. Treadwell's death, it would not have been difficult to collect, and would have meant to his survivors the difference between poverty and financial independence. Now it was barred by the lapse of time.

Miss Laura was waiting in eager expectation. Outwardly calm, her eyes were bright, her cheeks were glowing, her bosom rose and fell excitedly. Could he tell her that this seemingly fortunate accident was merely the irony of fate—a mere cruel reminder of a former misfortune? No, she could not believe it!

"It has made me happy, Henry," she said, while he still kept his eyes bent on the papers to conceal his perplexity, "it has made me very happy to think that I may not come to you empty-handed."

"Dear woman," he thought, "you shall not. If the note is not good, it shall be made good."

"Laura," he said aloud, "I am no lawyer, but Caxton shall look at these to-day, and I shall be very much mistaken if they do not bring you a considerable sum of money. Say nothing about them, however, until Caxton reports. He will be here to see me to-day and by to-morrow you shall have his opinion."

Miss Laura went away with a radiantly hopeful face, and as she and Graciella went down the street, the colonel noted that her step was scarcely less springy than her niece's. It was worth the amount of Fetters's old note to make her happy; and since he meant to give her all that she might want, what better way than to do it by means of this bit of worthless paper? It would be a harmless deception, and it would save the pride of three gentlewomen, with whom pride was not a disease, to poison and scorch and blister, but an inspiration to courtesy, and kindness, and right living. Such a pride was worth cherishing even at a sacrifice, which was, after all, no sacrifice.

He had already sent word to Caxton of his accident, requesting him to call at the house on other business. Caxton came in the afternoon, and when the matter concerning which he had come had been disposed of, Colonel French produced Fetters's note.

"Caxton," he said, "I wish to pay this note and let it seem to have come from Fetters."

Caxton looked at the note.

"Why should you pay it?" he asked. "I mean," he added, noting a change in the colonel's expression, "why shouldn't Fetters pay it?"

"Because it is outlawed," he replied, "and we could hardly expect him to pay for anything he didn't have to pay. The statute of limitations runs against it after fifteen years—and it's older than that, much older than that."

Caxton made a rapid mental calculation.

"That is the law in New York," he said, "but here the statute doesn't begin to run for twenty years. The twenty years for which this note was given expires to-day."

"Then it is good?" demanded the colonel, looking at his watch.

"It is good," said Caxton, "provided there is no defence to it except the statute, and provided I can file a petition on it in the county clerk's office by four o'clock, the time at which the office closes. It is now twenty minutes of four."

"Can you make it?"

"I'll try."

Caxton, since his acquaintance with Colonel French, had learned something more about the value of half an hour than he had ever before appreciated, and here was an opportunity to test his knowledge. He literally ran the quarter of a mile that lay between the colonel's residence and the court house, to the open-eyed astonishment of those whom he passed, some of whom wondered whether he were crazy, and others whether he had committed a crime. He dashed into the clerk's office, seized a pen, and the first piece of paper handy, and began to write a petition. The clerk had stepped into the hall, and when he came leisurely in at three minutes to four, Caxton discovered that he had written his petition on the back of a blank marriage license. He folded it, ran his pen through the printed matter, endorsed it, "Estate of

Treadwell *vs.* Fetters," signed it with the name of Ellen Treadwell, as executrix, by himself as her attorney, swore to it before the clerk, and handed it to that official, who raised his eyebrows as soon as he saw the endorsement.

"Now, Mr. Munroe," said Caxton, "if you'll enter that on the docket, now, as of to-day, I'll be obliged to you. I'd rather have the transaction all finished up while I wait. Your fee needn't wait the termination of the suit. I'll pay it now and take a receipt for it."

The clerk whistled to himself as he read the petition in order to make the entry.

"That's an old-timer," he said. "It'll make the old man cuss."

"Yes," said Caxton. "Do me a favour, and don't say anything about it for a day or two. I don't think the suit will ever come to trial."

Thirty-one

On the day following these events, the colonel, on the arm of old Peter, hobbled out upon his front porch, and seating himself in a big rocking chair, in front of which a cushion had been adjusted for his injured ankle, composed himself to read some arrears of mail which had come in the day before, and over which he had only glanced casually. When he was comfortably settled, Peter and Phil walked down the steps, upon the lowest of which they seated themselves. The colonel had scarcely begun to read before he called to the old man.

"Peter," he said, "I wish you'd go upstairs, and look in my room, and bring me a couple of light-coloured cigars from the box on my bureau—the mild ones, you know, Peter."

"Yas, suh, I knows, suh, de mil' ones, dem wid de gol' ban's 'roun' 'em. Now you stay right hyuh, chile. till Peter come back."

Peter came up the steps and disappeared in the doorway.

The colonel opened a letter from Kirby, in which that energetic and versatile gentleman assured the colonel that he had evolved a great scheme, in which there were millions for those who would go into it. He had already interested Mrs. Jerviss, who had stated she would be governed by what the colonel did in the matter. The letter went into some detail upon this subject, and then drifted off into club and social gossip. Several of the colonel's friends had inquired particularly about him. One had regretted the loss to their whist table. Another wanted the refusal of his box at the opera, if he were not coming back for the winter.

"I think you're missed in a certain quarter, old fellow. I know a lady who would be more than delighted to see you. I am invited to her house to dinner, ostensibly to talk about our scheme, in reality to talk about you.

"But this is all by the way. The business is the thing. Take my proposition under advisement. We all made money together before; we can make it again. My option has ten days to run. Wire me before it is up what reply to make. I know what you'll say, but I want your 'ipse dixit.' "

The colonel knew too what his reply would be, and that it would be very different from Kirby's anticipation. He would write it, he thought, next day, so that Kirby should not be kept in suspense, or so that he might have time to enlist other capital in the enterprise. The colonel felt really sorry to disappoint his good friends. He would write and inform Kirby of his plans, including that of his approaching marriage.

He had folded the letter and laid it down, and had picked up a newspaper, when Peter returned with the cigars and a box of matches.

"Mars Henry?" he asked, "w'at's gone wid de chile?"

"Phil?" replied the colonel, looking toward the step, from which the boy had disappeared. "I suppose he went round the house."

"Mars Phil! O Mars Phil!" called the old man.

There was no reply.

Peter looked round the corner of the house, but Phil was nowhere visible. The old man went round to the back yard, and called again, but did not find the child.

"I hyuhs de train comin'; I 'spec's he's gone up ter de railroad track," he said, when he had returned to the front of the house. "I'll run up dere an' fetch 'im back."

"Yes, do, Peter," returned the colonel. "He's probably all right, but you'd better see about him."

Little Phil, seeing his father absorbed in the newspaper, and not wishing to disturb him, had amused himself by going to the gate and looking down the street toward the railroad track. He had been doing this scarcely a moment, when he saw a black cat come out of a neighbour's gate and go down the street.

Phil instantly recalled Uncle Peter's story of the black cat. Perhaps this was the same one!

Phil had often been warned about the railroad.

"Keep 'way f'm dat railroad track, honey," the old man had repeated more than once. "It's as dange'ous as a gun, and a gun is dange'ous widout lock, stock, er bairl: I knowed a man oncet w'at beat 'is wife ter def wid a ramrod, an' wuz hung fer it in a' ole fiel' down by de ha'nted house. Dat gun could n't hol' powder ner shot, but was dange'ous 'nuff ter kill two folks. So you jes' better keep 'way f'm dat railroad track, chile."

But Phil was a child, with the making of a man, and the wisest of men sometimes forget. For the moment Phil saw nothing but the cat, and wished for nothing more than to talk to it.

So Phil, unperceived by the colonel, set out to overtake the black cat. The cat seemed in no hurry, and Phil had very nearly caught up with him—or her, as the case might be—when the black cat, having reached the railroad siding, walked under a flat car which stood there, and leaping to one of the truck bars, composed itself, presumably for a nap. In order to get close enough to the cat for conversational purposes, Phil stooped under the overhanging end of the car, and kneeled down beside the truck.

"Kitty, Kitty!" he called, invitingly.

The black cat opened her big yellow eyes with every evidence of lazy amiability.

Peter shuffled toward the corner as fast as his rickety old limbs would carry him. When he reached the corner he saw a car standing on the track. There was a brakeman at one end, holding a coupling link in one hand, and a coupling pin in the other, his eye on an engine and train of cars only a rod or two away, advancing to pick up the single car. At the same moment Peter caught sight of little Phil, kneeling under the car at the other end.

Peter shouted, but the brakeman was absorbed in his own task, which required clòse attention in order to assure his own safety. The engineer on the cab, at the other end of the train, saw an old Negro excitedly gesticulating, and pulled a lever mechanically, but too late to stop the momentum of the train, which was not equipped with air brakes, even if these would have proved effective to stop it in so short a distance.

Just before the two cars came together, Peter threw himself forward to seize the child. As he did so, the cat sprang from the truck bar; the old man stumbled over the cat, and fell across the rail. The car moved only a few feet, but quite far enough to work injury.

A dozen people, including the train crew, quickly gathered. Willing hands drew them out and laid them upon the grass under the spreading elm at the corner of the street. A judge, a merchant and a Negro labourer lifted old Peter's body as tenderly as though it had been that of a beautiful woman. The colonel, somewhat uneasy, he scarcely knew why, had started to limp painfully toward the corner, when he was met by a messenger who informed him of the accident. Forgetting his pain, he hurried to the scene, only to find his heart's delight lying pale, bleeding and unconscious, beside the old Negro who had sacrificed his life to save him.

A doctor, who had been hastily summoned, pronounced Peter dead. Phil showed no superficial injury, save a cut upon the head, from which the bleeding was soon stanched. A Negro's strong arms bore the child to the house, while the bystanders remained about Peter's body until the arrival of Major McLean, recently elected coroner, who had been promptly notified of the accident. Within a few minutes after the officer's appearance, a jury was summoned from among the bystanders, the evidence of the trainmen and several other witnesses was taken, and a verdict of accidental death rendered. There was no suggestion of blame attaching to any one; it had been an accident, pure and simple, which ordinary and reasonable prudence could not have foreseen.

By the colonel's command, the body of his old servant was then conveyed to the house and laid out in the front parlour. Every honour, every token of respect, should be paid to his remains.

Thirty-two

Meanwhile the colonel, forgetting his own hurt, hovered, with several physicians, among them Doctor Price, around the bedside of his child. The slight cut upon the head, the physicians declared, was not, of itself, sufficient to account for the rapid sinking which set in shortly after the boy's removal to the house. There had evidently been some internal injury, the nature of which could not be ascertained. Phil remained unconscious for several hours, but toward the end of the day opened his blue eyes and fixed them upon his father, who was sitting by the bedside.

"Papa," he said, "am I going to die?"

"No, no, Phil," said his father hopefully. "You are going to get well in a few days, I hope."

Phil was silent for a moment, and looked around him curiously. He gave no sign of being in pain.

"Is Miss Laura here?"

"Yes, Phil, she's in the next room, and will be here in a moment."

At that instant Miss Laura came in and kissed him. The caress gave him pleasure, and he smiled sweetly in return.

"Papa, was Uncle Peter hurt?"

"Yes, Phil."

"Where is he, papa? Was he hurt badly?"

"He is lying in another room, Phil, but he is not in any pain."

"Papa," said Phil, after a pause, "if I should die, and if Uncle Peter should die, you'll remember your promise and bury him near me, won't you, dear?"

"Yes, Phil," he said, "but you are not going to die!"

But Phil died, dozing off into a peaceful sleep in which he passed quietly away with a smile upon his face.

It required all the father's fortitude to sustain the blow, with the added agony of self-reproach that he himself had been unwittingly the cause of it. Had he not sent old Peter into the house, the child would not have been left alone. Had he kept his eye upon Phil until Peter's return the child would not have strayed away. He had neglected his child, while the bruised and broken old black man in the room below had given his life to save him. He could do nothing now to show the child his love or Peter his gratitude, and the old man had neither wife nor child in whom the colonel's bounty might find an object. But he would do what he could. He would lay his child's body in the old family lot in the cemetery, among the bones of his ancestors, and there too, close at hand, old Peter should have honourable sepulture. It was his due, and would be the fulfilment of little Phil's last request.

The child was laid out in the parlour, amid a mass of flowers. Miss Laura, for love of him and of the colonel, with her own hands prepared his little body for the last sleep. The undertaker, who hovered around, wished, with a conventional sense of fitness, to remove old Peter's body to a back room. But the colonel said no.

"They died together; together they shall lie here, and they shall be buried together."

He gave instructions as to the location of the graves in the cemetery lot. The undertaker looked thoughtful.

"I hope, sir," said the undertaker, "there will be no objection. It's not customary—there's a coloured graveyard—you might put up a nice tombstone there—and you've been away from here a long time, sir."

"If any one objects," said the colonel, "send him to me. The lot is mine, and I shall do with it as I like. My great-great-grandfather gave the cemetery to the town. Old Peter's skin was black, but his heart was white as any man's! And when a man reaches the grave, he is not far from God, who is no respecter of persons, and in whose presence, on the judgment day, many a white man shall be black, and many a black man white."

The funeral was set for the following afternoon. The graves were to be dug in the morning. The undertaker, whose business was dependent upon public favour, and who therefore shrank from any step which might affect his own popularity, let it be quietly known that Colonel French had given directions to bury Peter in Oak Cemetery.

It was inevitable that there should be some question raised about so novel a proceeding. The colour line in Clarendon, as in all Southern towns, was, on the surface at least, rigidly drawn, and extended from the cradle to the grave. No Negro's body had ever profaned the sacred soil of Oak Cemetery. The protestants laid the matter before the Cemetery trustees, and a private meeting was called in the evening to consider the proposed interment.

White and black worshipped the same God, in different churches. There had been a time when coloured people filled the galleries of the white churches, and white ladies had instilled into black children the principles of religion and good morals. But as white and black had grown nearer to each other in condition, they had grown farther apart in feeling. It was difficult for the poor lady, for instance, to patronise the children of the well-to-do Negro or mulatto; nor was the latter inclined to look up to white people who had started, in his memory, from a position but little higher than his own. In an era of change, the benefits gained thereby seemed scarcely to offset the difficulties of readjustment.

The situation was complicated by a sense of injury on both sides. Cherishing their theoretical equality of citizenship, which they could neither enforce nor forget, the Negroes resented, noisly or silently, as prudence dictated, its contemptuous denial by the whites; and these, viewing this shadowy equality as an insult to themselves, had sought by all the machinery of local law to emphasise and perpetuate their own superiority. The very word "equality" was an offence. Society went back to Egypt and India for its models; to break caste was a greater sin than to break any or all of the ten commandments. White and coloured children studied the same books in different schools. White and black people rode on the same trains in separate cars. Living side by side, and meeting day by day, the law, made and administered by white men, had built a wall between them.

And white and black buried their dead in separate graveyards. Not until they reached God's presence could they stand side by side in any relation of equality. There was a Negro graveyard in Clarendon, where, as a matter of course the coloured dead were buried. It was not an ideal locality. The land was low and swampy, and graves must be used quickly, ere the water collected in them. The graveyard was unfenced, and vagrant cattle browsed upon its rank herbage. The embankment of the railroad encroached upon one side of it, and the passing engines sifted cinders and ashes over the graves. But no Negro had ever thought of burying his dead elsewhere, and if their cemetery was not well kept up, whose fault was it but their own?

The proposition, therefore, of a white man, even of Colonel

French's standing, to bury a Negro in Oak Cemetery, was bound to occasion comment, if nothing more. There was indeed more. Several citizens objected to the profanation, and laid their protest before the mayor, who quietly called a meeting of the board of cemetery trustees, of which he was the chairman.

The trustees were five in number. The board, with the single exception of the mayor, was self-perpetuating, and the members had been chosen, as vacancies occurred by death, at long intervals, from among the aristocracy, who had always controlled it. The mayor, a member and chairman of the board by virtue of his office, had sprung from the same class as Fetters, that of the aspiring poor whites, who, freed from the moral incubus of slavery, had by force of numbers and ambition secured political control of the State and relegated not only the Negroes, but the old master class, to political obscurity. A shrewd, capable man was the mayor, who despised Negroes and distrusted aristocrats, and had the courage of his convictions. He represented in the meeting the protesting element of the community.

"Gentlemen," he said, "Colonel French has ordered this Negro to be buried in Oak Cemetery. We all appreciate the colonel's worth, and what he is doing for the town. But he has lived at the North for many years, and has got somewhat out of our way of thinking. We do not want to buy the prosperity of this town at the price of our principles. The attitude of the white people on the Negro question is fixed and determined for all time, and nothing can ever alter it. To bury this Negro in Oak Cemetery is against our principles."

"The mayor's statement of the rule is quite correct," replied old General Thornton, a member of the board, "and not open to question. But all rules have their exceptions. It was against the law, for some years before the war, to manumit a slave; but an exception to that salutary rule was made in case a Negro should render some great service to the State or the community. You will recall that when, in a sister State, a Negro climbed the steep roof of St. Michael's church and at the risk of his own life saved that historic structure, the pride of Charleston, from destruction by fire, the muncipality granted him his freedom."

"And we all remember," said Mr. Darden, another of the trustees, "we all remember, at least I'm sure General Thornton does, old Sally, who used to belong to the McRae family, and was a member of the Presbyterian Church, and who, because of her age and infirmities—she was hard of hearing and too old to climb the stairs to the gallery—was given a seat in front of the pulpit, on the main floor."

"That was all very well," replied the mayor, stoutly, "when the Negroes belonged to you, and never questioned your authority. But times are different now. They think themselves as good as we are. We had them pretty well in hand until Colonel French came around, with his schools, and his high wages, and now they are getting so fat and sassy that there'll soon be no living with them. The last election did something, but we'll have to do something more, and that soon, to keep them in their places. There's one in jail now, alive, who has shot and disfigured and nearly killed two good white men, and such an example of social equality as burying one in a white graveyard will demoralise them still further. We must preserve the purity and prestige of our race, and we can only do it by keeping the Negroes down."

"After all," said another member, "the purity of our race is not apt to suffer very seriously from the social equality of a graveyard."

"And old Peter will be pretty effectually kept down, wherever he is buried," added another.

These sallies provoked a smile which lightened the tension. A member suggested that Colonel French be sent for.

"It seems a pity to disturb him in his grief," said another.

"It's only a couple of squares," suggested another. "Let's call in a body and pay our respects. We can bring up the matter incidentally, while there."

The muscles of the mayor's chin hardened.

"Colonel French has never been at my house," he said, "and I shouldn't care to seem to intrude."

"Come on, mayor," said Mr. Darden, taking the official by the arm, "these fine distinctions are not becoming in the presence of death. The colonel will be glad to see you."

The mayor could not resist this mark of intimacy on the part of one of the old aristocracy, and walked somewhat proudly through the street arm in arm with Mr. Darden. They paid their respects to the colonel, who was bearing up, with the composure to be expected of a man of strong will and forceful character, under a grief of which he was exquisitely sensible. Touched by a strong man's emotion, which nothing could conceal, no one had the heart to mention, in the presence of the dead, the object of their visit, and they went away without giving the colonel any inkling that his course had been seriously criticised. Nor was the meeting resumed after they left the house, even the mayor seeming content to let the matter go by default.

Thirty-three

Fortune favoured Caxton in the matter of the note. Fetters was in Clarendon the following morning. Caxton saw him passing, called him into his office, and produced the note.

"That's no good," said Fetters contemptuously. "It was outlawed yesterday. I suppose you allowed I'd forgotten it. On the contrary, I've a memorandum of it in my pocketbook, and I struck it off the list last night. I always pay my lawful debts, when they're properly demanded. If this note had been presented yesterday, I'd have paid it. To-day it's too late. It ain't a lawful debt."

"Do you really mean to say, Mr. Fetters, that you have deliberately robbed those poor women of this money all these years, and are not ashamed of it, not even when you're found out, and that you are going to take refuge behind the statute?"

"Now, see here, Mr. Caxton," returned Fetters, without apparent emotion, "you want to be careful about the language you use. I might sue you for slander. You're a young man, that hopes to have a future and live in this county, where I expect to live and have law business done long after some of your present clients have moved away. I didn't owe the estate of John Treadwell one cent—you ought to be lawyer enough to know that. He owed me money, and paid me with a note. I collected the note. I owed him money and paid it with a note. Whoever heard of anybody's paying a note that wasn't presented?"

"It's a poor argument, Mr. Fetters. You would have let those ladies starve to death before you would have come forward and paid that debt."

"They've never asked me for charity, so I wasn't called on to offer it. And you know now, don't you, that if I'd paid the amount of that note, and then it had turned up afterward in somebody else's hands, I'd have had to pay it over again; now wouldn't I?"

Caxton could not deny it. Fetters had robbed the Treadwell estate, but his argument was unanswerable.

"Yes," said Caxton, "I suppose you would."

"I'm sorry for the women," said Fetters, "and I've stood ready to pay that note all these years, and it ain't my fault that it hasn't been presented. Now it's outlawed, and you couldn't expect a man to just give away that much money. It ain't a lawful debt, and the law's good enough for me."

"You're awfully sorry for the ladies, aren't you?" said Caxton, with thinly veiled sarcasm.

"I surely am; I'm honestly sorry for them."

"And you'd pay the note if you had to, wouldn't you?" asked Caxton.

"I surely would. As I say, I always pay my legal debts."

"All right," said Caxton triumphantly, "then you'll pay this. I filed suit against you yesterday, which takes the case out of the statute."

Fetters concealed his discomfiture.

"Well," he said, with quiet malignity, "I've nothing more to say till I consult my lawyer. But I want to tell you one thing. You are ruining a fine career by standing in with this Colonel French. I hear his son was killed to-day. You can tell him I say it's a judgment on him; for I hold him responsible for my son's condition. He came down here and tried to demoralise the labour market. He put false notions in the niggers' heads. Then he got to meddling with my business, trying to get away a nigger whose time I had bought. He insulted my agent Turner, and came all the way down to Sycamore and tried to bully me into letting the nigger loose, and of course I wouldn't be bullied. Afterwards, when I offered to let the nigger go, the colonel wouldn't have it so. I shall always believe he bribed one of my men to get the nigger off, and then turned him loose to run amuck among the white people and shoot my boy and my overseer. It was a low-down performance, and unworthy of a gentleman. No really white man would treat another white man so. You can tell him I say it's a judgment that's fallen on him to-day, and that it's not the last one, and that he'll be sorrier yet that he didn't stay where he was, with his nigger-lovin' notions, instead of comin' back down here to make trouble for people that have grown up with the State and made it what it is."

Caxton, of course, did not deliver the message. To do so would have been worse taste than Fetters had displayed in sending it. Having got the best of the encounter, Caxton had no objection to letting his defeated antagonist discharge his venom against the absent colonel, who would never know of it, and who was already breasting the waves of a sorrow so deep and so strong as almost to overwhelm him. For he had loved the boy; all his hopes had centred around this beautiful man child, who had promised so much that was good. His own future had been planned with reference to him. Now he was dead, and the bereaved father gave way to his grief.

Thirty-four

The funeral took place next day, from the Episcopal Church, in which communion the little boy had been baptised, and of which old Peter had always been an humble member, faithfully appearing every Sunday morning in his seat in the gallery, long after the rest of his people had deserted it for churches of their own. On this occasion Peter had, for the first time, a place on the main floor, a little to one side of the altar, in front of which, banked with flowers, stood the white velvet casket which contained all that was mortal of little Phil. The same beautiful sermon answered for both. In touching words, the rector, a man of culture, taste and feeling, and a faithful servant of his Master, spoke of the sweet young life brought to so untimely an end, and pointed the bereaved father to the best source of consolation. He paid a brief tribute to the faithful servant and humble friend, to whom, though black and lowly, the white people of the town were glad to pay this signal tribute of respect and appreciation for his heroic deed. The attendance at the funeral, while it might have been larger, was composed of the more refined and cultured of the townspeople, from whom, indeed, the church derived most of its membership and support; and the gallery overflowed with coloured people, whose hearts had warmed to the great honour thus paid to one of their race. Four young white men bore Phil's body and the six pallbearers of old Peter were from among the best white people of the town.

The double interment was made in Oak Cemetery. Simultaneously both bodies were lowered to their last resting-place. Simultaneously ashes were consigned to ashes and dust to dust. The earth was heaped above the graves. The mound above little Phil's was buried with flowers, and old Peter's was not neglected.

Beyond the cemetery wall, a few white men of the commoner sort watched the proceedings from a distance, and eyed with grim hostility the Negroes who had followed the procession. They had no part nor parcel in this sentimental folly, nor did they approve of it—in fact they disapproved of it very decidedly. Among them was the colonel's discharged foreman, Jim Green, who was pronounced in his denunciation.

"Colonel French is an enemy of his race," he declared to his sympathetic following. "He hires niggers when white men are idle; and pays them more than white men who work are earning. And now he is burying them with white people."

When the group around the grave began to disperse, the little knot of disgruntled spectators moved sullenly away. In the evening they might have been seen, most of them, around Clay Jackson's barroom. Turner, the foreman at Fetters's convict farm, was in town that evening, and Jackson's was his favourite haunt. For some reason

Turner was more sociable than usual, and liquor flowed freely, at his expense. There was a great deal of intemperate talk, concerning the Negro in jail for shooting Haines and young Fetters, and concerning Colonel French as the protector of Negroes and the enemy of white men.

Thirty-five

At the same time that the colonel, dry-eyed and heavy-hearted, had returned to his empty house to nurse his grief, another series of events was drawing to a climax in the dilapidated house on Mink Run. Even while the preacher was saying the last words over little Phil's remains, old Malcolm Dudley's illness had taken a sudden and violent turn. He had been sinking for several days, but the decline had been gradual, and there had seemed no particular reason for alarm. But during the funeral exercises Ben had begun to feel uneasy—some obscure premonition warned him to hurry homeward.

As soon as the funeral was over he spoke to Dr. Price, who had been one of the pallbearers, and the doctor had promised to be at Mink Run in a little while. Ben rode home as rapidly as he could; as he went up the lane toward the house a Negro lad came forward to take charge of the tired horse, and Ben could see from the boy's expression that he had important information to communicate.

"Yo' uncle is monst'ous low, sir," said the boy. "You bettah go in an' see 'im quick, er you'll be too late. Dey ain' nobody wid 'im but ole Aun' Viney."

Ben hurried into the house and to his uncle's room, where Malcolm Dudley lay dying. Outside, the sun was setting, and his red rays, shining through the trees into the open window, lit the stage for the last scene of this belated drama. When Ben entered the room, the sweat of death had gathered on the old man's brow, but his eyes, clear with the light of reason, were fixed upon old Viney, who stood by the bedside. The two were evidently so absorbed in their own thoughts as to be oblivious to anything else, and neither of them paid the slightest attention to Ben, or to the scared Negro lad, who had followed him and stood outside the door. But marvellous to hear, Viney was talking, strangely, slowly, thickly, but passionately and distinctly.

"You had me whipped," she said. "Do you remember that? You had me whipped—whipped—whipped—by a poor white dog I had despised and spurned! You had said that you loved me, and you had promised to free me—and you had me whipped! But I have had my revenge!"

Her voice shook with passion, a passion at which Ben wondered. That his uncle and she had once been young he knew, and that their relations had once been closer than those of master and servant; but this outbreak of feeling from the wrinkled old mulattress seemed as strange and weird to Ben as though a stone image had waked to speech. Spellbound, he stood in the doorway, and listened to this ghost of a voice long dead.

"Your uncle came with the money and left it, and went away. Only he and I knew where it was. But I never told you! I could have spoken at any time for twenty-five years, but I never told you! I have waited—

I have waited for this moment! I have gone into the woods and fields and talked to myself by the hour, that I might not forget how to talk—and I have waited my turn, and it is here and now!"

Ben hung breathlessly upon her words. He drew back beyond her range of vision, lest she might see him, and the spell be broken. Now, he thought, she would tell where the gold was hidden!

"He came," she said, "and left the gold—two heavy bags of it, and a letter for you. An hour later *he came back and took it all away,* except the letter! The money was here one hour, but in that hour you had me whipped, and for that you have spent twenty-five years in looking for nothing—something that was not here! I have had my revenge! For twenty-five years I have watched you look for—nothing; have seen you waste your time, your property, your life, your mind—for nothing! For ah, Mars' Ma'colm, you had me whipped—*by another man!*"

A shadow of reproach crept into the old man's eyes, over which the mists of death were already gathering.

"Yes, Viney," he whispered, "you have had your revenge! But I was sorry, Viney, for what I did, and you were not. And I forgive you, Viney; but you are unforgiving—even in the presence of death."

His voice failed, and his eyes closed for the last time. When she saw that he was dead, by a strange revulsion of feeling the wall of outraged pride and hatred and revenge, built upon one brutal and bitterly repented mistake, and labouriously maintained for half a lifetime in her woman's heart that even slavery could not crush, crumbled and fell and let pass over it in one great and final flood the pent-up passions of the past. Bursting into tears—strange tears from eyes that had long forgot to weep—old Viney threw herself down upon her knees by the bedside, and seizing old Malcolm's emaciated hand in both her own, covered it with kisses, fervent kisses, the ghosts of the passionate kisses of their distant youth.

With a feeling that his presence was something like sacrilege, Ben stole away and left her with her dead—the dead master and the dead past—and thanked God that he lived in another age, and had escaped this sin.

As he wandered through the old house, a veil seemed to fall from his eyes. How old everything was, how shrunken and decayed! The sheen of the hidden gold had gilded the dilapidated old house, the neglected plantation, his own barren life. Now that it was gone, things appeared in their true light. Fortunately he was young enough to retrieve much of what had been lost. When the old man was buried, he would settle the estate, sell the land, make some provision for Aunt Viney, and then, with what was left, go out into the world and try to make a place for himself and Graciella. For life intrudes its claims even into the presence of death.

When the doctor came, a little later, Ben went with him into the death chamber. Viney was still kneeling by her master's bedside, but strangely still and silent. The doctor laid his hand on hers and old Malcolm's, which had remained clasped together.

"They are both dead," he declared. "I knew their story; my father told it to me many years ago."

Ben related what he had overheard.

"I'm not surprised," said the doctor. "My father attended her when she had the stroke, and after. He always maintained that Viney could speak—if she had wished to speak."

Thirty-six

The colonel's eyes were heavy with grief that night, and yet he lay awake late, and with his sorrow were mingled many consoling thoughts. The people, his people, had been kind, aye, more than kind. Their warm hearts had sympathised with his grief. He had sometimes been impatient of their conservatism, their narrowness, their unreasoning pride of opinion; but in his bereavement they had manifested a feeling that it would be beautiful to remember all the days of his life. All the people, white and black, had united to honour his dead.

He had wished to help them—had tried already. He had loved the town as the home of his ancestors, which enshrined their ashes. He would make of it a monument to mark his son's resting place. His fight against Fetters and what he represented should take on a new character; henceforward it should be a crusade to rescue from threatened barbarism the land which contained the tombs of his loved ones. Nor would he be alone in the struggle, which he now clearly foresaw would be a long one. The dear, good woman he had asked to be his wife could help him. He needed her clear, spiritual vision; and in his lifelong sorrow he would need her sympathy and companionship; for she had loved the child and would share his grief. She knew the people better than he, and was in closer touch with them; she could help him in his schemes of benevolence, and suggest new ways to benefit the people. Phil's mother was buried far away, among her own people; could be consult her, he felt sure she would prefer to remain there. Here she would be an alien note; and when Laura died she could lie with them and still be in her own place.

"Have you heard the news, sir," asked the housekeeper, when he came down to breakfast the next morning.

"No, Mrs. Hughes, what is it?"

"They lynched the Negro who was in jail for shooting young Mr. Fetters and the other man."

The colonel hastily swallowed a cup of coffee and went down town. It was only a short walk. Already there were excited crowds upon the street, discussing the events of the night. The colonel sought Caxton, who was just entering his office.

"They've done it," said the lawyer.

"So I understand. When did it happen?"

"About one o'clock last night. A crowd came in from Sycamore—not all at once, but by twos and threes, and got together in Clay Johnson's saloon, with Ben Green, your discharged foreman, and a lot of other riffraff, and went to the sheriff, and took the keys, and took Johnson and carried him out to where the shooting was, and——"

"Spare me the details. He is dead?"

"Yes."

A rope, a tree—a puff of smoke, a flash of flame—or a barbaric orgy of fire and blood—what matter which? At the end there was a lump of clay, and a hundred murderers where there had been one before.

"Can we do anything to punish *this* crime?"

"We can try."

And they tried. The colonel went to the sheriff. The sheriff said he had yielded to force, but he never would have dreamed of shooting to defend a worthless Negro who had maimed a good white man, had nearly killed another, and had declared a vendetta against the white race.

By noon the colonel had interviewed as many prominent men as he could find, and they became increasingly difficult to find as it became known that he was seeking them. The town, he said, had been disgraced, and should redeem itself by prosecuting the lynchers. He may as well have talked to the empty air. The trail of Fetters was all over the town. Some of the officials owed Fetters money; others were under political obligations to him. Others were plainly of the opinion that the Negro got no more than he deserved; such a wretch was not fit to live. The coroner's jury returned a verdict of suicide, a grim joke which evoked some laughter. Doctor McKenzie, to whom the colonel expressed his feelings, and whom he asked to throw the influence of his church upon the side of law and order, said:

"It is too bad. I am sorry, but it is done. Let it rest. No good can ever come of stirring it up further."

Later in the day there came news that the lynchers, after completing their task, had proceeded to the Dudley plantation and whipped all the Negroes who did not learn of their coming in time to escape, the claim being that Johnson could not have maintained himself in hiding without their connivance, and that they were therefore parties to his crimes.

The colonel felt very much depressed when he went to bed that night, and lay for a long time turning over in his mind the problem that confronted him.

So far he had been beaten, except in the matter of the cotton mill, which was yet unfinished. His efforts in Bud Johnson's behalf—the only thing he had undertaken to please the woman he loved, had proved abortive. His promise to the teacher—well, he had done his part, but to no avail. He would be ashamed to meet Taylor face to face. With what conscience could a white man in Clarendon ever again ask a Negro to disclose the name or hiding place of a coloured criminal? In the effort to punish the lynchers he stood, to all intents and purposes, single-handed and alone; and without the support of public opinion he could do nothing.

The colonel was beaten, but not dismayed. Perhaps God in his wisdom had taken Phil away, that his father might give himself more completely and single-mindedly to the battle before him. Had Phil lived, a father might have hesitated to expose a child's young and impressionable mind to the things which these volcanic outbursts of passion between mismated races might cause at any unforeseen moment. Now that the way was clear, he could go forward, hand in hand with the good woman who had promised to wed him, in the work he had laid out. He would enlist good people to demand better laws, under which Fetters and his kind would find it harder to prey upon the weak.

Diligently he would work to lay wide and deep the foundations of prosperity, education and enlightenment, upon which should rest justice, humanity and civic righteousness. In this he would find a worthy career. Patiently would he await the results of his labours, and if they came not in great measure in his own lifetime, he would be content to know that after years would see their full fruition.

So that night he sat down and wrote a long answer to Kirby's letter, in which he told him of Phil's death and burial, and his own grief. Something there was, too, of his plans for the future, including his marriage to a good woman who would help him in them. Kirby, he said, had offered him a golden opportunity for which he thanked him heartily. The scheme was good enough for any one to venture upon. But to carry out his own plans, would require that he invest his money in the State of his residence, where there were many openings for capital that could afford to wait upon development for large returns. He sent his best regards to Mrs. Jerviss, and his assurance that Kirby's plan was a good one. Perhaps Kirby and she alone could handle it; if not, there must be plenty of money elsewhere for so good a thing.

He sealed the letter, and laid it aside to be mailed in the morning. To his mind it had all the force of a final renunciation, a severance of the last link that bound him to his old life.

Long the colonel lay thinking, after he retired to rest, and the muffled striking of the clock downstairs had marked the hour of midnight ere he fell asleep. And he had scarcely dozed away, when he was awakened by a scraping noise, as though somewhere in the house a heavy object was being drawn across the floor. The sound was not repeated, however, and thinking it some trick of the imagination, he soon slept again.

As the colonel slept this second time, he dreamed of a regenerated South, filled with thriving industries, and thronged with a prosperous and happy people, where every man, having enough for his needs, was willing that every other man should have the same; where law and order should prevail unquestioned, and where every man could enter, through the golden gate of hope, the field of opportunity, where lay the prizes of life, which all might have an equal chance to win or lose.

For even in his dreams the colonel's sober mind did not stray beyond the bounds of reason and experience. That all men would ever be equal he did not even dream; there would always be the strong and the weak, the wise and the foolish. But that each man, in his little life in this our little world might be able to make the most of himself, was an ideal which even the colonel's waking hours would not have repudiated.

Following this pleasing thread with the unconscious rapidity of dreams, the colonel passed, in a few brief minutes, through a long and useful life to a happy end, when he too rested with his fathers, by the side of his son, and on his tomb was graven what was said of Ben Adhem: "Here lies one who loved his fellow men," and the further words, "and tried to make them happy."

Shortly after dawn there was a loud rapping at the colonel's door:

"Come downstairs and look on de piazza, Colonel," said the agitated voice of the servant who had knocked. "Come quick, suh."

There was a vague terror in the man's voice that stirred the colonel strangely. He threw on a dressing gown and hastened downstairs, and to the front door of the hall, which stood open. A handsome mahogany burial casket, stained with earth and disfigured by rough handling, rested upon the floor of the piazza, where it had been deposited during the night. Conspicuously nailed to the coffin lid was a sheet of white paper, upon which were some lines rudely scrawled in a handwriting that matched the spelling:

Kurnell French:
Take notis. Berry yore ole nigger somewhar else. He can't stay in Oak Semitury. The majority of the white people of this town, who dident tend yore nigger funarl, woant have him there. Niggers by there selves, white peepul by there selves, and them that lives in our town must bide by our rules.

By order of
CUMITTY.

The colonel left the coffin standing on the porch, where it remained all day, an object of curious interest to the scores and hundreds who walked by to look at it, for the news spread quickly through the town. No one, however, came in. If there were those who reprobated the action they were silent. The mob spirit, which had broken out in the lynching of Johnson, still dominated the town, and no one dared to speak against it.

As soon as Colonel French had dressed and breakfasted, he drove over to the cemetery. Those who had exhumed old Peter's remains had not been unduly careful. The carelessly excavated earth had been scattered here and there over the lot. The flowers on old Peter's grave and that of little Phil had been trampled under foot—whether wantonly or not, inevitably, in the execution of the ghoulish task.

The colonel's heart hardened as he stood by his son's grave. Then he took a long lingering look at the tombs of his ancestors and turned away with an air of finality.

From the cemetery he went to the undertaker's, and left an order; thence to the telegraph office, from which he sent a message to his former partner in New York; and thence to the Treadwells'.

Thirty-seven

Miss Laura came forward with outstretched hands and tear-stained eyes to greet him.

"Henry," she exclaimed, "I am shocked and sorry, I cannot tell you how much! Nor do I know what else to say, except that the best people do not—cannot—could not—approve of it!"

"The best people, Laura," he said with a weary smile, "are an abstraction. When any deviltry is on foot they are never there to prevent it—they vanish into thin air at its approach. When it is done, they excuse it; and they make no effort to punish it. So it is not too much to say that what they permit they justify, and they cannot shirk the responsibility. To mar the living—it is the history of life—but to make war upon the dead!— I am going away, Laura, never to return. My dream of usefulness is over. To-night I take away my dead and shake the dust of Clarendon from my feet forever. Will you come with me?"

"Henry," she said, and each word tore her heart, "I have been expecting this—since I heard. But I cannot go; my duty calls me here. My mother could not be happy anywhere else, nor would I fit into any other life. And here, too, I am useful—and may still be useful—and should be missed. I know your feelings, and would not try to keep you. But, oh, Henry, if all of those who love justice and practise humanity should go away, what would become of us?"

"I leave to-night," he returned, "and it is your right to go with me, or to come to me."

"No, Henry, nor am I sure that you would wish me to. It was for the old town's sake that you loved me. I was a part of your dream—a part of the old and happy past, upon which you hoped to build, as upon the foundations of the old mill, a broader and a fairer structure. Do you remember what you told me, that night—that happy night—that you loved me because in me you found the embodiment of an ideal? Well, Henry, that is why I did not wish to make our engagement known, for I knew, I felt, the difficulty of your task, and I foresaw that you might be disappointed, and I feared that if your ideal should be wrecked, you might find me a burden. I loved you, Henry—I seem to have always loved you, but I would not burden you."

"No, no, Laura—not so! not so!"

"And you wanted me for Phil's sake, whom we both loved; and now that your dream is over, and Phil is gone, I should only remind you of where you lost him, and of your disappointment, and of—this other thing, and I could not be sure that you loved me or wanted me."

"Surely you cannot doubt it, Laura?" His voice was firm, but to her sensitive spirit it did not carry conviction.

"You remembered me from my youth," she continued tremulously but bravely, "and it was the image in your memory that you loved. And now, when you go away, the old town will shrink and fade from your memory and your heart and you will have none but harsh thoughts of it; nor can I blame you greatly, for you have grown far away from us, and we shall need many years to overtake you. Nor do you need me, Henry—I am too old to learn new ways, and elsewhere than here I should be a hindrance to you rather than a help. But in the larger life to which you go, think of me now and then as one who loves you still, and who will try, in her poor way, with such patience as she has, to carry on the work which you have begun, and which you—Oh, Henry!"

He divined her thought, though her tear-filled eyes spoke sorrow rather than reproach.

"Yes," he said sadly, "which I have abandoned. Yes, Laura, abandoned, fully and forever."

The colonel was greatly moved, but his resolution remained unshaken.

"Laura," he said, taking both her hands in his, "I swear that I should be glad to have you with me. Come away! The place is not fit for you to live in!"

"No, Henry! it cannot be! I could not go! My duty holds me here! God would not forgive me if I abandoned it. Go your way; live your life. Marry some other woman, if you must, who will make you happy. But I shall keep, Henry—nothing can ever take away from me—the memory of one happy summer."

"No, no, Laura, it need not be so! I shall write you. You'll think better of it. But I go to-night—not one hour longer than I must, will I remain in this town. I must bid your mother and Graciella good-bye."

He went into the house. Mrs. Treadwell was excited and sorry, and would have spoken at length, but the colonel's farewells were brief.

"I cannot stop to say more than good-bye, dear Mrs. Treadwell. I have spent a few happy months in my old home, and now I am going away. Laura will tell you the rest."

Graciella was tearfully indignant.

"It was a shame!" she declared. "Peter was a good old nigger, and it wouldn't have done anybody any harm to leave him there. I'd rather be buried beside old Peter than near any of the poor white trash that dug him up—so there! I'm so sorry you're going away; but I hope, sometime," she added stoutly, "to see you in New York! Don't forget!"

"I'll send you my address," said the colonel.

Thirty-eight

It was a few weeks later. Old Ralph Dudley and Viney had been buried. Ben Dudley had ridden in from Mink Run, had hitched his horse in the back yard as usual, and was seated on the top step of the piazza beside Graciella. His elbows rested on his knees, and his chin upon his hand. Graciella had unconsciously imitated his drooping attitude. Both were enshrouded in the deepest gloom, and had been sunk, for several minutes, in a silence equally profound. Graciella was the first to speak.

"Well, then," she said with a deep sigh, "there is absolutely nothing left?"

"Not a thing," he groaned hopelessly, "except my horse and my clothes, and a few odds and ends which belong to me. Fetters will have the land—there's not enough to pay the mortgages against it, and I'm in debt for the funeral expenses."

"And what are you going to do?"

"Gracious knows—I wish I did! I came over to consult the family. I have no trade, no profession, no land and no money. I can get a job at braking on the railroad—or may be at clerking in a store. I'd have asked the colonel for something in the mill—but that chance is gone."

"Gone," echoed Graciella, gloomily. "I see my fate! I shall marry you, because I can't help loving you, and couldn't live without you; and I shall never get to New York, but be, all my life, a poor man's wife—a poor white man's wife."

"No, Graciella, we might be poor, but not poor-white! Our blood will still be of the best."

"It will be all the same. Blood without money may count for one generation, but it won't hold out for two."

They relapsed into a gloom so profound, so rayless, that they might almost be said to have reveled in it. It was lightened, or at least a diversion was created by Miss Laura's opening the garden gate and coming up the walk. Ben rose as she approached, and Graciella looked up.

"I have been to the post-office," said Miss Laura. "Here is a letter for you, Ben, addressed in my care. It has the New York postmark."

"Thank you, Miss Laura."

Eagerly Ben's hand tore the envelope and drew out the enclosure. Swiftly his eyes devoured the lines; they were typewritten and easy to follow.

"Glory!" he shouted, "glory hallelujah! Listen!"

He read the letter aloud, while Graciella leaned against his shoulder and feasted her eyes upon the words. The letter was from Colonel French:

"My dear Ben:

I was very much impressed with the model of a cotton gin and press which I saw you exhibit one day at Mrs. Treadwells'. You have a fine genius for mechanics, and the model embodies, I think, a clever idea, which is worth working up. If your uncle's death has left you free to dispose of your time, I should like to have you come on to New York with the model, and we will take steps to have the invention patented at once, and form a company for its manufacture. As an evidence of good faith, I enclose my draft for five hundred dollars, which can be properly accounted for in our future arrangements."

"O Ben!" gasped Graciella, in one long drawn out, ecstatic sigh.

"O Graciella!" exclaimed Ben, as he threw his arms around her and kissed her rapturously, regardless of Miss Laura's presence. "Now you can go to New York as soon as you like!"

Thirty-nine

Colonel French took his dead to the North, and buried both the little boy and the old servant in the same lot with his young wife, and in the shadow of the stately mausoleum which marked her resting-place. There, surrounded by the monuments of the rich and the great, in a beautiful cemetery, which overlooks a noble harbour where the ships of all nations move in endless procession, the body of the faithful servant rests beside that of the dear little child whom he unwittingly lured to his death and then died in the effort to save. And in all the great company of those who have laid their dead there in love or in honour, there is none to question old Peter's presence or the colonel's right to lay him there. Sometimes, at night, a ray of light from the uplifted torch of the Statue of Liberty, the gift of a free people to a free people, falls athwart the white stone which marks his resting place—fit prophecy and omen of the day when the sun of liberty shall shine alike upon all men.

When the colonel went away from Clarendon, he left his affairs in Caxton's hands, with instructions to settle them up as expeditiously as possible. The cotton mill project was dropped, and existing contracts closed on the best terms available. Fetters paid the old note—even he would not have escaped odium for so bare-faced a robbery—and Mrs. Treadwell's last days could be spent in comfort and Miss Laura saved from any fear for her future, and enabled to give more freely to the poor and needy. Barclay Fetters recovered the use of one eye, and embittered against the whole Negro race by his disfigurement, went into public life and devoted his talents and his education to their debasement. The colonel had relented sufficiently to contemplate making over to Miss Laura the old family residence in trust for use as a hospital, with a suitable fund for its maintenance, but it unfortunately caught fire and burned down—and he was hardly sorry. He sent Catherine, Bud Johnson's wife, a considerable sum of money, and she bought a gorgeous suit of mourning, and after a decent interval consoled herself with a new husband. And he sent word to the committee of coloured men to whom he had made a definite promise, that he would be ready to fulfil his obligation in regard to their school whenever they should have met the conditions.

One day, a year or two after leaving Clarendon, as the colonel, in company with Mrs. French, formerly a member of his firm, now his partner in a double sense—was riding upon a fast train between New York and Chicago, upon a trip to visit a western mine in which the reorganised French and Company, Limited, were interested, he noticed that the Pullman car porter, a tall and stalwart Negro, was watching him furtively from time to time. Upon one occasion, when the colonel was alone in the smoking-room, the porter addressed him.

"Excuse me, suh," he said, "I've been wondering ever since we left New York, if you wa'n't Colonel French?"

"Yes, I'm Mr. French—Colonel French, if you want it so."

"I 'lowed it must be you, suh, though you've changed the cut of your beard, and are looking a little older, suh. I don't suppose you remember me?"

"I've seen you somewhere," said the colonel—no longer the colonel, but like the porter, let us have it so. "Where was it?"

"I'm Henry Taylor, suh, that used to teach school at Clarendon. I reckon you remember me now."

"Yes," said the colonel sadly, "I remember you now, Taylor, to my sorrow. I didn't keep my word about Johnson, did I?"

"Oh, yes, suh," replied the porter, "I never doubted but what you'd keep your word. But you see, suh, they were too many for you. There ain't no one man can stop them folks down there when they once get started."

"And what are you doing here, Taylor?"

"Well, suh, the fact is that after you went away, it got out somehow that I had told on Bud Johnson. I don't know how they learned it, and of course I knew you didn't tell it; but somebody must have seen me going to your house, or else some of my enemies guessed it—and happened to guess right—and after that the coloured folks wouldn't send their children to me, and I lost my job, and wasn't able to get another anywhere in the State. The folks said I was an enemy of my race, and, what was more important to me, I found that my race was an enemy to me. So I got out, suh, and I came No'th, hoping to find somethin' better. This is the best job I've struck yet, but I'm hoping that sometime or other I'll find something worth while."

"And what became of the industrial school project?" asked the colonel. "I've stood ready to keep my promise, and more, but I never heard from you."

"Well, suh, after you went away the enthusiasm kind of died out, and some of the white folks throwed cold water on it, and it fell through, suh."

When the porter came along, before the train reached Chicago, the colonel offered Taylor a handsome tip.

"Thank you, suh," said the porter, "but I'd rather not take it. I'm a porter now, but I wa'n't always one, and hope I won't always be one. And during all the time I taught school in Clarendon, you was the only white man that ever treated me quite like a man—and our folks just like people—and if you won't think I'm presuming, I'd rather not take the money."

The colonel shook hands with him, and took his address. Shortly afterward he was able to find him something better than menial employment, where his education would give him an opportunity for advancement. Taylor is fully convinced that his people will never get very far along in the world without the good will of the white people, but he is still wondering how they will secure it. For he regards Colonel French as an extremely fortunate accident.

And so the colonel faltered, and, having put his hand to the plow, turned back. But was not his, after all, the only way? For no more now than when the Man of Sorrows looked out over the Mount of Olives, can men gather grapes of thorns or figs of thistles. The seed which the colonel sowed seemed to fall by the wayside, it is true; but other eyes have seen with the same light, and while Fetters and his kind still dominate their section, other hands have taken up the fight which the colonel dropped. In manufactures the South has gone forward by leaps and bounds. The strong arm of the Government, guided by a wise and just executive, has been reached out to crush the poisonous growth of peonage, and men hitherto silent have raised their voices to commend. Here and there a brave judge has condemned the infamy of the chain-gang and convict lease systems. Good men, North and South, have banded themselves together to promote the cause of popular education. Slowly, like all great social changes, but visibly, to the eye of faith, is growing up a new body of thought, favourable to just laws and their orderly administration. In this changed attitude of mind lies the hope of the future, the hope of the Republic.

But Clarendon has had its chance, nor seems yet to have had another. Other towns, some not far from it, lying nearer the main lines of travel, have been swept into the current of modern life, but not yet Clarendon. There the grass grows thicker in the streets. The meditative cows still graze in the vacant lot between the post-office and the bank, where the public library was to stand. The old academy has grown more dilapidated than ever, and a large section of plaster has fallen from the wall, carrying with it the pencil drawing made in the colonel's schooldays; and if Miss Laura Treadwell sees that the graves of the old Frenches are not allowed to grow up in weeds and grass, the colonel knows nothing of it. The pigs and the loafers—leaner pigs and lazier loafers—still sleep in the shade, when the pound keeper and the constable are not active. The limpid water of the creek still murmurs down the slope and ripples over the stone foundation of what was to have been the new dam, while the birds have nested for some years in the vines that soon overgrew the unfinished walls of the colonel's cotton mill. White men go their way, and black men theirs, and these ways grow wider apart, and no one knows the outcome. But there are those who hope, and those who pray, that this condition will pass, that some day our whole land will be truly free, and the strong will cheerfully help to bear the burdens of the weak, and Justice, the seed, and Peace, the flower, of liberty, will prevail throughout all our borders.

Reader's Companion

1. *The Colonel's Dream* is in large part a story of migration: the relocation of our protagonist, a white southerner, to the North after the region's defeat in the Civil War; and his return to his land of origin after more than two decades. As the narrator describes the geography of the South upon the colonel's return home, "listless negroes dozing on the curbstone" and "pigs sleeping in the shadow of the old wooden market house" are listed among the "things" that characterize Clarendon's landscape. Similarly, in announcing his joy at his quick acquisitions in Clarendon, the colonel absentmindedly declares, "I have been in Clarendon two days; and I have already bought a dog, a house, and man." What clues does the Colonel's statement offer concerning his attitude toward black life? What might Chestnutt be suggesting with such statements?

2. Upon his return, the colonel is reunited with Peter, the young black boy (now neglected older man) given to him as a child by his father as a companion and helper. The more prosperous gentleman laments and muses over the pitiable condition of "old Peter." In attempting to isolate reasons for the remarkable differences in their fates, the narrator suggests, "[t]he colonel had prospered because, having no Peters to work for him, he had been compelled to work for himself." After reading the novel, would you agree that the absence of black labor was the main reason for Colonel French's prosperity? Why or why not? What other factors were at play?

3. Throughout the novel, a nagging tension between the present, the future, and the past is the subject of much discussion. What do you make of the upwardly mobile Garciella's statement to Ben that she loves the south "like my old black mammy"? How are similar attitudes concerning the relationship between race and progress displayed in other points in the story?

4. Toward the middle of the book, Colonel French discovers that the greed of Fetters has spiraled so dangerously out of control that white women and children have been set to work in conditions "worse than slaves." Discuss the significance of this statement, keeping in mind the prevalence of the debt system in the novel that effectively renders black men as property once again.

5. The colonel's mill scheme serves as employment for many black and a few white men in Clarendon. The whites' refusal to work "under" a black foreman is consistent with the white community's discomfort over the decision to bury old Peter in the

French family plot. Yet old black individuals have been frequently paired with young whites in southern culture. How is old Peter's and young Phil's relationship representative of acceptable pairings of white and black in (southern) American life? What does this suggest about dominant perceptions of African Americans?

6. In a similar vein, assess the negro barber William Nichols's declaration to Colonel French that he "loves the aristocracy," and his comment that if he'd "be'n bawn white" he would have been an aristocrat. What contradictions of nineteenth-century American life is Chestnutt exposing here? Why is it important that these comments be made to the colonel?

7. Colonel French is thwarted in his early attempt to liberate Bud Johnson from Fetters's plantation. His wife, Catharine, is disappointed in the turn of events but has faith that the Colonel will ultimately prove successful. As the narrator suggests, "[i]n her simple creed, God might sometimes seem to neglect his black children, but no harm could come to a negro who had a rich white gentleman for friend and protector." That Bud Johnson dies only confirms the ironic tone of this statement. What do you think Chesnutt is suggesting with that remark?

8. Viney's deathbed declaration that she purposely kept silent for twenty-five years about the fate of the money so important to the Dudley men raises important questions about race and female sexuality. What's the significance of Viney's subversive act? How would you characterize the nature of Viney and old man Dudley's relationship? Why is it important that they die almost simultaneously?

9. For many in the novel, the North is credited with having corrupted the colonel's southern sensibilities concerning race. By novel's end, he returns to New York, choosing to bury his son and old Peter side by side—fulfilling a wish for his son that was rejected in Clarendon. What do you make of the presentation of the North as a relative racial utopia?

About the Author

Born in 1858 to mixed race parents, Charles Waddell Chesnutt is considered the first African-American writer to be seriously regarded by the general American literati. Earning a living as a court stenographer and lawyer, he published many short stories and three novels—*The House behind the Cedars* (1900), which focused on racial passing, *The Marrow of Tradition* (1901), which dealt with racial violence, and *The Colonel's Dream*. Three other novels, *Mandy Oxendine* (written in the 1890s), *Paul Marchand, F.M.C.* (finished in 1921), and *The Quarry* (finished in 1928) were deemed to be too controversial to be printed during Chesnutt's time, but have recently resurfaced and are in print.

Though he was light enough to pass for white, Chesnutt refused to sever his connection to African-American causes and communities, and was an integrationist and civil rights leader. In 1928, the NAACP awarded him the Spingarn Medal for distinguished literary contributions to African Americans. Chesnutt died in 1932.